INVASION USA

WILLIAM W. JOHNSTONE

with
FRED AUSTIN

INVASION USA

PINNACLE BOOKS
Kensington Publishing Corp.
http://www.kensingtonbooks.com

PINNACLE BOOKS are published by

Kensington Publishing Corp.
850 Third Avenue
New York, NY 10022

All Kensington Titles, Imprints, and Distributed Lines are available at special quantity discounts for bulk purchases for sales
promotions, premiums, fund-raising, and educational or insti-
tutional use. Special book excerpts or customized printings can
also be created to fit specific needs. For details, write or phone
the office of the Kensington special sales manager: Kensington
Publishing Corp., 850 Third Avenue, New York, NY 10022,
attn: Special Sales Department, Phone: 1-800-221-2647.

Pinnacle and the P logo Reg. U.S. Pat. & TM Off.

First Printing: January 2006

10 9 8 7 6 5 4 3 2 1

Printed in the United States of America

*"Contrary to popular belief, my books are
not about killing people.
They're about killing the right people."*
—William W. Johnstone

*"God grants liberty only to those who love it,
and are always ready to guard and defend it."*
—Daniel Webster

*Although there is a town in Arizona
called Little Tucson, the community of the same name
in this novel is completely fictional, as are its citizens.
There is no Sierrita County in Arizona.*

Only the outrage is real.

—William W. Johnstone
Fred Austin
December 2005

Prologue

The town of Little Tucson, Arizona, lies twenty miles north of the United States/Mexico border, seventy-five miles south/southwest of Tucson. The Chamber of Commerce signs on the highway at the edges of town used to say WELCOME TO LITTLE TUCSON—HOME OF 8,034 FRIENDLY PEOPLE—AND A FEW OLD GRUMPS! Several years ago, when the Chamber decided to replace the signs, the members voted to change the old-fashioned greeting as well. Based on the fact that the citizens of Little Tucson are a mixture—forty percent Anglo, sixty percent Hispanic—and get along well because they're all hard-working, God-fearing folks, a microcosm of the finest America has to offer, when the new signs went up they had a new motto on them as well: WELCOME TO LITTLE TUCSON—HOME OF 8,034 FRIENDLY PEOPLE WORKING TOGETHER.

If you were just driving through, Little Tucson would look like a nice little town, like a million others you'll find across the good old U.S. of A. That was certainly true once.

But not anymore.

1

Monday, 8:19 a.m.

Burton Minnow walked toward the front of his shop, ready to unlock the door and flip the sign in the window around so it announced to the world that Minnow Printing was open for business. Eight-thirty in the morning until six in the evening, Monday through Friday, closed Saturday and Sunday.

Burt knew he was probably losing some customers by being closed on Saturday, what with the way folks did business on the weekends these days. Heck, he could probably open on Sunday afternoon for a while and a few people would come in to get something printed. But he'd been keeping the same hours for nearly forty years, and he was just too old to change his routine. Saturdays were for sleeping late and working around the house; Sundays meant going to church and then coming home to have dinner with his wife Justine, followed by a long, lazy afternoon of reading the big Sunday paper from Tucson and watching a little football or baseball on TV, depending on which season it was. Shoot, a man couldn't beat a day like that. A little extra business that might not even materialize just wasn't worth giving it up.

Burt had a push broom in his left hand, keys in his right. A few minutes earlier, he had parked his car behind the shop, as usual, and come in through the back door to turn the lights on. After he unlocked the front door, he would sweep off the sidewalk in front of the shop. Little Tucson was an old community, old enough so that it had real sidewalks that ran for five blocks along both sides of Main Street, and along some of the cross streets, too. Each business owner who had space in the buildings along Main Street was responsible for sweeping off his or her section of the sidewalk. Burt took pride in keeping his part clean, just as he took pride in doing a good printing job for a reasonable price.

He slid the key into the lock and turned it. He had already disarmed the alarm when he came in the back. Little Tucson might look like a throwback to the fifties and sixties in some ways, but the people who lived here were aware that those days were long gone. All the businesses had alarms; some of them even had bars on the windows. The old-timers like Burt didn't like it, but they had to face facts. The world was more dangerous than it used to be.

The lock snapped back and Burt pocketed his keys and pushed the door open, expecting to step out onto the sidewalk and exchange waves with Ignacio Guiterrez, who was usually opening up the barber shop across the street about this time, and Louly Parker, who worked at Brannon Auto Parts in the next block, just across one of the side streets.

Most days, Louly opened the auto parts store for Tom Brannon. Some folks might have speculated about a good-looking, young single woman working so closely with a married man, but not anybody who'd been around Little Tucson for very long. They all knew that Tom was still madly in love with his wife Bonnie, even after being married for thirty years, and Bonnie felt the same about him. They were almost like a couple of kids, frisking around the way they did, and Louly Parker, despite being twenty-five years old, tall, redheaded, and stacked, couldn't ever come between them even if she wanted to, which she didn't because she was a good church-going gal herself.

Burt didn't see Ignacio or Louly when he stepped out. The sidewalks up and down the street were pretty much deserted, in fact. Burt grunted. That was odd.

He stopped short, still clutching the broom, as movement to his left caught his eye. Turning in that direction, he saw two young Hispanic men, both around twenty years old, wearing dark T-shirts, baggy pants, and running shoes that probably cost more than Burt's first car. One of them held a can of spray paint, moving his hand back and forth so that the red paint formed an elaborate design on the big plate glass window in the front of Burt's shop. Burt hadn't opened the window blinds yet, so he hadn't seen what was going on.

"Good gravy!" he exclaimed involuntarily. "What are you boys doin'?"

They glanced at him, arrogant sneers on their faces, the tagger pausing for a second in his work before going back to it. The hiss of the paint leaving the can sounded loud in the hot, still, early morning air.

Burt took a step toward them, holding the broom with both hands now. "Do I know you boys?" he asked. "Are you from around here? You'd better quit that. It's already gonna be a chore cleanin' off all that paint."

He didn't think he had ever seen the two young men before. Little Tucson didn't have a lot of people moving in, but naturally the population changed some over time. It had been a long time since Burt had been able to say honestly that he knew everybody in town. Maybe these boys just didn't realize that folks in Little Tucson didn't go in for this sort of foolish vandalism.

As they continued to ignore him and the one with the paint kept spraying it on the window, Burt shook the broom handle at them without thinking about what he was doing. "Stop that now!" he said. "I don't want to have to call the sheriff on you boys, but I will if I have to."

The one who wasn't painting looked at Burt again and finally spoke. "Stick that broom up your ass, *viejo.*"

Burt just stared at him for a couple of seconds, shocked by what the youngster had said to him. Then he lifted the broom and took a step closer, saying, "Why, you—" He stopped before he used a racial slur. Even though he was mad, he wasn't going to do that.

The boy smiled and turned more toward Burt, pulling up the front of his T-shirt as he did so. Sticking up from the waistband of the baggy trousers was the butt of some sort of fancy pistol. Burt's eyes widened, and he knew suddenly that he had made a bad mistake. He had assumed that these boys were from around here and that he could handle them. Now he realized he was wrong.

They were *Mara Salvatrucha*—M-15.

Still smiling, the one with the gun pulled it out and fired three shots, *bam, bam, bam,* into Burton Minnow's belly. Burt had been in a few fights when he was a young man, and it felt like a giant fist had punched him three times in the stomach. He dropped the broom and doubled over as he staggered backward a few steps. He was in front of the door to his shop when he collapsed. The worst pain he had ever known in his life engulfed him as he lay there with his blood leaking out onto the unswept sidewalk.

With a final flourish, the tagger finished his design on the window. The shooter stuck the gun back in the waistband of his trousers. They grinned at each other, and the expressions made it clear that gunning down an old man in broad daylight, on Little Tucson's Main Street, meant little or nothing to them. They weren't worried about it.

No one tried to stop them as they sauntered away, turned a corner, and disappeared. Behind them, Burt Minnow forced his eyes open, too numb from loss of blood and impending death to feel much of anything anymore. His lips moved, forming his wife's name. Somewhere nearby, footsteps pounded on the sidewalk, people coming to help at last, but too late.

Much too late.

2

Tuesday, 3:35 a.m.

Madison Wheeler shifted a little in bed, unsure of what had disturbed him. Maybe his wife Cindy was in the mood for some lovin'. She got that way sometimes in the middle of the night, Lord knew why, but Madison sure as hell wasn't gonna argue with her. A fella could sleep anytime.

But Cindy wasn't snuggled against his back, reaching over his hip to fish around inside his shorts. In fact, she seemed to be sound asleep, lying on her left side facing away from him.

Now that he had been pulled up out of slumber, he knew he would have a hard time dozing off again. And since he was awake anyway, might as well take a chance . . .

He rolled toward her and pressed his groin against her comfortably wide rump, slipping his hand around at the same time to cup her right breast through the thin fabric of her nightgown. She stirred and wiggled her butt against him, not in a sensuous way but just getting comfortable. It had an effect on him anyway.

"Madison?" she murmured sleepily. "That you?"

"Who else?" he asked.

"Oh . . . you never know. It's hard for a girl to keep track of all her lovers."

They both chuckled. Madison rubbed his thumb over her hardening nipple. "You're a shameless woman."

"And you're a horny ol' goat."

"I am *not* old."

She made a purring sound and twitched her butt again, but this time it was deliberate. Madison told himself he was a lucky man tonight. Sometimes Cindy told him to quit pawin' her and go back to sleep. To tell the truth, she probably said no more often than she said yes under these circumstances, which was understandable because they had two kids, a boy in high school and a girl in junior high, and their activities kept Cindy pretty busy on top of her part-time job at the Alomar Real Estate office in Little Tucson, so naturally she was tired and needed her sleep at night. But Madison worked hard, too, keeping their ranch running and at least semi-profitable, and he knew that sometimes a little middle-of-the-night nooky was just as refreshing as sleep. So he was willing to risk being told no because the times that Cindy *did* say yes were so good they made everything else worthwhile.

She rolled over toward him and kissed him. He pulled up her gown and rubbed her thigh. Lord, how this woman made him want her! Despite their banter, there had never been anybody else for either of them ever since they had gotten married seventeen years earlier and he had brought her out here to live on the ranch he inherited from his parents. Madison didn't know if there were really such things as matches made in heaven, but this one had sure been made somewhere good.

He was just about to slip a finger under her panties when a zooming roar shook the house and made them both exclaim in unison, "What the hell!"

Madison sat up and threw the sheet back. He swung his legs out of bed and stood up while Cindy sat up and pulled her gown back down. "What in the world was that?" she asked.

He reached for his blue jeans, which he had left draped over the chair beside the bed. "Sounded like an airplane, and it was flyin' mighty low. It must've flown over earlier, a little higher, because somethin' woke me up and I'll bet that was it."

"You think it's having engine trouble?"

That engine had sounded fine to Madison, but he wasn't what you'd call an expert on such things. Some of his friends who owned ranches in the area had planes and swore they were invaluable for checking on the far reaches of their spreads, but Madison had never gone in for that, at least not yet.

"I don't know, but I'll go see," he told his wife. He sat down on the edge of the bed to pull socks and boots on, then picked up the shirt he had left lying on the floor and shrugged into it.

"Be careful," Cindy called after him as he headed for the door. She snapped on the bedside lamp. Madison waved without looking around as he left the bedroom.

The doors of the kids' rooms were open. The plane flying so low over the house must have spooked them, too. Justin asked from the door of his room, "What's goin' on, Dad?" while Danielle just looked worried.

"I don't know," Madison replied to his son's question, "but I'm gonna find out. Make sure that plane didn't go down somewhere close by."

"You want me to go with you?"

"No, just go back to bed. I don't expect this'll amount to much of anything. Plane's probably landed in Tucson by now."

It was true that he didn't hear the engine anymore. The plane must have flown on . . .

Either that, or crashed.

He hadn't heard a crash, but he might not have with the house closed up and the air conditioners running. To ease his mind about it—and because he knew Cindy would worry if he didn't—he'd go and have a look around.

Stopping briefly in his den, he took an old lever-action Winchester out of the gun cabinet and loaded it from a box of cartridges he fished out of his desk drawer. The rifle was darn near an antique, but it worked just fine, was accurate over a good long distance, and had plenty of stopping power. Not that he expected to need a weapon. Anybody who had grown up on the range as he had, though, knew that you didn't go pokin' around at night without taking a gun along.

As he walked through the kitchen toward the back door, he jumped a little as something cold and wet prodded the back of his hand. Then he laughed quietly and said, "Dang it, Skeeter, you like to scared me out of a year's growth."

In the dimness of the room he couldn't see the

dog, but he knew Skeeter's stub of a tail would be wagging a mile a minute. Skeeter was part blue heeler and part something else, one of those dogs that's so ugly you can't help but love him. He padded after Madison as the rancher went on to the door and said, "You want to come with me and see about that plane?"

By way of answer, Skeeter dashed outside when Madison unlocked the door and opened it. The mutt bounded toward the pickup and ran around it, always eager to take a ride.

"Hold on," Madison called to him. "I don't know if I'm goin' anywhere."

With the rifle tucked under his left arm, he walked toward the barn and the old windmill beyond it. The blades turned lazily in the night breeze, but they weren't connected to anything anymore. A modern pump kept the corral tank filled. Madison hadn't been able to bring himself to tear down the old windmill, though. His granddaddy had built it, many years ago.

Besides, if you wanted a vantage point where you could see anything in this mostly flat valley between the Sierrita Mountains and the Baboquivari Range, you had to have something to climb up on. Madison leaned the Winchester against the base of the windmill and went up the ladder.

He clambered onto the platform at the top, beside the gently turning blades, and gazed around. It was a dark night, with plenty of stars but only a thin sliver of moon. He saw the cluster of lights ten miles to the east that marked the location of Little Tucson. There were other lights scattered around over the mostly dark countryside, and Madison knew most of them, knew which of his neighbors' ranches was marked by which light. Back when he and Cindy had first been married, when money was tight, they had climbed up here a lot of evenings and spent hours looking around and talking. That was cheaper entertainment than driving into town and going to the show.

So it wasn't any problem for Madison to pick out the lights that weren't supposed to be there. They were moving through his south pasture, maybe two miles from the house. Headlights, no doubt about it. Something *was* going on down there.

And with a surge of anger, he decided that he was going to see what it was. Nobody had a right to be driving around his place in the middle of the night.

He climbed down, picked up the rifle, and opened the pickup door. Skeeter jumped inside without being told and moved over on the seat to let Madison slide behind the wheel. "Thanks," Madison said dryly. "I thought for a second there you planned on drivin'."

He started the truck and drove away from the house, catching a glimpse in the side mirror of the back door opening and light from the kitchen spilling out. He saw Cindy's silhouette as she stood there watching him drive away and wondered if she'd wanted to tell him something. It could wait until he got back, he supposed.

A dirt track led down to the south pasture. The pickup bumped over it. Despite the darkness, Madison drove without lights. He knew every foot of this ground and didn't need them. For some reason, he thought it might be important not to announce his presence until he found out what was going on.

A cattle guard rattled under his wheels as he crossed into the big, fenced pasture. This wasn't fertile country; it took quite a few acres to grow enough grass to feed his stock. He irrigated as much as he could from the branch of the Santa Cruz River that ran through his property, but a fella could take only so much water without causing his neighbors to do without. Madison was the sort of man who believed in looking out for his neighbors just like he did for himself.

The headlights were only a couple of hundred yards away now. They had stopped moving but still burned, even though the vehicle they were attached to had halted. The twin cones of brilliance reached out and washed over an airplane, a Cessna Caravan turbo-prop. Madison wasn't sure how come that information had popped into his head so readily. It took him a second to remember that his friend and fellow rancher Warren Hendrix had one just like it. This wasn't Warren's plane, though.

Men trooped back and forth in the glow of the headlights, moving between the plane and the automobile. Madison was close enough to see that it was a van now. He put the pickup in neutral, cut the engine, and coasted to a stop in silence.

Madison was not by nature a profane man, but as he stared through the windshield of the pickup, he breathed, "Goddamn M-fifteens."

Like everyone else in this part of the country, he had heard of *Mara Salvatrucha*, the deadly gang composed mainly of El Salvadorans and Guatemalans that had moved into the area along the U.S./Mexico border and taken over nearly all the illegal activity. An outgrowth of earlier, similar gangs, they were the worst of the lot so far, hundreds of the most violent criminal lowlifes to ever draw breath. Thieves, murderers, bank robbers, drug dealers, smugglers of illegal aliens, they took full advantage of the porous borders between the countries and went wherever they wanted, doing as they pleased and taking whatever struck their fancy. Little Tucson and the area around it had been spared the worst of M-15's depredations so far, but Madison Wheeler thought that might be changing. Just the day before, two men suspected of being members of the gang had shot and killed poor old Burt Minnow, right on the sidewalk in front of his printing shop in town. Now, those were members of the gang walking around Madison's south pasture, he was fairly certain of that, and they were unloading a huge shipment of drugs from the plane that had landed there, bringing the poison up from below the border.

How dare they! Fury filled Madison at the thought of these scum using *his* land this way. He picked up the rifle from the floorboard and then reached up to pop the bulb out of the dome light. When he opened the door, the light stayed dark. He slid out and Skeeter followed him, jumping to the ground. Leaving the pickup door open, Madison rested the Winchester's barrel on the sill of the rolled-down window. He reached into the cab and pulled the knob that turned on the headlights.

They blazed into life, stabbing out into the darkness and washing over both the plane and the van, as well as the men clustered around them. "Hold it!" Madison yelled as he levered a round into the chamber. "I'll shoot the first man who moves!"

He had the drop on them, sure enough. And at a range of fifty or sixty yards, he could carry out his threat. He was a fine shot with the old Winchester.

Sure, they outnumbered him by at least ten to one, but he had the element of surprise on his side.

Still, maybe he should have called 911 *first*, he thought as he glanced at the cell phone lying on the pickup seat. It was still within reach, but he was going to have to stretch to get it . . .

Suddenly, Skeeter growled furiously behind him.

Madison stiffened as a voice said in heavily-accented English, "I swear, sometimes I think you gringos are just too damn stupid to live. So, I kill you."

Madison tried to turn, but he was only halfway around when flame tore a gaping hole in the night. The banging of a million hammers filled the air as bullets spewed from the muzzle of an automatic weapon and slammed into the side of the pickup. Some of the slugs had ripped through Madison's body first, flesh and bone and blood not even slowing them down on their high-velocity path. Madison's body came apart under the terrible onslaught of lead like a giant bag of blood bursting at the seams. He died so quickly that he didn't have time to feel anything, which was probably a blessing.

More automatic weapons opened up as the gunners who had been posted on guard in the low-lying brush of the pasture tried to shoot the dog. Skeeter scooted under the pickup, which was still being hosed down by the M-15 killers. One of the bullets found the gas tank, and the vehicle suddenly exploded in a giant ball of fire. The flames consumed what was left of Madison Wheeler's body, which had slumped back through the open door against the front seat. The gunners laughed uproariously and traded quips about the man and his dog being barbecued like goats. They walked leisurely toward the plane and the van, where the work of unloading the massive drug shipment had resumed.

In the brush, Skeeter crawled along on his belly, his canine brain torn between survival and hatred for the men who had killed his master and friend. He had popped out from under the other side of the pickup just in time to escape the explosion, although he hadn't gotten away unscathed. His hindquarters were burned, much of the short gray and black hair being singed off by the flames. His legs still worked, though, so he had been able to make it into the brush without being spotted. Instinct kept him low as he crawled away.

He paused once, looked back, and whined. Then, as the wind carried the scent of the men to his nose, he snarled quietly, the sound low and full of hate.

He might be just a dog, but he knew pure evil when he smelled it.

3

The doors of the Little Tucson Savings Bank had just been unlocked for the day by Al Trejo, the security guard. Mrs. Ernestine Montgomery, eighty-eight, was waiting to come in, so Al held the door for her. Since it was the first of the month, he wasn't surprised to see her. Mrs. Montgomery always showed up on the first to go into the safe-deposit room and get some bonds out of her box, which she then cashed in and deposited into her account. She had been following that routine for years, and Al didn't expect her to stop any time soon. She was spry for her age and still drove all over the place. Drove better than a lot of younger people did, too, in Al's opinion.

"Good morning, Mrs. Montgomery," he greeted her.

"Good morning, Albert." She always called him that, and had ever since he was in her second-grade class at Little Tucson Elementary School, nearly forty years ago.

"Gonna be a hot one today."

"Yes, it certainly will. What do you expect from Arizona in June?"

Al laughed. "Yeah, you're right about that."

Mrs. Montgomery moved on toward the counter, and Al looked out the glass door toward Main Street. The bank building sat behind a small parking lot, rather than right up beside the street like many of the older buildings in town. It was a low, sprawling structure of beige brick, made to look sort of like old-fashioned adobe. A narrow cactus garden, enclosed in concrete curbs, divided the parking lot from the street.

Al liked working at the bank. After retiring from the Army—twenty years as an MP, and a damn good one if he said so himself—he had come home and worked for a couple of years as a deputy for Sheriff Buddy Gorman. Then this security guard job had opened up, and Al had taken it. He wasn't a young man anymore. Chasing around after bad guys over the whole county was a little more responsibility than he wanted. Making sure the Little Tucson Savings Bank stayed safe was more his speed these days.

Most of the time, the bank wasn't even very busy. Today would be a little different, being the first of the month. Quite a few retirees lived in and around Little Tucson, and they would be bringing in their Social Security checks to cash. A lot of people who got paid on the first would show up, too, especially at lunchtime and in the drive-through lanes later in the afternoon. Al didn't mind. More customers meant things wouldn't get boring.

Several more customers came into the bank. Al went behind his desk in the corner of the lobby and sat down. From there he could still see part of the parking lot, so he idly took note of the Ford Explorer that pulled up in one of the empty places. Two men got out while the driver stayed behind the wheel.

He should have noticed that, of course. Nine times out of ten, such a thing would have set off alarm bells in his head. But today he was thinking about the tragedy that had occurred out at the Wheeler ranch a couple of nights earlier. Madison Wheeler, who was a customer at the bank and had been a few grades behind Al in school, had been killed, and his wife and kids had barely escaped injury or even death when a van full of bastards had driven past their house and sprayed it with automatic-weapons fire. Cindy Wheeler, who would never be mistaken for a shrinking violet, had popped a few rounds after the van with a pistol, but she hadn't done any damage as far as she knew. She and Justin and Dani were staying in Little Tucson's lone motel at the moment, while the sheriff's department, the Border Patrol, and the DEA investigated the incident on the ranch.

That was a waste of manpower, in Al's opinion. He could have told all those hot-shot investigators exactly who was responsible for the atrocity—*Mara Salvatrucha.* Those M-15 sons of bitches were moving in on Little Tucson. Al hated them so much it made him sick to think that they shared the same Latin blood. Well, not exactly the same, he amended. They were from Guatemala and El Salvador for the most part, although they probably had some Mexicans working for them. Al's grandparents had been naturalized American citizens, and he was a member of the second generation of his family born north of the border. But he considered himself both American and Mexican—a citizen of the world, really, since he had traveled all over it during his Army years—and was proud of the heritage of both cultures.

So with all of those thoughts filling his head, especially his anger over what the M-15s had done to Madison Wheeler, and Burt Minnow before that, he wasn't paying as close attention to his job as he should have been and let two of the bastards walk into the bank right under his nose.

Carla May Willard glanced into the front seat of her red Nissan as she leaned over the car seat buckled into the back seat. "Andy!" she said as she saw her seven-year-old son scooting out of the car. "Get back in there!"

Her daughter Emily, who was fifteen months old, kicked and waved her chubby arms around, making it more difficult for Carla to strap her into the car seat. In exasperation, Carla blew back a lock of brunette hair that had fallen over her face. She finished tightening the straps so that Emily could ride safely. As she straightened from the task, pain twinged in her lower back. Damn it, she was only twenty-eight years old, she thought as she paused to rub her back for a second. She shouldn't have all these aches and pains yet.

That was what being a mother did for you, she supposed. Stole your youth and made you so tired you didn't give a damn about anything except getting through another day.

"Get in the car, Andy," she snapped as she opened the driver's door of the Nissan.

He had run off into the yard of the neat little

brick house. "I don't wanna go!" he called back to her.

"Well, you're going whether you want to or not, so get in here *right now*."

Andy was only seven, but he knew not to argue when his mother used that tone of voice. With an exaggerated sigh, he came over to the car, climbed through the open front door, and sat down hard on the seat.

"Close your door," Carla told him.

He slammed it and pouted.

"And buckle your seat belt."

"It's hard. I have trouble with it."

"Do it anyway." Carla started the car and checked the rearview mirror before she backed out onto the street. She caught a glimpse of her face. She was still pretty. Wasn't she? Her hair wasn't bad, and her body was still okay. You couldn't really tell she'd had two kids. Her husband Danny—ex-husband now—had been a fool to leave her. She could have made him happy. Well, it was his loss, she told herself, as she did at least half a dozen times a day. She had only been single for eight months. She would find somebody else. The fact that she was nearly thirty and had two kids and all the statistics she read in the women's magazines were working against her didn't matter. There was always Ray Torres, the owner of the insurance agency where she worked. She had seen him looking at her with interest in his eyes more than once. Of course, he was married, but she knew for a fact that he was having trouble with his wife and his marriage probably wouldn't last. Maybe she ought to give him a little encouragement, try to speed things up . . .

"We're gonna be late," Andy said.

"I thought you didn't even want to go."

"Yeah, but if you're gonna make me go to Bible School, I don't wanna be late."

"All right, all right, we're going." Carla backed from her driveway onto the street, then put the Nissan in drive and started toward the Little Tucson Baptist Church, which was about two miles away on the other side of town. She glanced at the clock on the dashboard. 9:15. Vacation Bible School started at 9:30. They had plenty of time to get where they were going.

The two men who walked into the bank were young, Hispanic, and dressed stylishly in baggy T-shirts and jeans. Al Trejo didn't really pay any attention to them until they walked past his desk toward the counter. He didn't remember ever seeing them in the bank before, and that brought a worried frown to his face. Al glanced through the glass of the front door at the Explorer the men had gotten out of. He saw the man behind the wheel and the faint ripple of heat rising from the engine.

The Explorer was still running.

There could have been other explanations, of course, but to Al's mind all the factors had come together and could mean only one thing—the bank was about to be robbed. He started to his feet, his hand reaching toward the holstered gun on his hip, his mouth opening to shout at the two young men.

They must have been keyed up, expecting trouble. One of them turned swiftly toward Al, reached under his shirt, and pulled out a compact machine gun. The weapon flared and sent a short burst stitching across Al's chest. The shout died in the security guard's throat, forever unvoiced. He was thrown backward by the impact of the slugs as they ripped through his lungs and pulped his heart, killing him almost instantly. His body hit the plate glass wall between the lobby and the office of Walt Lauderdale, the vice-president of the bank, and smashed on through it, showering glass down around him. Al never felt the shards cut him.

The second robber had his gun out now, too. He bounded over to the counter where a couple of tellers were working. Mrs. Montgomery stood in front of the counter with the bonds she was going to cash in and deposit. The robber elbowed her roughly out of the way, knocking her off her feet. Her eighty-eight-year-old hip shattered as it hit the tile floor, and she cried out in pain.

The robber leaned over the counter and stuck the muzzle of his automatic weapon in the face of Sheila Garcia, the older of the two tellers, and said, "Don't try nothin' funny, bitch, or I'll splatter your brains all over the place. Move back so you can't step on no alarm button."

The other robber, the one who had killed Al Trejo, leveled his weapon at Walt Lauderdale through the shattered glass and ordered, "Come outta there, man, unless you wanna die."

Walt did as he was told, walking shakily into the lobby with his hands held where the gunman could see them. The robber shouted, "Down on the floor!" He turned his attention to the handful of stunned customers who looked at him with expressions of mingled horror and sickness. "Everybody get down! On your bellies!"

At the counter, the other robber took a folded canvas bag from under his shirt and threw it at Sheila, who caught it instinctively. "Fill it up," he told her. "Nothing smaller than twenties." He took out another bag and tossed it to the other teller, Maria Esquivel. "You, too, bitch."

Maria tried to catch the bag but fumbled it. She reached down to the floor to pick it up, and while she was bent over her finger touched the button that set off the silent alarm. She was standing far enough back in her cubicle that she didn't think the robber would suspect she had triggered the alarm. As she straightened, her eyes touched the framed pictures that stood by her work station of her husband and her two babies. Lord forgive her if what she had just done cost those dear ones their wife and mother, she thought.

But these animals couldn't be allowed to get away. They had murdered Al Trejo, one of the nicest men Maria had ever met, and now they were looting the bank of its customers' hard-earned money. Somebody had to stop them.

Maria knew she had done all she could, though. She opened her drawer and began stuffing bills into the canvas bag while the M-15 brutes continued to wave their guns around and shout threats and obscenities.

Deputy Fred Kelso was in the sheriff's cruiser at the edge of town, waiting for travelers on their way through not to notice that the speed limit dropped right at the city limits. Not that Little Tucson was a speed trap or anything like that. The speed limit went from sixty miles per hour to fifty, which was not a significant drop. Now, if it had gone from sixty to thirty, say, *that* would be a speed trap.

But nobody seemed to be driving through this morning, and Fred was getting sleepy. He yawned and looked at the dashboard clock. 9:19. It was too early for anybody to be in much of a hurry to get anywhere.

The voice that came over the radio was loud and excited. The dispatcher, Cecil Rhodes—everybody called him Dusty, of course—had to be practically yelling into the microphone.

"Bank robbery!" Cecil yelped, forgetting all about codes and proper radio procedure in his excitement. "We got a bank robbery! Silent alarm, silent alarm!"

Little Tucson had two banks, the First State and the Savings Bank. Fred grabbed the mike, keyed it, and said, "Settle down, Cecil! Which bank?"

"The Little Tucson Savings Bank!"

That was at the other end of Main Street. Fred figured he could make it in two minutes. The cruiser's engine was already running. He slammed it in gear and hit his flashers as the tires peeled out. He left the siren off, though. No need to let the bad guys know he was coming.

"I'm on my way," he told Cecil. "Better call Buddy on the landline, just in case he ain't monitorin' the radio."

Sheriff Buddy Gorman would be at home by now, having worked an all-night shift. Buddy wasn't the sort of boss who dodged the hard shifts and kept all the cushy ones for himself. He took his turn, regular as clockwork.

Fred racked the microphone and concentrated on his driving. There wasn't much traffic on the streets of Little Tucson at this time of the morning, but there was some and the last thing he wanted to do was get into an accident on his way to the scene of a major crime. Little Tucson and vicinity didn't have all that many major crimes to start with.

Not until lately, anyway.

But there had already been two murders this week, and now the bank was being robbed. Had to be those bastards from M-15. If somebody had done something about the troubles along the border a long time ago . . . if somebody had tried to put a stop to the illegal activities of the earlier incarnations of the gang before it got so powerful . . . then the evil sons o' bitches might not feel they could waltz in anywhere and get away with whatever they wanted. The country hadn't seen such arrogance on the part of criminals since the days of Al Capone and his fellow mobsters.

It had taken Eliot Ness and the Untouchables to bring that crime wave under control. But if things had been then like they were now, Eliot Ness would have been reined in by the Feds and slapped with lawsuits by the ACLU. Capone would have laughed in the faces of the Untouchables, knowing that his victims were their own worst enemies because they had turned their fates over to a bunch of incompetent, uncaring bureaucrats who were more worried about political correctness than about right and wrong. Yeah, Eliot Ness would have been up a creek, all right.

But as Fred Kelso pressed down on the cruiser's accelerator and sent the powerful car rocketing along Main Street, he thought that maybe, just maybe, he had a chance to make a difference, just as Ness had done.

He entered the block where the Little Tucson Savings Bank was located at 9:24.

Thirty seconds earlier, Carla May Willard turned her Nissan onto Main Street. She saw flashing lights several blocks away and slowed down as she realized they were coming toward her. Even though Main Street was four lanes wide, two going in each direction, she pulled toward the sidewalk to give the emergency vehicle plenty of room. She couldn't tell yet if it was a police car, ambulance, or fire truck.

Then the lights turned sharply off to the left side of the road. They were on a police car, Carla saw, but it wasn't coming toward her anymore, so she sped up. She didn't want Andy to be late for Bible School, either, although it wouldn't be any big deal if he came in a few minutes later than the other kids, she supposed. Still, it never hurt to keep him happy, because if he was cranky he could make her life a living hell.

Two men came running out of the bank's front door and piled into a Ford Explorer just as Fred skidded the cruiser into the parking lot. He couldn't block both exits, so he slammed on the brakes and brought the car to a stop so that it slanted across the opening that would be easier for the Explorer to use. To get out the other way, the driver would have to back up awkwardly and avoid several parked cars.

Fred hoped the tactic would give him a slight advantage.

He caught only a glimpse of the robbers before they disappeared into the big vehicle with its darkly tinted windows. That was enough, though, to tell him that each man was carrying a canvas bag—and a gun. He hoped that nobody had gotten hurt inside the bank, but he knew he couldn't count on that. The members of M-15 were notorious for being trigger-happy. They shot first and didn't give a damn who got hurt. Fred knew he couldn't afford to take chances or give them any sort of break. He drew his sidearm as he threw open the door of the cruiser. Crouching behind the door, he aimed at one of the Explorer's rear tires and opened fire.

The Explorer's driver didn't try to back around and use the exit on the far side of the parking lot. Instead he got out of the space quickly and gunned the vehicle toward the deputy's cruiser. Fred kept firing, aiming at the windshield now as the Explorer came at him. He saw the glass spiderweb under the impact, but it didn't shatter. The driver twisted the wheel and sent the Explorer bumping over the curb and across the cactus garden toward the street. A tall saguaro went down under the impact of the Explorer's grill.

One of the robbers was in the back seat now, firing toward Fred as the Explorer turned broadside to him. The high-powered slugs slammed into the door of the cruiser but didn't penetrate it. However, the bullets knocked it back against Fred, and it hit him so hard he was stunned and lost his balance as he crouched there. He slid down to the pavement. His legs stuck out from under the cruiser door.

Bullets chewed into them, tearing flesh and breaking bone. Fred jerked and jittered and screamed as the rounds practically sawed his legs off at the thighs. The gunner quit firing as the Explorer's rear wheels bounced over the cactus garden and the powerful vehicle surged onto the street.

Fred slumped to the side, falling out from behind the car door. He didn't know if he had any bullets left in his service revolver or not, but he managed somehow to lift the heavy weapon, steady it with both hands and pull the trigger, as he felt himself losing consciousness. The gun blasted, so he tried again, operating purely on instinct now. Dimly, he heard the explosion of another shot.

Then he didn't hear anything. He had passed out from shock and loss of blood.

He had no way of knowing that his final bullet had struck the rear window of the Explorer, penetrated cleanly, zipped past the ear of the robber in the back seat, hit the headrest of the driver's seat, gone through that, and caught the driver in the back of the head, shattering his skull and boring on through to burst out the front in a grisly shower that coated the inside of the windshield with blood and brain matter. The man slumped to the side and turned the wheel as he did so, sending the Explorer rocketing straight at the sidewalk.

Carla let out a little cry of surprise as she saw the big vehicle suddenly careen over onto her side of the road. Instinctively, she slammed on the brakes to keep the Explorer from hitting her head-on. She knew her little Nissan would crumple like tinfoil in a crash like that. Andy yelled in alarm as he was thrown forward against the seat belt. Thank God she had forced him to buckle it.

In front of her, the Explorer jumped the curb, crossed the sidewalk, and slammed into a store-front that housed the office of a certified public accountant and notary public. The building's front wall collapsed around it in an avalanche of glass, broken masonry, twisted metal, and dust. Carla sat there in her stopped car, its engine still ticking over, and stared at the destruction. She wondered if the Explorer's driver had suffered a heart attack. Something had caused him to lose control of the vehicle. She reached for her purse, thinking she would get out her cell phone and call 911.

Before she could get her hands on the phone, two men came running out of the cloud of dust that seemed to envelop half the block. They carried bags and something else—guns, Carla realized with a shock. Their faces were streaked with blood from cuts they had received in the wreck.

And worst of all, they were running straight toward *her*.

Too late, she tried to throw the Nissan into reverse and get out of there. The men were already beside the car, waving their guns at her and yelling in Spanish. One of them yanked the back door open and jumped in. "Emily!" Carla shrieked. "Don't hurt my baby!"

The other man jerked the front passenger door open and shouted at Andy, "Get out!"

"Leave us alone!" Andy yelled back at him. "Mom! Mom! Do something!"

The man grabbed Andy's arm and twisted. Andy

cried out in pain. Carla said, "Leave him alone!" and leaned over to swat at the man.

He jammed the muzzle of the bulky gun he held against the side of Andy's head. "Tell him to get out, or I'll kill him."

Carla never would have guessed that she could be so scared, so consumed with horror, and still keep functioning somehow. She knew she had no choice but to cooperate. "Andy," she said, trying to keep her voice calm, "get out."

"But Mom—"

"I'll be all right, but you have to do like I told you and get out." She knew she *wouldn't* be all right. These madmen would likely kill her. But that would be fine as long as they didn't hurt her children. All her frustration, and her weariness were forgotten now. All that mattered was that her children survive this insane ordeal. As Andy shakily unbuckled his seat belt and started to get out of the car, Carla added, "Take your little sister with you."

"No time," the man said. He grabbed Andy again and pulled him out of the car, Andy yelling as he fell heavily to the sidewalk and rolled over a couple of times. The man lunged into the front seat, jabbed the gun toward Carla, and grated, "Drive!"

She took her foot off the brake, put it on the gas, and stepped down hard on it. The Nissan surged forward.

In the back seat, Emily wailed, not sure what was going on but able to tell that something was very wrong.

Carla's hands were so tight on the steering wheel she thought it might break in her grip. She knew the men had to be criminals of some sort, which meant she and Emily were now hostages. Hostages almost always died in these sorts of things, didn't they? But the ones who survived cooperated with their captors. She said, "I'll do anything you want, take you anywhere you want to go. Just don't hurt my baby."

"Shut up," the man in the front seat snapped at her. "Make a block and then go back east." He reached over and jerked the wheel in her hands. "Now!"

Carla spun the wheel and skidded through the turn. She made a block, turned again and then again, came back out on Main Street and headed east. In the rearview mirror, she saw smoke and dust and running people and flashing lights. She hoped the lights meant that the police were coming after her.

She drove fast but not recklessly. Main Street was also the highway that ran through Little Tucson. As Carla drove past the Baptist church, she saw the cars in the parking lot and knew that Vacation Bible School had started for the day. And Andy was late. She bit back a sob. She didn't want to annoy the gunmen by being weepy.

A cold ball of fear rolled around in her stomach. No one seemed to be following them. Was it possible that in all the confusion, the authorities didn't know that the two gunmen had carjacked her? Maybe nobody was even looking for her. Maybe no help was on the way.

No, that couldn't be. Andy would tell them what had happened. That is, he would if he could talk. He had been lying awfully still on the sidewalk the last time Carla had seen him. Maybe he had hit his head when the man threw him down and was knocked out. Maybe he was—

She wouldn't let herself think anything worse than that. She couldn't. She prayed that her son was all right. She hadn't prayed for a long time, not since the night Danny had walked out on her. That night she had gotten drunk for one of the few times in her life, and even though she knew it was wrong, she had asked God to smite the heartless son of a bitch. He had it coming for leaving her and the kids.

God hadn't answered that prayer, of course . . . or maybe He had answered it by leaving Danny unharmed. Carla didn't know. All she cared about now was that He answer this one by making sure that Andy and Emily were all right, no matter what happened to her.

They had left the town behind and were headed now for the Sierrita Mountains. Once they got up in the mountains, there were lots of little roads where the men could force her to turn off the highway. It got isolated in a hurry up there. No one would be around, no witnesses to whatever the men wanted to do.

The one in the back leaned over the seat and asked the inevitable question of the one in front. "You think we got time to fuck her?"

"Yeah, man, we make the time, fine piece o' gringa ass like this."

Carla's pulse hammered inside her skull. Of course they were going to rape her. She had known that in the back of her mind all along. They were criminals, evil men. They wouldn't hesitate.

"What about the little one?" the man in back asked.

Carla had to struggle mightily to keep from giving in to hysteria. Emily was just a baby. Surely even men as heartless as these wouldn't do anything sick to a little baby.

"We don't need her, man. Toss her out the window."

"No!" Carla screamed. The wheel jerked in her hands and the Nissan fishtailed back and forth across the road.

"Shit!" the man in front bellowed as he reached for the wheel, grabbed it, and brought the car back under control. He smacked the gun in his hand against the side of Carla's head. "You crazy bitch! I was jokin'! Nothin's gonna happen to your baby as long as you do what we say." He kept steering. "Now settle down, damn it!"

Carla took a deep breath and forced her frenzied nerves to cooperate. Her head hurt, and she felt a thin trickle of blood worm its way along her cheek from the little cut that the gun had opened up when the man hit her. "All right," she said. "All right. You know I'll do whatever you say. You don't have to threaten me, or hurt me or my baby."

"Okay." The man let go of the wheel. "The first side road you come to, turn off. My amigo and I wanna screw you. That all right with you?"

"Y-yes."

"Make her say it," the one in back put in.

"You heard him. Tell us what you want."

I want you both to die and burn in hell for all eternity!
Carla said, "I want you to . . . to screw me. Both of you."

"That's just what we're gonna do, baby."

A dirt road turned off to the left about a hundred yards ahead of the Nissan. Carla began to slow down. This was good, she told herself. In a bizarre way, it was a lucky break for her that the carjackers couldn't wait to rape her. They hadn't reached the mountains yet, so it was just possible that someone passing by on the highway might see her car parked on the dirt road and come to investigate. She told herself she was crazy for thinking there was even a chance, but the human mind was a stubborn thing. It refused to give up hope.

"Of course, after we're done with you, we may have to go ahead and kill you and the kid," the man in front added casually. "But you treat us nice and make us both happy, we will make it quick."

Carla's vision blurred as tears welled up in her eyes. There *was* no hope. She was going to die, and Emily was going to die, because no one would show up to save them. She turned onto the dirt road. She was going to her death, but she was too numb now to even do anything to try to stop it. In a matter of minutes—long, agonizing, degrading minutes— these beasts would be through with her, and they would kill her and Emily with as little thought or concern as stepping on an ant. How could this happen? How could the world be so cruel and unfair? Why weren't there any heroes left to come along and save the day in the nick of time?

Why?

4

On the CD player in the F-150's dashboard, Chris LeDoux sang about how the cowboy was still out there ridin' fences. "You just can't see him from the road," Tom Brannon sang along when the song got to that part.

He knew he couldn't carry a tune in a bucket. His wife Bonnie had told him that often enough. Brannon didn't care. He liked singing along with his favorite songs. But out of consideration for others, he confined it to the times when he was alone in the pickup.

He was east of town, driving toward Little Tucson. He had been out to see his folks, who still lived by themselves on the family spread at the edge of the Sierritas even though they were getting on in years. Herbert Brannon had to use a walker to get around most of the time now. His wife Mildred took care of him and wouldn't hear any talk about putting Herb in a home or some such foolishness like that. But her health wasn't as good as it had once been, either. Tom didn't know what he was going to do about the situation, but the time was coming when he would have to do *something*. He had a couple of older sisters, but one of them lived up in Flagstaff and the other over in California, in Bakersfield. He was the one still close to home, so he was the one who had inherited the job of looking after their folks. He tried to check in on them at least three times a week.

The spread wasn't a working ranch anymore, of course. All the stock had been sold off long ago. But it was home to Herb and Millie, and naturally they didn't want to leave it, even though it would have been easier on Tom if they lived closer to town. He had a business to run, too. Luckily, he had a good manager in Louly Parker and a couple of dependable part-time employees. They kept the auto parts store running pretty smoothly. Of course, business wasn't what it had once been. Ever since the Sav-Mart had moved in on the western edge of town, Tom's sales had declined. He had enough loyal customers to keep him going, though, at least until they all died off. When that happened . . . well, he could always go to work for SavMart himself. If they didn't need anybody in the auto parts department, he could stand at the door and say howdy to folks when they came in. He wondered idly if he ought to practice asking, "Need a buggy?"

That was when a flash of red caught his eye, and he noticed the little car parked on the dirt road, a couple of hundred yards north of the highway.

A frown creased Brannon's forehead. He saw a faint haze of dust hanging in the air along the dirt road. The red car had just driven along there and stopped within the last few minutes. Brannon had to wonder what the driver was doing out there. There was nothing around at that spot, no reason for anybody to stop.

Brannon kept his left hand on the wheel of the F-150 and in a habitual gesture ran his right hand over the close-cropped sandy hair that was starting to turn gray in places. He had kept the short haircut ever since he came back from Vietnam. It was simple, and Tom Brannon was a man who liked simple things. That was one reason he had never left Little Tucson except for a few years at the university in Tempe and his hitch in 'Nam. He was a small-town man, always had been, always would be.

And folks from small towns still looked out for their neighbors, even in this day and age when it seemed like nobody trusted anybody. Maybe whoever was in that little red car was having trouble. Wouldn't hurt to go take a look.

Brannon turned the F-150 onto the dirt road.

He was less than halfway to the car when he realized that he recognized it. He slowed to a stop. The car was a Nissan and had a distinctively shaped bumper sticker on the rear bumper. Even though Brannon couldn't read the words from this distance, he knew the bumper sticker came from the Torres Insurance Agency. The Nissan belonged to Carla May Willard. A week earlier, Brannon had sold her a bulb for her license plate light so the car would pass the annual safety inspection. He had gone outside the store and replaced the bulb for her, too, so she wouldn't have to fool with trying to do it herself. Just a friendly gesture. He liked Carla May, and there had been a time when it had looked like she would wind up being his daughter-in-law. She had dated his son Brian all through junior and senior year in high school and they had talked about getting married after they got through with college.

Of course, it hadn't worked out that way. Carla May—she had been Carla May Stevens at the time—had gotten mixed up with that no-account Danny Willard. Brannon could have told her that she was making a mistake. She would have been a lot better off with Brian, and that was just unbiased fact, not opinion. Young people had to work out these things for themselves, though. A couple of years later, Carla May had married Danny. She stuck it out for eight years, putting up with the drinking and the running around with other women that the whole town knew about, and likely she would have still been married to him if he hadn't up and left her.

When Danny left town, Brannon had thought about calling Brian up in Phoenix and sort of casually mentioning that Carla May was single again. In the end, though, he had decided not to meddle in his son's life. Brian would hear sooner or later that Carla May was divorced, and if he wanted to do something about it, he would.

Those thoughts flashed through Brannon's brain in a matter of seconds even though they had nothing to do with the question of what Carla May's car was doing parked out here in the middle of nowhere. It looked to be empty, yet it hadn't been there long. Carla May couldn't have gone very far.

Then Brannon's eyes, still very keen despite his fifty-four years, spotted movement inside the car. A little hand waved in the air in the back seat.

Good Lord! The baby's still strapped into her carseat, Tom thought. Now he *knew* something was wrong. Carla May would never go off and leave little Emily alone in the car like that. The day was already heating up. Kids died from being left in cars like that. Brannon gunned the F-150 forward.

He brought the pickup to a stop behind the Nissan and got out quickly. At least the windows were down in the car; that was something, anyway. Emily couldn't have gotten too hot already. She smiled up at Brannon as he reached in the open window and tickled a finger under her chin. "Where's your mama?" he asked. The car was empty except for the toddler.

"Gone wi' men," Emily gurgled.

Brannon looked in the front seat. His eyes narrowed as he spotted a small drop of red on the upholstery. Was that blood? His gut told him that something was very wrong here.

"What men?" he asked Emily. "Where?"

She stuck her thumb in her mouth and didn't answer. But she lifted her other arm and pointed.

Brannon turned toward a clump of paloverde that sat fifty or sixty yards off the dirt road. He knew there was a dry wash on the other side of the trees. The wash ran full of water every time it rained, and enough of that moisture was trapped under the ground to keep the trees alive.

"You stay here," he told Emily unnecessarily. The child couldn't get out of the carseat, so she wasn't going anywhere. Brannon stepped back to the F-150, reached into the cab, and took a tire iron out from under the seat.

He walked with long strides toward the paloverde trees and the dry wash beyond them. His pulse raced. He had seen his share of action in Vietnam, but that was a long time in the past. He was in good shape, always kept active, did plenty of hunting and fishing, and when his kids were young he had hiked with them all over this part of the country. He thought he could handle himself all right in case of trouble. But it had been a lot of years since he'd had any proof of that.

He worried about what he was going to find when he got to the wash. Carla May could have been kidnapped and brought out here by somebody who intended to rape and murder her. Brannon hated to think that such a thing could happen in this generally peaceful area he had always called home, but he wasn't wearing rose-colored glasses. This was an era in which bad things happened all the time, in just about any place you could think of. Why, just a few days earlier, members of that M-15 gang had killed two of Brannon's friends and customers. Louly had even witnessed one of the killings, just as she was about to open up the auto parts store. She had seen Burt Minnow gunned down in front of his printing shop.

There was just no telling what might happen these days.

Brannon stiffened as he neared the trees and heard sobbing. His hand tightened on the tire iron.

Moving quickly but silently, he glided into the trees, a big, fair-haired man, light on his feet for his size, maybe a little thicker through the middle than he had once been. He wore jeans and a faded blue shirt with the sleeves rolled up. He was about as common-looking a man as you could find. Stick him in a crowd and nobody would notice him.

There was no crowd out here now. Just Tom Brannon. Just one man.

He crouched near the edge of the wash and looked past the trunk of a paloverde. The wash was about six feet deep, with a relatively flat, sandy bottom. Carla May was sprawled down there with a man on top of her, his bare ass bobbing up and down as he pumped away between her thighs. A gun lay on the ground beside them. Brannon recognized it as a high-powered machine pistol, though he couldn't have said who the manufacturer was.

Another man stood over them, watching avidly. He had the same sort of gun in his hands. More than likely, he was supposed to be keeping a lookout, but he was too interested in what his friend was doing to Carla May. He didn't even glance toward Brannon.

Carla May still wore a short-sleeved blouse, but her captors had ripped the rest of her clothes off of her. She lay there stiffly, sobbing, as her attacker finished up. He pushed himself off of her and got to his feet a little shakily, leaving his gun lying on the ground. As he reached down to pull his jeans up, he said something in Spanish to the other one. Brannon was fluent in the language, and his jaw tightened in anger as the two men laughed at the vile comment. The second one set his gun down and reached for his belt, eager to undo his trousers and take his turn with their helpless victim.

This was the time, Brannon knew. Neither of them was holding a gun, but that wouldn't last very long. He had to *move.*

Coming up out of his crouch, he lifted the tire iron over his head in both hands and sprang out into the wash. He didn't yell or anything but rather attacked in silence. He drove the heel of his right boot into the small of one man's back and swung the tire iron at the other man's head.

That one turned and managed to fling an arm up to block the blow. The tire iron struck it solidly with most of Brannon's two hundred pounds behind the blow. The man's forearm snapped like a stick, breaking with a sharp crack. He screamed and staggered back.

Brannon landed awkwardly on the floor of the wash, stumbling a couple of steps before he caught his balance. He twisted around and saw that his kick had knocked the first man onto his hands and knees. Brannon lunged after him, slashing downward with the tire iron. The tool slammed into the man's side. Brannon hoped it broke some ribs. As the man collapsed, Brannon hit him again, aiming at his head this time. He fully intended to cave in the bastard's skull, but his aim was off a little and the blow was only a glancing one. It still landed hard enough to open up a gash and knock the man senseless.

Whirling, Brannon saw that the man with the broken arm had recovered enough to be going for the guns. Brannon was closer, though. He slung the tire iron at the guy, making him duck. That gave Brannon time to scoop up one of the guns. He hoped there was no trick to firing it, like some safety that was hard to find.

He didn't have to worry about that. The gun chattered and roared when he pulled the trigger.

It also nearly got away from him. He had to steady it with both hands. Dirt flew in the air near the feet of the man with the broken arm as a stream of bullets plowed a furrow in the floor of the wash.

The man reversed course with frantic agility to avoid running right into the torrent of lead. He scrambled toward the bank of the wash. Brannon hosed another burst after him but missed again. He grimaced. If he'd had his deer rifle or his old Army automatic, that son of a bitch would be on the ground with lead in him by now.

As it was, though, the man disappeared over the bank. Brannon went after him, reluctant to let him get away. But the man was sprinting toward the mountains, never looking back as he cradled his injured arm against his chest with his other hand. He was injured and unarmed, and Brannon decided that he was no longer an immediate threat. The way he was taking off for the tall and uncut, he looked like he might not stop until he got to New Mexico.

Besides, one of the scumbags was still here, and there was no telling when he might regain consciousness. Brannon had to do something about him.

And about Carla May, as well. She had scooted over to the edge of the wash and now sat there with her legs drawn up and her back pressed against the bank, watching Brannon with wide, horror-filled eyes. When he took a step toward her, she cried out and flinched. He realized that she might not recognize him.

"Carla May," he said in a quiet but urgent voice. "Carla May, it's all right. You know me. I'm Tom Brannon. Brian's dad, remember? I put a light bulb in your license plate light last week?"

She stared at him for a long moment. Finally, some of the blind terror faded from her eyes and was replaced by awareness. "M-Mr. Brannon?" she managed to gasp.

"That's right," he told her. "You're okay now, Carla May. Nobody's going to hurt you anymore."

Her eyes widened again. "Emily!"

"She's fine. She's still in the car. Might be frettin' a little by now, but she ought to be all right."

Carla May pushed herself unsteadily to her feet. Brannon made a point of not looking at her naked lower body. She turned and started trying to climb up the bank. He stepped to her side, grasped her arm, and helped her.

When she reached the top, she ran toward the car. Brannon let her go. She had to see for herself that her baby was all right. He picked up the second gun and the tire iron and quickly carried them back to the pickup. He left the guns there but kept the tire iron with him as he got a brand-new roll of duct tape out of the back and returned to the wash. The one he had knocked out hadn't regained consciousness yet, but he was starting to stir a little.

Brannon worked quickly. He used almost the entire roll of tape to bind the man's wrists and ankles. For good measure, he slapped a strip of it over the guy's mouth. If the bastard regained consciousness, Brannon didn't want to have to listen to anything he had to say. Then, grunting from the effort, he picked the man up, carried him over to the bank, and wrestled him to the top. Then he dumped him on the ground, took hold of his feet, and dragged him over to the F-150, not being gentle about it. The muffled sounds the man made told Brannon that he had come to and didn't appreciate being dragged over the rough, rocky ground.

Tough shit.

Carla May had gotten Emily out of the carseat

and stood next to the Nissan holding and kissing her and crying. Brannon lowered the pickup's tail-gate, lifted his prisoner, and rolled him into the bed. There was a fifty-pound bag of dog food in the back of the truck. Brannon picked it up and set it across the man's midsection. That would keep him from getting too feisty. With his mouth taped up like that and a fifty-pound weight on his stomach, he would have to work hard enough just to breathe. He'd be too busy with that to think much about trying to escape.

Brannon hopped down from the pickup and got a folded blanket from behind the seat. He went over to Carla May and wrapped it around her waist. "Come on back to the truck," he said. "I'll take you and the baby to town."

"M-my car . . ."

"It'll be okay out here until somebody can come out and get it."

Brannon put a hand on her shoulder and was glad to see that she didn't flinch. She had been through a hellish ordeal, but she was a strong girl, even if she didn't always make the wisest decisions. He thought she would be all right. He hoped that was so.

Before they got to the pickup, Brannon heard sirens. He looked toward the highway and saw a whole convoy of flashing lights speeding eastward from the direction of Little Tucson. A sheriff's car was in the lead, and someone inside it must have spotted the F-150 and the Nissan because the cruiser swung into the dirt road in a sharp turn that sent the back end drifting a little. The rest of the flashing lights followed.

"Something happen in town this morning?" Brannon asked.

Carla May shook her head. "I don't know."

Brannon looked at the approaching cars and said, "I reckon we're about to find out."

5

Buddy Gorman had this dream sometimes where he was outside, usually in the front yard of his house, and he heard an odd honking sound coming from the sky that made him tilt his head back and look up. He spotted something in the distance, like a dark smudge floating in the air, and as the noise grew louder, the smudge came closer, and then Buddy saw that it was a flock of ducks or geese or some sort of big birds, coming up from the south and headed north. Winter was over. There were so many the sky became black with them, and the honking was so loud that Buddy had to raise his voice so that his wife and kids, who were with him in the front yard, could hear him as he said, "They're going home. Look at that, they're going home."

This dream had really happened, years earlier when Buddy's children were young. There hadn't been so many birds that they blotted out the sun, of course, and their honking hadn't been quite so deafening in real life, but that was just how things got exaggerated when you dreamed about them later on. Buddy always felt good when he woke up after having that dream. It was like for a little while he had been transported out of himself, back to a happier time in his life. Not that he was unhappy now, but there had been something about those days, something that smacked of infinite possibilities . . .

He didn't feel good at the moment, dream or no dream, because the ringing of the phone had jerked him awake, and he always hated that. His hand shot out and grabbed the cordless off its base on the bedside table. He had it halfway to his ear before he came awake enough to realize that Jean was probably getting it elsewhere in the house. The phone rang again, though, so Buddy thumbed the button, brought it to his ear, and said thickly, "Hello?"

A moment later he was sitting up straight in bed, all the sleepiness jolted out of him by what he had just heard. A thin bar of sunlight came around the edge of the closed blinds over the bedroom window and slanted across the foot of the bed. Buddy squinted against the brightness and took a deep breath as he listened to Cecil Rhodes babble. Finally he said, "Take it easy, Dusty. I'm on my way."

He broke the connection before the agitated dispatcher could say anything else. As he stood up he reached for his pants.

By the time he walked into the kitchen three minutes later, fully dressed except for the top couple of buttons on his shirt being undone and the gunbelt he carried in his left hand, Jean had a cup of coffee ready for him. As she handed it to him, she said, "You got, what, an hour's sleep?"

"Maybe," Buddy said. "I'll be all right, though."

"I saw it was the office on the caller ID, that's why I didn't pick up. What's wrong?"

Buddy took a sip of the coffee and then set the cup on the kitchen table. As he buckled on the belt and its holstered service revolver, he said, "Bank robbery. Shots fired."

Jean's blue eyes widened. "You're kidding!"

"Wouldn't kid about a thing like that, honey."

He picked up the coffee to take with him. As he turned toward the door she caught hold of his arm for a second and looked worriedly at him. "Be careful."

He nodded and said, "Always am." Then he leaned over and brushed a quick kiss across his wife's lips.

He snagged the ball cap from the hook beside the back door as he went out. A lot of lawmen in the Southwest wore Stetsons, if they wore any sort of hat at all. Buddy Gorman wore a Cubs cap because he had been born in Chicago and lived there until he was in the eighth grade, when his family had moved to Arizona. He was still a Cubs fan, just like he still had a bit of a Chicago accent despite living down here for a lot of years.

A tall, lanky man with graying dark hair, he pulled the cap on his head and walked quickly to the sheriff's car parked in the driveway next to the house. He put the coffee cup in the holder on the console, started the car, and backed out. As soon as he hit the street, he had the lights and siren going, and his foot was heavy on the gas.

He'd tried to keep his tone light with Jean, but from the sound of what Dusty had told him, this was bad, really bad. The silent alarm had gone off at the Little Tucson Savings Bank, and Fred Kelso had been on his way to respond. Dusty didn't know what had happened after that, but citizen reports began to come in of shots being fired and a big wreck on Main Street and—Lord have mercy!—an officer down. That could only be Fred, and despite the fact that the temperature was in the nineties already and not even ten o'clock yet, Buddy Gorman felt the cold touch of fear in his gut.

The Sierrita County Sheriff's Department was small—Buddy himself, two full-time deputies, Fred Kelso and Wayne Rushing, four reserve deputies, and a couple of volunteer dispatchers. Their responsibilities covered the entire county, including the town of Little Tucson, which had a constable but no police department. The town contracted with the county for law enforcement and emergency services.

Because of that smallness, the members of the department felt a special bond with each other, like they were family as much as coworkers. Buddy would have been worried about Fred even without that, of course, but Fred was almost like a little brother to him. Still a little raw at the job, maybe a bit too gung ho at times, but with all the makings of a good cop.

And according to the reports, he was down, maybe wounded. Maybe dead. Buddy didn't know.

But he would soon, because he was getting close to the bank. He swung the car around a corner into Main Street.

His foot hit the brake, bringing the cruiser to a screeching halt as he saw the back end of a Ford Explorer sticking out from the ruined front of Hank Becerra's accounting office. That would be the bad wreck Dusty had told him about. A county ambulance was already on the scene, red lights flashing brightly even in the brilliant sunshine. A couple of EMTs knelt on the sidewalk next to a young boy who sat there crying. Buddy didn't recognize the kid right away.

He left the engine running and jumped out of the car. As he hurried over to the boy and the two paramedics, he called, "What happened?"

Before either of the EMTs could answer, the boy looked up at Buddy and yelled, "They took her! They made her drive off with them!"

The boy had quite a bit of blood on his face from a gash on his forehead. As he tried to scramble to his feet, one of the paramedics took hold of his arm and forced him to remain seated on the concrete sidewalk. "Take it easy, son. That's a pretty bad knock you got on the head."

Buddy leaned over, resting his hands on his knees, and asked, "Who are you talking about, son?"

"My mom! The guys who wrecked that truck! They took her and my baby sister!"

Hostages, Buddy thought, and the coldness inside him grew even chillier. Even without knowing the details, he could make a good guess as to what had happened. The guys in the Explorer must have robbed the bank. They were fleeing when they wrecked, so they grabbed the first car to come along and forced the driver to help them escape. This boy's mother had been in the wrong place at the wrong time.

"What's your name, son?"

"A-Andy."

"What's your last name?"

He sniffled. "Willard."

"And your mother?"

"C-Carla Willard. Carla May, some people call her."

Buddy kept his voice calm and level. "And you say your sister is in the car, too?"

Andy Willard nodded. "Y-yeah. Her name's Emily. She's in a carseat."

"How many men were there?"

"T-two, I think. That's all I saw. One of 'em grabbed me and threw me out of the car."

"What kind of car is it?"

"It's red." He had to stop to think. "A Nissan. A little one. That's all I know."

Buddy squeezed his shoulder. "Thanks, Andy. You've been a big help. You let these nice paramedics take care of you now, all right?"

Andy nodded shakily.

"One more thing," Buddy said. "Those two guys . . . did they have guns?"

Andy's head bobbed up and down. "Uh-huh. Big guns. Like pistols, but funny-looking."

Buddy could only guess the kid was talking about automatic weapons. That didn't surprise him. These days, the bad guys had more firepower than the cops.

As Buddy straightened, Andy sobbed loudly and said, "I'm late for Bible School."

Aren't we all? Buddy thought.

One of the paramedics stood up and said quietly to him, "There's one in the Explorer. The driver."

Buddy nodded. "Anybody hurt in the building?"

"Nope. They were all lucky. The Explorer took out one of the secretary's desks when it came through the wall, but she was in the back of the office making some copies when it happened."

There was that to be thankful for, Buddy told himself as he moved closer to the Explorer, stepping over some rubble so that he could glance through the driver's side window. The glass was shattered. He saw the figure slumped over the steering wheel. The guy's head was a bloody mess. Buddy couldn't tell if the injury had been caused by the wreck or by something else. That would be determined later. For now, the most important thing was that the guy was dead.

So there had been three of them. A wheelman and two who went into the bank. Those two had survived the crash and carjacked Carla May Willard.

Buddy hurried back to his car. As he drove toward the bank a couple of blocks away, he got on the radio and told Dusty to find out the license plate number of a red Nissan belonging to Carla May Willard and then get out an APB on it.

There was an ambulance in front of the bank, too, as well as a fire truck. Two paramedics were about to load a gurney into the back of the ambulance. Buddy jumped out of his car and hurried over to see who they had.

His jaw tightened at the sight of Fred Kelso's pale, drawn face above the sheet that was pulled up to his neck. At least the sheet wasn't over his face. He was still alive.

"Whattaya got?" Buddy asked the paramedics.

"His legs are shot to hell, Sheriff," one of them replied. "He nearly bled out before we got here and got him stabilized. Doesn't look like he was hit in the body, though, so he's got a chance."

Buddy nodded curtly. "Take good care of him. I don't suppose he said anything?"

The EMT shook his head. "He was out cold when we got here. He may not ever wake up, Sheriff."

Buddy didn't want to think about that. He turned toward the door of the bank.

When he stepped inside, he saw that Wayne Rushing, his other full-time deputy, was already there. Buddy hadn't seen Wayne's car outside, but Wayne lived only a few blocks away. He could have run over here on foot when he heard the shooting. He was supposed to be off duty right now, and in fact he wore a pair of blue jeans instead of his uniform trousers. He had his uniform shirt on, though, and a Stetson cuffed to the back of his head. He was talking to some of the bank employees, who huddled together, still in shock.

Buddy stopped at the sight of a body lying on the tile floor. Someone had thrown a suit jacket over the man's head and shoulders. Buddy's teeth grated together as he recognized the security guard uniform—Al Trejo. From the blood on the front of his shirt and the way he wasn't moving, Buddy knew he was dead.

Buddy had to close his eyes for a second. Al had worked for him as a deputy. They had been close, still got together for a beer fairly often, and they'd been planning to go hunting together in the fall.

Now Al would never drink another beer. Buddy would never hear his boisterous laugh again. Rage filled the sheriff. What sort of bastards could have done this?

He thought he knew the answer.

"Get me up to speed, Wayne," he snapped as he

went over to the deputy, carefully walking around Al Trejo's body on the way.

Quickly, Wayne laid out the information he had already gathered from the witnesses. It had played out pretty much like Buddy suspected. Two men— young, Hispanic, strangers to Little Tucson—had walked into the bank while a third man had stayed outside in the vehicle. Al must have suspected something, because he had jumped to his feet and reached for his gun. One of the bastards shot him. Then the two of them cleaned out the bank. The people who worked in the bank weren't sure what had happened outside. They hadn't seen it, but they had heard a lot of shots.

That would have been Fred trying to apprehend the robbers, Buddy knew. He wondered if the autopsy on the dead man in the Explorer would find a bullet somewhere in him. Buddy found himself hoping that was the case. He hoped that Fred had gotten off at least one good shot before he was gunned down.

The radio clipped on Buddy's belt crackled. Dusty Rhodes said, "Got a report of a red Nissan matchin' the description of Miz Willard's goin' east out of town about fifteen minutes ago, Sheriff."

Buddy acknowledged. He looked around and saw that one of the reserve officers had come into the bank. "Make sure this scene stays secure, Luis," he said to the man. "Come on, Wayne."

They hurried out of the bank. The other three reserve officers had just pulled up in their cars, civilian vehicles that had portable flashers set on top of them. Buddy pointed to one of the reserves. "Inside with Luis, Harry. Francisco, Lauren, follow

Wayne and me. We're looking for a red Nissan that headed east out of town a little while ago."

"You want one of the ambulances to come along, too, Sheriff?" Lauren Henderson asked. She had been a police officer in Phoenix before moving down here and was one of the more experienced members of his force. Buddy would have liked to have her as a full-time deputy, but she didn't want to be more than a reserve.

"What about the one down at Becerra's?" he asked.

"The kid's okay. They're not going to transport him to the hospital, even though he'll need to have a doctor examine him later. They can come along."

Buddy nodded. "Let them know and then follow the rest of us."

Lauren hurried off to take care of that. Buddy asked Wayne if he had his car here, and when the deputy shook his head no, the sheriff said, "Ride with me, then."

Within moments, they were out of town, traveling at high speed toward the Sierrita Mountains. When Buddy glanced in the rearview mirror, he saw that not only were the two reserves' cars and the ambulance following him, but one of the fire trucks was, too.

That was all right, he supposed. There was no telling what they would find out here.

He just hoped Carla May Willard and her baby were still alive.

6

Tom Brannon was relieved to see the sheriff's car in the lead of the little convoy. He and Buddy Gorman had been friends since high school. Buddy had moved to Little Tucson from Chicago, and it had been quite a shock for him, going from a huge, bustling city in the Midwest to a small, sleepy town not far from the Mexican border. He'd had a hard time fitting in if Tom Brannon hadn't spotted him reading a Doc Savage paperback on their first day of freshman year. Tom loved Doc, so they had struck up a friendship. The fact that Tom was an athlete and well-liked had opened a lot of doors for Buddy. He had wound up one of the most popular kids in school—despite the fact that he wouldn't give up that darned Chicago Cubs cap.

They had been in the Army together, had watched each other's back in 'Nam, and had come home together, Buddy to join the sheriff's department as a deputy, Tom to work on the family ranch and then later open up the auto parts store on Main Street. As

Buddy got out of his car and hurried toward the pickup, Tom felt like everything would be all right.

"Mrs. Willard, are you okay?" Buddy asked immediately.

She jerked her head in a nod. "My boy," she said. "Andy? Is he—"

"He's fine," Buddy told her with a smile. "Got a cut on his head, and you'll need to let a doctor take a look at him to make sure there's nothing the paramedics missed, but he ought to be fine. He told us what happened. That's a good boy you've got."

"I . . . I know. Sometimes I forget, but . . . I know." Carla May started to cry again.

Buddy looked a little wall-eyed, Tom thought. Like most men, he didn't quite know how to deal with a sobbing, wailing female. He motioned for Lauren Henderson to take over. She put an arm around Carla May's shoulders and gently led her toward the ambulance, where the paramedics could check her out.

Quietly, Tom said to Buddy, "They'll need to do a rape kit on her. One of those bastards was just finishing up when I got here."

Buddy nodded. "Poor gal. That'll mean an HIV test and all that worry, too." He rubbed his chin. "Speaking of those bastards . . . where are they? And how are you mixed up in this, Tom?"

He answered the second question first. "Just an innocent bystander. I was driving into town from my folks' place and saw Carla May's car parked out here. I didn't recognize it at first, but I thought something might be wrong, so I drove up here to check."

"Always got to be the Good Samaritan, don't you?" Tom shrugged, and jerked a thumb over his shoulder. "It's mighty lucky for Carla May that I was. One of 'em's in the back of my pickup." When Buddy moved his hand toward the butt of the revolver on his hip, Tom went on, "He's not going anywhere. Got a fifty-pound bag of dog food on top of him."

Buddy smiled faintly. "That'll work. What about the other one?"

"Gone," Tom said with a shake of his head. "I hated to let him get away, but I had Carla May to think of. Also, I'd knocked out the other one and figured I'd better get him trussed up while I had the chance. Didn't want him comin' to and jumping me."

"No, I'd say you did the right thing. How'd you knock him out?"

"Tire iron. Used it to bust the other one's arm, too."

Buddy frowned at him. "You know, from what I've heard, those fellas were armed with automatic weapons."

"Yeah." Tom opened the door of the F-150. "There they are. I picked 'em up and put 'em on the seat. Figured you'd need them."

The sheriff stared at the machine pistols for a long moment and then shook his head. "You went up against a couple of stone killers packing that much firepower with just a tire iron?"

"Well, I'd have preferred a cannon, say, but the tire iron was handy."

Buddy Gorman laughed. "I never have been able to decide if you're the bravest man I know, Tom, or the biggest damn fool."

Tom looked at the prisoner in the back of the

pickup. "What did they do, besides kidnapping and raping Carla May?"

"Robbed Little Tucson Savings." A grim look came over Buddy's face. "They killed Al Trejo, and shot up one of my deputies, too."

Brannon felt heartsick. "Damn it, Buddy."

"I know."

"I guess it was Fred Kelso who got shot, since Wayne's here with you."

"That's right."

"How is he?"

"Don't know," Buddy said. "He was hit pretty bad, but the paramedics seemed to think he has a chance."

"Lord, I hope so." Tom glanced toward the back of the pickup. "I'm startin' to wish I'd bashed the guy's head in, like I thought about doing."

"It's a good thing you didn't. We'll need him to testify. Plus you might have gotten in trouble for doing something like that."

Tom's eyes narrowed. "You mean *I* could get in trouble for busting the skull of a murdering, bank-robbing rapist?"

"Yeah, it's a hell of a note, ain't it? But you know things aren't like they used to be, Tom. The criminals have all the rights now, not the victims."

Tom Brannon just shook his head.

Wayne Rushing and Francisco Montero hauled the taped-up killer out of the back of Brannon's pickup and put him in the rear seat of the sheriff's car. Buddy said, "Follow us on into town, Tom. You'll have to make a statement."

"Sure. Louly can handle things at the store until I can get there."

"You may have more things to worry about than working at the store."

"How do you figure?" Tom asked with a frown.

"You're going to be a hero. You captured a bank robber and killer and rescued a woman. Gonna be lots of spotlights focused on you for a while, pal."

"There's no need for that," Tom insisted.

"But that's the way it'll be, like it or not. The worst of it, though, is the fact that the fella there probably belongs to M-15."

Brannon's eyebrows went up. "That gang from below the border?"

"They're not below the border anymore," Buddy said. "They're here, and after today, they're gonna have one hell of a grudge against you, Tom."

Enrique Colon tried not to let his face reveal just how much pain he was in. A doctor had set his broken arm and put a cast on it, but it still hurt like *El Diablo*. He had asked for something to ease the pain, but the doctor had refused, saying that Señor Montoya wanted to talk to him while his brain was still clear. Enrique didn't know how clear his brain really was at the moment. How could any man think straight when he hurt so much?

Two men came into the back room of the cantina where Enrique waited. One of them motioned curtly for him to stand up. He got to his feet, swallowing hard as he did so. He didn't know the men's names, but he recognized their faces and the black T-shirts and black jeans they wore. They were Señor Montoya's personal bodyguards and assistants. His *segundos.* Both were lean and dark-faced and moved with the easy, deadly grace of jaguars.

Enrique had good reason to be afraid of jaguars. One had nearly gotten him when he was just a boy back in El Salvador, near the village where he had grown up. It would have if he hadn't been just a little faster on his feet than his younger brother . . . Sometimes, even after more than twenty years, he woke up at night sweating because he thought he could still hear Pablo's screams.

"Upstairs," one of the men grunted as they led Enrique out of the back room. He went with one of them in front of him and the other behind. They made him nervous, and he wished he was anywhere else now, instead of in this cantina in Nogales, just across the border from Arizona.

The thumping beat of the music from the main room penetrated easily, even back here in the rear of the building. So did the thick, cloying smell of marijuana smoke. The customers smoked pot openly, and so did a lot of the cantina's employees. They all knew the law wouldn't bother them. This place belonged to Ernesto Luis Montoya, and what little law there was in Nogales knew perfectly well that they were to steer clear of it.

When the three men reached the top of the stairs, they found themselves in a short hallway that ended in a heavy wooden door. Thick and dark with age, the door looked like something that might have been found in an old mission, established hundreds of years ago by the stubborn priests who first brought European civilization to this raw, savage land. One of the jaguar-men, as Enrique thought of them, reached and clasped the brass handle on the door. He pulled it open and motioned with his eyes for Enrique to go inside.

Swallowing again, Enrique did so. The jaguar-men moved into the room behind him. The door closed with a solid thump, and to Enrique's surprise, he could no longer hear the music. The marijuana smell was gone, too, dispersed by the ceiling fan that turned lazily overhead.

The room was dim, with dark paneling on the walls and thick drapes over the windows that completely shut out the afternoon light. It might as well have been midnight outside. Enrique blinked as he waited for his eyes to adjust. His arm still hurt, but his nervousness kept him from thinking about it too much. For the first time, he had been summoned to a meeting with Señor Montoya, the leader of *Mara Salvatrucha.* He didn't like the feeling very much.

The room was expensively furnished, with heavy, overstuffed chairs and thick carpets on the floor. On one side of the room was a huge desk. On the wall behind it were computers and screens, so much equipment that it looked to Enrique like the control room of a spaceship like in *Star Wars.*

A giant-screen television was across from the desk, with big speakers around it. A home theater, they called it. Enrique knew there was a powerful satellite receiver on the roof of the cantina. Señor Montoya could watch anything he wanted, from anywhere in the world. The big TV was dark at the moment, though, as were the computer monitors. The only light in the room came from a shaded lamp on the desk. The man sitting behind the desk leaned back in his big leather chair so that the light from the lamp fell only on his legs. His torso and his head were in the shadows. Enrique could make them out in the reflected glow, but not clearly.

"Enrique Colon," a deep, powerful voice said. Like the voice of God must sound, Enrique thought. Or maybe the Devil.

"Si, Señor Montoya," Enrique said quickly, eager to please.

"Tell me what happened in Little Tucson."

"We . . . we went there to rob the bank, as you instructed, Señor." He wished he didn't seem so tentative. That looked bad in front of Señor Montoya. "Armando stayed in the car. Porfirio and I went into the bank. The guard realized what we were about to do, so I shot him." There was a note of pride in his voice. He wanted Señor Montoya to think that he was a bad hombre, a ruthless killer. In point of fact, it had been Porfirio who had gunned down the security guard, but Señor Montoya didn't have to know that.

Enrique paused, thinking that perhaps Señor Montoya would tell him that he had done well, but instead the man behind the desk just said, "Go on."

"We got the money, and we ran out to the Explorer, but one of the bitch tellers must have triggered an alarm somehow. We should have killed them all, first thing."

"It's too late for that now. What happened?"

"A police car came up and blocked the exit. Armando drove over the curb and through, like a cactus garden, you know . . . Anyway, the policeman was shooting at us, so we shot back at him. I'm sure we killed him."

"Then why didn't you get away successfully?"

The icy-voiced question made Enrique want to squirm. It was amazing how Señor Montoya could make someone feel like that. Enrique was a tough man. He had raped his first girl at twelve, killed his first man at fourteen. He had killed at least a dozen since then, and he couldn't even count all the women he had raped. Yet just a few words from Señor Montoya could make the blood in his veins turn to ice.

"The policeman, he must have made a lucky shot. Armando was hit in the back of the head. It killed him instantly, and he wrecked the Explorer. Porfirio and I had to grab another car to get away. A woman came along with her kids, so we made her drive us."

"An attractive woman?"

"Very attractive, Señor." Enrique couldn't keep a boastful note from creeping into his voice. "After we got out of town, we stopped to rape her. She cried out in passion when I fucked her."

That was another lie, of course; the woman hadn't made a sound other than an occasional whimper.

Señor Montoya said, "Let me get this straight. You stopped to rape this woman only a few miles out of Little Tucson, with two bags of money in the car and the authorities perhaps on your trail?"

"There was nobody chasing us, Señor. We were certain of that, otherwise we never would have stopped. And we planned to kill the woman and take her car as soon as we were through with her."

"Then what happened to prevent that?"

"This gringo," this crazy gringo, he came out of nowhere, and he hit me with something that broke my arm." Enrique touched the cast and winced, although truthfully the arm didn't hurt any worse now than it had before. "Then he hit Porfirio in the head and probably killed him."

"You don't know?"

Enrique shook his head. "I'm sorry, Señor, but I had no chance to help him or to stay and make sure he was dead. The gringo, he got hold of Porfirio's gun, and he almost shot me. I barely escaped with my life."

"But you didn't escape with the money." The accusatory words stung like a lash.

Señor Montoya's eyes seemed to glow in the shadows.

"No, Señor," he said. "I could not get back to the car, where the money was. As I said, I barely escaped—"

"Yes, with your life, I know." Finally, Señor Montoya leaned forward so that the light fell on his face. It was a handsome face in a way, with rugged, powerful features below thick, dark hair, the cheeks faintly pitted from some childhood illness, the eyes dark and deep-set and blazing. What Enrique saw in those eyes made him shudder, and he knew in that moment why people sometimes called Señor Montoya *El Babania Comida*—the Eater of Babies. At this moment, he looked like he was fully capable of making a meal out of an infant.

Just like a jaguar that stole out of the jungle to bring death and terror to those unfortunate enough to cross its path.

"And what makes you think," Montoya went on, "that your life is worth more to me than the money you ran off and left behind, Enrique?"

Struggling to find his voice, Enrique said, "Señor,

I . . . I apologize. I know it was wrong to lose the money—"

"It was wrong to leave Porfirio behind, too. If he is alive, he can testify against us. I don't fear the American law, but I don't like needless complications."

"Señor, Porfirio would never—"

"And there is the woman you kidnapped, too," Montoya went on as if Enrique had not spoken. "And this crazy gringo who attacked you. They are all what the Americans call loose ends." Montoya shook his head slowly. "I don't like loose ends, Enrique. What should I do with them?"

Enrique gulped. "C-cut them off, Señor?"

"Exactly." Montoya leaned back again. "You, too, are a loose end." He nodded to his *segundos.*

Enrique cried out in pain as the jaguar-men grabbed him. The one on his right jostled his broken arm. Enrique screamed even louder. No one outside this soundproofed room would hear him though.

Montoya got up, his movements sleek and unhurried. He opened a drawer in the desk and took out a machete. Enrique could tell by looking at it that the blade was razor-sharp. He writhed and struggled, but especially with his broken arm, he was no match for the animal strength of the two men who held him.

"You made a mistake, Enrique," Montoya said as he came around the desk. "And mistakes cannot be tolerated."

He plunged the machete into Enrique's throat and with a swift, incredibly powerful downward stroke cut the man open from neck to nuts. Enrique lived long enough to scream again and watch in horror as his bloody insides slopped onto the carpet. Darkness closed in around him.

Montoya shook his head slowly. "Such a mess," he said. "I really should learn not to give in to these impulses. Now the carpet may have to be replaced."

His two men stood there, stolid, silent, still clutching the arms of the eviscerated thing that barely looked human now.

"Take that out of here and get rid of it," Montoya snapped. "Then send someone to Little Tucson. I don't want any of those witnesses talking. Shut them up. If necessary, they are to be killed." He paused, thinking momentarily about the crazy gringo Enrique had mentioned. Montoya had to wonder about a man like that. What gave him the *cojones* to attack two well-armed killers, just to protect a woman? It might be interesting to talk to such a man . . .

Montoya said, "That's all," and his men left the room, dragging what was left of Enrique Colon.

7

Considering that there could have easily been a massacre inside the Little Tucson Savings Bank, Buddy Gorman thought the town had gotten off relatively easy. Al Trejo was dead—and that fact still broke Buddy's heart—while Fred Kelso was seriously wounded and his condition still weighed on Buddy's mind. The doctors at the Sierrita County Hospital gave Fred a fifty-fifty chance of surviving. There was some discussion about taking him by helicopter to a larger hospital in Tucson or Phoenix, but after a video consultation with doctors there, it was decided to leave him be since he was stable and the local doctors were doing everything that they could. He was still in a coma and had not regained consciousness since the bank robbery early that morning.

Mrs. Montgomery had a broken hip and would be laid up for a long time. A doctor had checked Andy Willard and pronounced that except for the cut on his head, he was fine. There was no sign of concussion. His mother Carla was bruised and shaken up, of course, but the damage to her had been more psychological and spiritual than physical—other than the threat of AIDS or pregnancy.

Tom Brannon was fine, not a scratch on him from his encounter. Buddy still had to shake his head when he thought about Tom jumping those two bastards with only a tire iron for a weapon.

Tom was waiting outside Buddy's office now, sitting on one of the plastic chairs in the hall with his wife Bonnie beside him. She had come into town right away when Tom called her to let her know what had happened. Bonnie Brannon was a tall, slender woman with a long, thick mane of brown hair. There might be a few streaks of gray in it, but a person would have to look hard to see them. She didn't look old enough to have two grown children.

Even through the big window in Buddy's office that looked out on the rest of the sheriff's department, Buddy had been able to hear Bonnie reading the riot act to Tom. He shouldn't have taken such a crazy chance. He could have gotten himself killed. He should have thought about her, even if he didn't care what happened to him.

Then Tom had said something too quietly for Buddy to hear the words, but from the look of it, he had spoken only a couple of simple sentences. Buddy would have been willing to bet that they had something to do with Carla May Willard, because Bonnie Brannon had quieted down immediately. Her husband had saved Carla's life, without a doubt, as well as the life of her daughter, and no argument Bonnie could make would top that one.

Buddy stood up and went to the door, easing it open. He wasn't looking forward to his conversation, but the sooner he had it, the better. He said,

"Tom, could you and Bonnie come in here for a few minutes?"

They stood up and came inside the office while Buddy went back behind the desk. Without sitting down himself, he motioned them into chairs and picked up a folder from his desk. He handed it across to Tom.

"We were lucky," Buddy said. "The guy you grabbed spent some time in jail in San Diego. Four months on an assault charge, which got his fingerprints in the system. His name is Porfirio Mendez."

Tom had opened the folder and studied the documents inside, one of which had Mendez's mug shots glaring out from it. "He's from Guatemala," Tom said, sounding a little surprised.

Buddy nodded. "Most of the members of M-15 are from either Guatemala or El Salvador."

"M-15," Bonnie said. "I've heard of them. They're the same people who . . . who killed poor old Burt Minnow and Madison Wheeler."

Buddy nodded again. "That's right."

Bonnie looked scared, and he didn't blame her. She had good reason to be. This part of Arizona had been pretty quiet and peaceful until recent years. There has been some smuggling of drugs and illegal immigrants, of course, as there was along any border, but on a small scale. The coming of *Mara Salvatrucha* had changed everything. Those folks didn't do anything on a small scale, and they killed indiscriminately, wantonly, ruthlessly. Anyone who got in their way or inconvenienced them even a little was considered fair game. They were worse than animals.

"I sent queries about Mendez to the authorities

in Mexico and Guatemala, and I've gotten answers back from them already," Buddy went on. "That's mighty fast for those agencies to work. They don't have a reputation for efficiency."

"That must mean that Mendez is well known to them," Tom commented.

"You could say that. He may have only done four months jail time in the U.S., but he's been in and out of Guatemalan and Mexican jails since he was fifteen, on charges ranging from petty theft to murder. He got off on the murder rap—by that time he was known to be a member of M-15, and probably nobody really wanted to convict him anyway. They were just going through the motions. But he was sent away numerous times on drug-related charges, as well as rape." He hated to say it in front of Bonnie, but she had a right to know, as well as Tom. "Rape is one of the gang's main weapons. If they have a grudge against somebody, they like to strike back at him through his female relatives."

Tom and Bonnie exchanged a glance. She said, "You're warning us, aren't you, Buddy? You're saying that *I'm* in danger as much as Tom is."

Buddy shrugged. "Mendez has a couple of broken ribs and a concussion, plus he's been arrested for murder, bank robbery, assault, attempted rape, kidnapping, car theft, and anything else we can think of that might stick. It's possible that because he failed in the job he was given, his bosses in M-15 might just cut him loose. It's more likely, though, that they'll want revenge for the man they lost, and they'll want Mendez out of jail."

"That last part's not going to be easy," Tom put in. "There are plenty of witnesses."

"Witnesses can be intimidated. Their memory gets foggy. They change their testimony. They leave town and go so far and so fast that they can't be found."

"There's nothing wrong with my memory . . . and I'm not going anywhere," Tom said.

"I know," Buddy said with a nod. "And I'm counting on that. We'll do everything we can to keep you safe, but you've got to do your part, Tom. Keep your eyes open . . . wide open."

Tom nodded.

"I know you've got hunting rifles and shotguns at home. You might want to put one in your pickup, and in Bonnie's car, too."

"I don't want to carry a rifle or a shotgun in my car, Buddy," Bonnie said.

"Now, Bonnie, this is serious," Buddy began. "You might need to defend yourself—"

She hefted her purse and said, "In that case, I've got a perfectly good .38 automatic right here."

Buddy just stared at her for a second and then said, "Oh."

A faint smile tugged at the corners of Tom's mouth. "Bonnie's probably as good a shot as I am." His expression grew serious again. "But she doesn't have the experience that I have when it comes to handling a gun while somebody else is shooting at you."

"Vietnam was a long time ago, Tom," she said crisply. "It's not like you've been engaging in weekly gunfights since then."

"No . . . but some things you never really forget."

"Like how to ride a bicycle?"

Tom grunted. "Yeah. Like how to ride a bicycle."

Buddy hoped for Tom's sake that he remembered more than that. Before this was over, he might need more deadly skills than bicycle riding.

They left the sheriff's office and the courthouse a short time later, stepping from the air-conditioned coolness into the heat of an Arizona afternoon in June. "Buddy's not going to need you for anything else?" Bonnie asked as she paused beside the door of her Chevy Blazer, which was parked next to her husband's F-150. Their long marriage was a testament to the idea that a Ford person and a Chevy person *could* get along, if they had a strong enough incentive to do so.

Tom shook his head in reply to her question. "No, I've already given my statement and signed it. I'll have to testify when Mendez's case comes up before the grand jury, but that's probably the next thing I have to do. And it won't be for a while, since he's in the hospital, too."

"I hope Mrs. Montgomery recovers all right," Bonnie said with a worried frown. "It can be pretty bad to break a hip at her age."

"She'll be fine," Tom said confidently. "There's nobody tougher than that old lady."

Bonnie unlocked and opened the door of her SUV. "Are you going to the store?"

"Reckon I'd better. Louly's probably heard lots of wild stories by now about what happened. I'll go by and put her mind at ease, see if she can handle things for the rest of the day. Then I'll come on home."

"Don't neglect the store on my account. I'll be

fine. You don't have to come home and babysit me."

That was just like her, still touchy about certain things, even after all these years. She didn't want anybody thinking she couldn't take care of herself. That fierce, stubborn independence could be annoying at times—but it was also one of the reasons Tom Brannon had fallen in love with her and still loved her with a depth and intensity that could take his breath away.

"Babysitting you wasn't what I had in mind," he told her. "I'm just a mite tired after capturing some Guatemalan gang member and rescuing a fair damsel."

"Don't joke about it, Tom," Bonnie said quickly. "You can't begin to know what Carla May has gone through, that poor girl."

He ran his hand over his head and nodded. "Yeah, I reckon you're right about that. I didn't mean anything by what I said."

Bonnie stepped closer to him and lifted a hand to rest it on his cheek. "I know you didn't." She came up on her toes to kiss him, although she didn't have to raise herself much. She was almost as tall as he was. "I think I'll go by her house and see how she's doing. You think that would be all right?"

"I don't see why not. See you at home later?"

"Sure."

They got in their respective vehicles and drove off, Tom hanging back so that Bonnie could pull out of the parking lot first. Then they turned in different directions, Bonnie toward the edge of town where Carla lived, Tom toward the business district.

As he drove, he felt worry gnawing lightly at his

guts. He could have gone with Bonnie and called
Louly at the store. That way he would have known
that Bonnie was safe.

On the other hand, they couldn't stay together
24/7. They would have to be apart some of the
time. He couldn't dump all the responsibility for
the business on Louly, and there were his parents
to think about, too. He couldn't neglect them.

That brought up a fresh worry. His folks lived several
miles out of town, and Buddy Gorman had said that
M-15 liked to strike back at their enemies through
family. Was it safe for his mom and dad to be out there
by themselves? Tom wondered if they should come
and stay with him and Bonnie for a while. They would
put up an argument, of course, especially his dad.
Herb Brannon had lived in that ranch house all his
life. Getting him to budge from it might require dy-
namite. Tom smiled at the thought.

The Explorer that had driven through the front of
the accountant's office was gone now—along with
the body of the dead gang member inside it—but
there was still plenty of evidence of the destruction
that had taken place. The sidewalk was blocked off
with yellow crime-scene tape. Sheets of plywood had
been nailed up over the gaping hole left behind by
the crash. Part of Main Street had been blocked off
with orange cones, leaving only one lane of traffic
getting through in that direction. Tom drove past,
shaking his head at the devastation.

That crime-scene tape was getting to be a famil-
iar sight in downtown. Earlier in the week, it had
marked off the spot where Burt Minnow had been
murdered. Tom had seen the dark stain on the
sidewalk left by the old man's blood. A city work

crew had gotten most of the stain up, but if you knew where to look, you could still see it, mute testimony to the senseless slaying that had occurred there. Tom felt a pang of sorrow as he drove past the spot. Burt had been a friend and a neighbor ever since Tom had opened the auto parts store. It was still hard to believe he was gone.

Tom turned into the side street, went along it to an alley that led behind the block of businesses, and parked back there in an open, graveled area where employees parked so as to leave the spaces along Main Street open for customers. He unlocked the rear door and went inside, past the restroom and the tiny lounge, through the big area behind the counter that was filled with shelves and bins where parts from light bulbs and fuses to brake drums and air cleaners were kept. Radiator hoses of all shapes and sizes hung from hooks on the walls and had to be gotten down with a long pole made for that purpose. Heavy steel racks along one side of the building were filled with tires. The parts counter bisected the main room. Up front were more shelves containing car wax, radios and speakers, motor oil, brake fluid, air fresheners, even fuzzy dice to hang from the rearview mirror. In this part of the country, where people didn't think twice about driving ninety or a hundred miles to go shopping or take in a movie, their vehicles were mighty important to them. Brannon Auto Parts tried to provide anything folks might need for their cars and trucks, at a reasonable price. Not as cheap as SavMart, of course, but most of Tom's customers were regulars who had been shopping with him for

years and didn't have any interest in going elsewhere just to save a few cents.

When he came in, Louly Parker was behind the
counter ringing up some windshield wiper blades
for a customer. Her long red hair was pulled back
in a ponytail, and her jeans were tight enough to
hug the curves of her bottom. Tom was an extremely happily married man, but that didn't mean
he couldn't recognize an excellent female behind
when he saw one. When he had first hired Louly,
some of his predominantly male, middle-aged customers had been a little unsure about buying auto
parts from such a young, pretty gal. They had realized fairly quickly, though, that Louly knew engines
inside and out. The only girl in a family of four
brothers who had endlessly rebuilt hot rods, she
had learned everything there was to know about
cars at an early age—including how not to let boys
get too fresh in the back seat.

Of course, other customers had been more than
happy to have Louly wait on them. Tom suspected
some ol' boys came in and bought stuff they didn't
really need, just so they could shoot the breeze with
Louly for a while. That was all right, too.

The fella buying windshield wipers was the only
customer in the store at the moment. As soon as he
was gone, Louly turned to Tom, threw her arms
around him, and gave him a big hug. He patted her
on the back. She put a hand on his chest and
pushed, putting some distance between them. She
said, "What the hell, Tom. You're the Lone Ranger
now or something?"

Tom grinned. "How does a kid like you know anything about the Lone Ranger?"

"I had to show my daddy how to work his DVD player so he can watch all the episodes he's bought on disc. Don't change the subject. You could've gotten yourself killed, charging in on those bank robbers like that. Then what would I have done for a job?"

"Gone to work for SavMart, I guess, like everybody else in the world."

Louly rolled her eyes. "No thanks. I like this place."

"I'll sell it to you and retire."

"One of these days I'll take you up on that offer."

The banter was well-worn and concealed the affection between them.

"Have you found out anything about those guys?" Louly went on. "I've heard people say they belonged to that M-15 outfit."

Tom's expression grew more serious as he nodded. "That's right. Sheriff Gorman identified the one who was captured, and he's definitely M-15."

Louly shivered. "From everything I've seen and heard, that's one scary bunch. They killed poor old Burt Minnow like he was nothing to them, like somebody swatting a fly."

"Yeah, I'll be staying closer to home for a while, since they may be holding a grudge against me. You think you're up to working some longer hours?"

Without hesitation, she nodded. "You're worried about Bonnie, aren't you?"

"Well, yeah. More about her than about me, to tell you the truth."

"That doesn't surprise me a bit. I'll be here whenever you need me, Tom."

He gave her a friendly pat on the shoulder, a gesture that would have gotten him in trouble a lot of places. Thankfully, political correctness had only a tenuous grip on Little Tucson; people didn't see sexual harassment everywhere they looked.

"Thanks. I don't think you'll have any trouble here—"

"If I do, there's a baseball bat under the counter."

Tom smiled, but he knew a baseball bat wouldn't be much protection against the likes of M-15. Louly would only be here during the day, though, and he didn't think the gang would retaliate in broad daylight.

Then he reminded himself of what had happened this morning at the bank, and earlier in the week to Burt Minnow, and he wasn't so sure.

"I'm going to see about getting the guys to come in more often, so you won't have to be working by yourself any."

"That's not necessary, but if it makes you feel better, I won't argue with you."

"Good. You shouldn't argue with your boss."

"Especially one as stubborn as you," she teased back at him.

He went into the small, crowded office and made some calls. Sal Guerrero, one of his part-timers, agreed to come in and work the rest of the day with Louly, and he and Mitch Hobson would split the shifts until further notice so that Louly would never be alone in the store. That made Tom feel a little better. He left, heading for home.

Bonnie had planned to stop by Carla May Willard's house, but she might be home, too, by the time he got there, Tom thought.

8

Carla leaned her forehead against the cool tile of
the wall inside the shower and let the water cascade
down over her. She closed her eyes and stood there,
soaking in the heat and steam. After a moment the
shakes hit her again, and she had to grab hold of
the bar that ran around the inside of the shower.
Her hands gripped it tightly, squeezing harder and
harder, and that helped control the shuddering.

But it just grew worse, and finally Carla sagged
against the wall and let herself slide down it until
she was sitting on the floor of the shower. The water
hit the top of her head and streamed over her face,
plastering down her hair. She kept shaking, her
breathing ragged as she sobbed. Tears welled from
her eyes and were immediately washed away.

She wished that the memories could be washed
away so easily.

Even before she had gotten to the hospital, while
she was riding in the back seat of Lauren Henderson's sheriff's department cruiser, she had been
dreaming of a shower. She felt so incredibly filthy,

and not just from rolling around on the sandy bottom of that wash. This filth stained her both inside and out, and she couldn't wait to wash it off.

Lauren had made it clear in a firm but reasonably gentle manner that she couldn't clean up until the doctor had examined her and evidence had been gathered. *Evidence.* That was a delicate way of putting it, when what they really did was to swab that bastard's semen out of her vagina, comb her pubic hair so they could recover any hairs or bits of skin he'd left behind on her, and scrape under her fingernails in hopes of finding skin or blood samples there, even though she had told Lauren she hadn't clawed the man. It was just procedure, covering all the bases. The son of a bitch had gotten away, but the authorities might get their hands on him someday and they wanted all the DNA evidence they could get so they could convict him.

Carla didn't care if he was convicted or not. She wanted him dead, not in prison.

At least the other one had been caught. Tom Brannon had seen to that. Mr. Brannon had shown up before the second man had had a chance to rape her. Why couldn't it have been just a little earlier?

And why didn't she feel any cleaner when she had been under this shower for a long time, so long that the hot water was starting to run out?

The bathroom door opened, and Deputy Henderson's voice asked, "Mrs. Willard? Are you okay in there?"

Carla forced her voice to work. "Y-yeah. I'm fine. I . . . I'll be right out."

"Okay. No rush. I just wanted to be sure you were all right."

The deputy had brought Carla home and offered to stay and keep an eye on Andy and Emily while Carla got cleaned up at last. She was grateful for that. She just wasn't up to looking after her kids right now. She would have to find somebody to help her, maybe her mother. Although that would mean that Carla would have to put up with her mother's endless carping about how she never should have married Danny Willard.

That was absolutely right, of course. If Danny hadn't been such a worthless bum, she wouldn't have been carjacked, kidnapped, raped, and almost killed. If he hadn't abandoned them, she might not have been driving along Main Street right at that particular moment. Yes, there was no doubt about it. It was all Danny's fault.

The shakes had subsided somewhat. Carla pulled herself to her feet and shut off the now cold water coursing from the shower head. She opened the stall and stepped out, picking up a thick towel from the back of the toilet and wrapping herself in it.

After she had dried off and put on a robe, she left the bathroom and went into the dining room of her modest home. Deputy Henderson was sitting there, playing some sort of board game with Andy, who seemed fine despite the bandage on his head. Carla was surprised to see Bonnie Brannon in the dining room as well. She was sitting cross-legged on the floor, rolling a ball back and forth with Emily.

Mrs. Brannon smiled up at her and said, "Hello, Carla May." At least she had the good sense not to ask her how she was doing. That wasn't surprising. Carla had always thought Mrs. Brannon was smart and sweet. She should have married Brian, she told herself. Then Mr. and Mrs. Brannon would have been her in-laws, and everything would have been all right. None of the bad things would have happened to her.

Carla started to cry again.

"Lord, here we go again," Lauren Henderson muttered under her breath, then immediately regretted it. Of course Carla Willard was upset. She had been kidnapped, raped, and terrorized. She had every right to cry. Thankfully, she didn't appear to have heard Lauren's comment.

Bonnie Brannon had, though, and she shot a quick frown of disapproval in Lauren's direction. Lauren shrugged and made a face as if to say she was sorry. And she was, of course.

Carla's crying set off the two kids. Bonnie got off the floor, cuddling Emily in her arms as she did so, and as she went over to Carla, she said to Lauren, "Why don't you take Andy out in the backyard for a little while?"

Lauren nodded. "That's a good idea. I hear Andy's got a dog, and I'd like to see it. Okay, Andy? You'll show me your puppy, won't you?"

He sniffled and wiped the back of his hand across his nose, but he nodded in answer to her question and walked slowly toward the back door.

Lauren hesitated. Quietly, she said to Bonnie, "Sheriff Gorman told me to keep an eye on—"

"It's all right, you'll just be in the backyard. And if the sheriff gives you any trouble, just let me know. Buddy Gorman and my husband have been friends for years."

"Well . . . okay." Lauren stepped out into the backyard with Andy, who knelt down and called a short-legged, long-bodied dachshund pup from its doghouse in a corner of the fenced-in yard. Lauren smiled and said, "A wiener dog! I love wiener dogs."

"His name is Frankie."

"For Frankfurter?" Lauren guessed.

"Yeah," Andy said with a grin. His eyes still had some tears in them, but he was all right again now.

"How old is he?"

"I don't know. I've only had him a couple of weeks. My mom got him for me 'cause I did good in school this year. She was afraid I wasn't gonna pass, so she said she'd get me a dog if I did. I was afraid she wasn't gonna keep her promise, but she did."

Andy picked up a rubber ball that was lying on the ground and tossed it across the yard. The dachshund pup went after it, short legs churning rapidly. Andy laughed and clapped his hands as Frankie retrieved the ball and brought it back to him.

Lauren looked down at the boy and the dog and shook her head. When she saw something this innocent, it was hard to believe the evil that was *Mara Salvatrucha* could exist in the same world. Surely that was some bizarre alternate universe.

But it wasn't, of course. The evil was here and now, and it wasn't content to lurk in its own dark corners. It was eager to crawl out into the light, to befoul and pollute and ruin the rest of the world for the good people who had worked so hard to make decent lives for themselves. Ever since she had become aware of that evil, Lauren had longed to smash it, to drive it back into its hole and bury it so deep that it could never see daylight again. That desire was one reason she had gone into law enforcement.

The fact that she got to pack heat didn't hurt, either.

The back door opened, and Bonnie Brannon came out, still carrying Emily. Carla followed them. She had put on some jeans and a shirt and wore flip-flops on her feet. Her eyes were still a little red and swollen, but she looked a little more composed now. Lauren hoped that the condition lasted. Carla had a couple of kids who were depending on her to be strong.

"If you need to get back to work, Deputy, I can stay here for a while," Bonnie said. "Carla's called her mother, and she's going to come stay with her for a while."

Lauren nodded. "That's a good idea. But I can stay as long as I need—"

"It's all right, really," Carla broke in. "I appreciate everything you've done for me, Deputy, but I think it would be better if . . . if you went on back to work. Having you here . . . well, it's just a reminder of . . . of what happened."

Lauren felt a flash of irritation, but then she realized that Carla didn't really mean to sound ungrateful. She just wanted to get a sense of normalcy back in her life, and she couldn't do that as long as Lauren was hanging around in uniform, with a service revolver holstered on her hip.

"All right, that's fine. But if there's any problems, any sign that something's not right, call the sheriff's department and somebody will be here right away."

Carla nodded. "I will. And thank you again."

Lauren reached down to pet the dachshund. "So

long, Andy," she said to the little boy. "Take good care of Frankie."

"I will," he said. "I already promised my mom I'd feed him and change his water and clean up his poop."

Lauren tried not to grin. "Well, if you do all that, I'm sure everything will be fine."

She nodded to Carla and Bonnie, then went back through the house and out to her car parked in front. As she pulled away, she felt a tingle of apprehension. Members of M-15 didn't get caught and put in jail very often. Hardly ever, in fact. So this case was going to get a lot of publicity, and the gang probably wouldn't like that. The leaders wouldn't want one of their men convicted and sent to prison. That might make them look weak to the other members of the gang. They would do *something*, Lauren thought. She was convinced of it.

The question was what form the evil would take this time, and how far would it poke its ugly nose into the light?

Tom and Bonnie Brannon lived about a mile east of Little Tucson, on an asphalt road that curved around on itself through a wide-flung residential area sprawled along the banks of a small creek that ran most of the year but often dried up in the middle of summer. There were half a dozen houses on the road, none of them in sight of the others. The Brannon house was an old, Spanish-style dwelling, with adobe walls, a red tile roof, and a tree-shaded patio in the center of the house. It wasn't as old as it looked, having been built in the 1940s. The original owners had kept it up well, and ever since Tom and Bonnie had bought the place in the seventies, they had taken good care of it, too. It was a cool little oasis in what was often a sea of sweltering heat. Tom always felt a sense of relief when he came home, as if he were withdrawing from the hectic pace of the real world into a haven of peace and relaxation.

He felt no relief today, though, because when he drove up the first thing he noticed was that Bonnie's Blazer wasn't parked in the two-car garage attached to the house.

That didn't have to mean anything, Tom told himself. She might have stayed longer than he expected at Carla May's house. Or she could have driven out to SavMart to pick up some groceries.

He parked the pickup in the garage and went inside, pausing in the kitchen to put his fists in the small of his back, press hard, and stretch his spine. It had been a long day and he wasn't as young as he used to be. Some of his muscles were starting to ache a little from the strain he had subjected them to during the fight with the two gang members. He had a right to expect that, jumping around like Captain America as he had.

He thought about getting the phone book, looking up Carla May's number, and calling her house to see if Bonnie was still over there. The problem with that idea was that if he did, Bonnie would think he was checking up on her—and rightly so, because that would be exactly what he was doing. Maybe it would be better to wait a while longer, he decided.

Hell with it. He was going to call Carla May's house and just see if Bonnie was there. If she didn't like it, tough.

Before he could pick up the phone, though, he heard a noise in the garage, a heavy thump as if something had fallen over. It wasn't the door of Bonnie's Blazer, he knew that. He would have heard the engine as the SUV pulled in.

Nobody had any reason to be messing around in there. Tom stood stiff and still for a long moment, listening intently, but he didn't hear anything else.

The door leading from the kitchen into the garage was close enough for him to reach. He put his hand out and turned the lock button on the doorknob. That wouldn't keep anybody out who really wanted in, but it might slow them down for a few seconds. Then, moving quietly, he headed for his den.

The gun cabinet in there held two shotguns and three rifles. They were locked up and unloaded, of course. Tom went into the den, took a ring of keys from his pocket, and unlocked the cabinet. There was an unhurried efficiency to his movements as he took down a pump shotgun, unlocked a drawer in his desk, took out a box of shells, and loaded the gun. He dropped a handful of extra shells in the pocket of his shirt. Then he moved back to the kitchen, holding the shotgun level just above his waist.

No one was there. The door appeared to be undisturbed. Tom heard something in the garage, though—the sound of an object scooting along the floor. Somebody was moving things around in there.

Planting a bomb, maybe?, he wondered.

Holding the shotgun with his right hand, he reached out with his left and unlocked the kitchen door again. He grasped the knob and took a deep breath. Then he twisted the knob, flung the door open, and lunged through it into the garage, sweeping the shotgun from side to side as his eyes searched for a target.

He heard a startled yelp and saw movement from the corner of his eye. His finger was already tightening on the trigger as he snapped the barrel in that direction.

He eased off on the pressure just in time to stop the shotgun from blasting as he recognized the muscular, hairy body and bushy tail of his dog Max. The big mutt was part golden retriever and part something else. Tom stared as Max recovered from his surprise and came toward him, tail wagging. Tom's nerves were still stretched so tight they were jangling.

Next to the wall, a paint can lay on its side. Tom realized that Max had knocked it off a stack of similar cans and had been pushing it along the cement floor of the garage with his nose. There was no telling why the dog had been doing such a thing; to his canine brain, it must have made sense.

"Damn it, Max, I almost blasted you." Tom's voice was shaky. Max nuzzled his left hand as he let the shotgun hang at his side in the right. After a second, though, Max returned to the stack of paint cans. He pawed at it, and another of the cans fell.

Tom frowned. Max was acting like there was something behind those cans. Maybe he ought to take a look.

As he stepped closer, he heard a buzzing sound. It was instantly recognizable, and Tom snapped, "Max! Get away from there!"

Max looked at him and whined but backed off as Tom had told him to do. Tom set the shotgun on the workbench that ran along the wall to his left and took a garden hoe from the hooks where it hung on the wall. He moved closer to the cans and reached out with the hoe to pull a couple of them farther away from the wall.

That gave the big rattlesnake that had crawled behind them enough room to coil up and shake the rattle on the end of his tail that much harder. The snake's head lifted a little. Its tongue flickered in and out.

Tom felt a chill as he looked at the creature. He hated snakes with a passion. That was one bad thing about living in southern Arizona. A person could almost get used to the heat, but Tom knew he would never get used to the snakes.

"Stay back, Max," he said. He raised the hoe and brought it down in a swift, accurate stroke. The sharp edge of the blade caught the rattler just behind the head and pinned it to the floor. The long, muscular body whipped around wildly. Tom moved the hoe back and forth until the blade grated on the cement. The snake's head was completely severed from its body. That didn't stop the body from coiling and writhing, and the rattler's mouth opened and closed as instinct made it try to bite something, anything. Max darted forward, and Tom yelled at him, telling him again to stay back. "Just because the damn thing's dead doesn't mean it can't still bite you. The snake doesn't *know* it's dead yet."

The body's contortions were lessening, though, and the biting motions slowed down as well. Tom made sure Max stayed away until all signs of life had left the snake. Then he used the hoe to pick up the head and carried it around back to the trash barrel.

He would put some trash in there later and burn it. He went back to the body and chopped the rattle off the tail. The rattle had fourteen segments to it. One year for each segment meant the snake was an old son of a bitch. Tom set the rattle on his workbench to let it dry out. When it was dry, he would put it in the glass jar on one of the shelves that held the rattles from all the snakes he had killed over the years. He kept the grisly souvenirs as a reminder to always watch where he was stepping.

You never knew when something venomous might be waiting to bite you.

He picked up the snake's body, carried it around back, and slung it into the brush along the creek for the scavengers. As he started to turn back toward the house he heard an engine, and by the time he reached the garage, Bonnie was pulling the Blazer inside. *Now* the relief he normally felt on coming home flooded through Tom.

Bonnie got out of the SUV, looked at the shotgun on the workbench and the hoe in Tom's hand, and she frowned slightly as she asked, "What's going on here?"

"Just killing a serpent in the garden of Eden," he told her.

9

Cipriano and Leobardo Asturias were brothers; that much was obvious to anyone who looked at them. They might have been taken for twins, but Cipriano was really two years older. They were born and raised in a small village near the Mayan ruins of Tikal, on the northern plains of Guatemala. It was an area of great poverty and hardship. People farmed and sometimes harvested chicle from the trees, which was used to make chewing gum for the gringos far to the north in *los Estados Unidos*. From the time Cipriano and Leobardo were mere children, they had worked, spending long hours each day using machetes to hack at the hard trunks of sapodilla trees, making the cuts from which the sap drained. When the buckets that caught the sap were full, Cipriano and Leobardo and the other workers would carry them to the long, covered huts in the village where the sap would be dried and kneaded into chicle. For this they were paid only a few centavos a day. Or rather, their parents were paid a few centavos for the work that Cipriano and

Leobardo did. This money supplemented what their mother earned by selling her body. Most of it went to buy liquor for her and her husband, who had accidentally chopped off half of one foot several years earlier and now lay about growing grossly fat and yelling at his wife because she couldn't manage to fuck more than ten or twelve men every day. She swilled down mescal and screamed back at him that there weren't more than ten or twelve men in the village who could get it up well enough to fuck her—and he certainly wasn't one of them.

Cipriano and Leobardo stood this life for as long as they could. One evening when Cipriano was twelve and Leobardo was ten, they waited until their parents had passed out from drinking, and then, with the skills they had acquired in the sapodilla forest, they used their machetes to chop their parents into small pieces. By morning, they were well on their way to Guatemala City, walking determinedly along the road that led through the mountains toward the sea.

It was in Guatemala City, several months later, that they met Ernesto Luis Montoya, who at seventeen was already a pimp, a drug smuggler, and a freelance assassin. Montoya took the Asturias brothers under his wing, sensing something useful in them. They talked very little and seemed to have no need of conversation between themselves. It was as if they sensed each other's thoughts. One night, though, Cipriano's iron control slipped slightly and he told Montoya what he and Leobardo had done to their parents. Then and there, Montoya knew he had made the right decision. With two such able assistants, he would rise quickly in the criminal ranks. With two such *segundos*, he would go far.

It was a dream that had come true. Montoya was now the unquestioned leader of *Mara Salvatrucha,* a gang the likes of which had never before been seen. And Cipriano and Leobardo were his avenging angels, the tools of his righteous wrath. None dared stand against them.

Least of all some weak, pathetic gringos. If they knew what was good for them, they would leave the place called Little Tucson. If not, *Mara Salvatrucha* would scour them from the face of the earth.

Cipriano had passed along Señor Montoya's orders to a gunner named Humberto Rojas. Rojas was to take as many men with him as he wanted and go north from Nogales to Little Tucson, where he would confront the woman who had caused all the trouble for Porfirio and Enrique. Only Porfirio was still alive, and he was in the Sierrita County jail, having been released from the hospital late that afternoon. M-15 had an informant who worked at the hospital, a nurse with family south of the border. She had proven to be very cooperative once some of the gang had paid a visit to her mamá and chopped off a couple of the old lady's fingers. She had called a number in Nogales and passed along the information as soon as Porfirio was moved from the hospital to the jail.

It was a shame they had not been able to move more quickly. If a raid on the hospital could have been put together in time, that would have been the simplest solution. Just take Porfirio out of there and bring him back across the border. While Montoya could muster a large enough force to attack the jail itself, that was an extreme measure. It would be better to secure Porfirio's release through legal means, once all the witnesses had either recanted or disappeared. *Mara Salvatrucha* had several attorneys on the U.S. side who worked for the gang.

Humberto Rojas was confident in his ability to handle any problem, especially where gringos were concerned. They were all foolish and lacked *cojones.* He took only two men with him as he crossed the border at Nogales and headed northwest toward Little Tucson.

Doris Stevens had brassy blond hair, a big chest, a three-pack-a-day cigarette habit, a whiskey drawl, and four ex-husbands. She'd made plenty of mistakes in her life, God knew that was true, but she had learned a lot, too, and she wasn't shy about passing along that acquired wisdom to her daughter.

"Didn't I tell you you could do better?" she said to Carla. "Didn't I say that Danny Willard was a no-account troublemaker?"

"Yes, Mama," Carla said with a bored, hostile edge to her voice. She had been listening to this same shit ever since her mother had gotten there.

Doris pointed at her daughter with the two fingers that held her cigarette. "Your problem is you do too much of your thinkin' with what's between your legs."

"Mama!" Carla hissed, jerking her head toward the dining room, where Andy and Emily were finishing up their supper of peanut butter and jelly sandwiches Doris had made for them. Carla hoped her mother hadn't dropped too many cigarette ashes in the peanut butter. "The kids'll hear."

Doris waved a hand as she sat in one of the living

room chairs, across from where Carla perched on the sofa with her legs drawn up underneath her. "Oh, hell, they don't know what I'm talkin' about. That kinda stuff just goes right over their heads. I'm just sayin', you saw Danny as a big, strappin', handsome boy and got the urge to lay down on your back. And you just don't do your best thinkin' on your back, darlin'."

Carla wondered briefly just how much psychological damage it would do to her children if they saw her choke the living hell out of their grandmother. Then she shoved the idea aside and said meekly, "You're right, Mama." Sometimes if she just agreed with everything her mother said, eventually Doris would shut up.

Doris puffed on her cigarette for a minute and then said, "What you should've done was marry Brian Brannon. Hell, he was a lot nicer, and his daddy owns his own business." A confidential tone came into Doris's voice, as if they were girlfriends or something equally ludicrous. "You know, between the times when I was married to your daddy and your Uncle Buster, I thought I might just set my cap for Tom Brannon. Now there is one hell of a good-lookin' man. I swear, he's a dead ringer for Jeff Chandler."

"Who?"

Doris stared at her. "Jeff Chandler? The movie star?"

Carla just shook her head.

"Lord," Doris said with an exasperated sigh. "Your generation's the most ignorant one I ever saw."

"Wasn't Mr. Brannon already married by the time you and Daddy were divorced?"

"Well, yeah . . . but I figured I could take him away from that wife of his if I really wanted to. Skinny little thing like her, with hardly any tits at all. Not like these bazooms, I tell you." Doris used both hands to cup her massive breasts.

Carla closed her eyes and rested her head on the sofa cushion. What in the world had she been thinking when she called her mother? Didn't the old bat care the least little bit about the ordeal her daughter had gone through less than twelve hours earlier?

On the other hand, maybe being driven crazy was a good thing. It was a distraction, anyway.

The thump of car doors outside made Carla jerk her head up. Her eyes flew open. "Somebody's here!" she said, hysteria creeping into her voice.

"Don't get in an uproar," Doris scolded her. "Probably just some folks comin' to see you. Maybe Tom Brannon." Her hand went to her hair and patted the stiffly hairsprayed curls. She got up as the doorbell rang and said, "I'll get it."

"Mama, be careful—" Carla started to say.

"Now, don't go lettin' one bad thing get you all skittish," Doris said over her shoulder as she reached for the doorknob. She turned it and opened the door without even looking through the peephole first.

Carla saw the two men standing there on the other side of the screen door, and her hand went to her mouth in horror. They were both stocky and Hispanic, and for a second she had the wild idea that one of them was the man who had raped her. Then she realized that he was a stranger, but it didn't matter. He grabbed the handle of the screen door and yanked it open. Carla screamed as she bolted up from the sofa. "Andy!" she cried. "Get Emily and run! Out the back!"

Andy knew the backyards of this neighborhood. He could slip away in the darkness with Emily, and at least her children would survive, no matter what happened to her.

"Goddamn it!" Doris bleated, but she didn't have time to get anything else out before the man in the lead planted a hand right in the middle of her bosom and shoved. She flew backward, tripped over a coffee table, and went down hard on the floor.

Carla brought up the pistol she had pulled from behind the sofa cushion. She'd kept it close at hand ever since Deputy Henderson and Bonnie Brannon left. It was only a little .32 that had belonged to Danny. He had left it behind when he abandoned his family, probably because it was a Saturday night special and a piece of crap. But it was the only gun Carla had, and she intended to empty every bullet in it before she let these bastards put their hands on her.

She was too slow, though. The man who had pushed her mother down was suddenly right in front of her. His hand flashed up, closed over the pistol's cylinder, and wrenched the gun out of her grip. Carla cried out in fear and anger as she lost her last line of protection.

The man backhanded her, knocking her onto the sofa. He dropped to one knee and pressed a forearm like a bar of iron across her throat, pinning her there. Carla gasped for breath as she saw the other man haul her mother to her feet, then draw back a fist and slam a punch to her mouth. Blood flew from Doris's pulped lips. She was stunned, and when the man let go of her she crumpled limply to the floor.

Carla thought that things couldn't possibly get any worse, but she was wrong. Andy came stumbling into the room, being pushed from behind by a third man, who must have gone around to the back to stop anyone from getting away. Andy had Emily in his arms, and both of them were crying.

The man leaning his forearm across Carla's throat put his face close to hers and hissed, "Your kids are scared. They're scared we're gonna hurt you. They're right. We're gonna hurt you, and then we're gonna hurt them. The old lady, too."

"D-don't!" Carla managed to gasp out. "I'll d-do anything you say. Anything!"

"Damn right you will." With the hand that held the little pistol, the man took hold of Carla's shirt and ripped it down the front, sending the buttons flying. He pulled it back, exposing her bra, and said, "Lupe."

The man who had punched Doris stepped over and took a switchblade out of one of the pockets of his baggy jeans. He flicked the blade open, slid the tip under Carla's bra, between her breasts, and pulled the knife sharply upward, cutting the bra in half. The tip of the blade had scratched her skin slightly, leaving a little mark between her breasts where blood seeped out.

The man holding her down used his gun hand to flip the bra back, baring her breasts. He ran the pistol over them. The metal prodded painfully at her flesh. He lifted the pistol and then rested the barrel against her left nipple.

The man whispered, "There's only one way you can save yourself and your kids."

"Any . . . anything!"

"Leave."

She struggled to focus her eyes on him, surprised by the single word he had just spoken.

"Wh-what?"

"Leave," he repeated. "Get out of town. Leave Little Tucson today."

"Wh-where do you want me to go?"

"Don't care. Just so you ain't here. Just run, and don't stop."

Understanding was beginning to seep into Carla's stunned, terrified brain, just as the blood was slowly seeping out of the cut on her chest. These men hadn't come here to rape and kill her, although if she didn't cooperate they might certainly do just that. They just wanted her to leave so that she couldn't testify against their fellow gang member, the bank robber who was now behind bars in the county jail. That was fine.

The man had eased up a little on her throat. She was able to speak more easily as she rasped, "You mean if we leave town and don't come back, you won't kill us?"

"That's right. You a smart little bitch. Cute, too."

"We'll go," she said without hesitation. "I . . . I promise."

"You gimme your word?"

"Yes. I swear! Just . . . just leave us alone!"

"You know, I almost believe you. You just got to convince me a little more that you're tellin' the truth."

"What do you want?" Carla asked desperately.

Without answering her, the man turned his head and said, "Lupe, cut the little boy's ear off. Either one, it don't matter."

"No!" Carla screamed. "Oh, God, no, don't hurt him! Don't touch him! We'll go! We'll pack up and leave tonight! My God, please! We'll go and never come back!"

"Hold on, Lupe," the man said. He leered down into Carla's face and went on, "You'll hide where the law can't ever find you and drag you back here?"

"Y-yes! I swear it! I . . . I know some people I can call."

The idea had just occurred to her. Back in the days before Danny left, she had toyed with the idea of leaving him. She had done some poking around on the Internet and found a group in Phoenix that helped women get away from abusive husbands. It was an underground organization that would hide a woman and her kids and help them get new identities, so that her husband would never be able to find them and force them to return. Sure, it was for women who were in real danger—but if she didn't qualify, who did? It didn't matter that the threat came not from her husband but rather from an evil gang that was spreading out insidiously all along the border.

Her voice was a little stronger as she went on, "We'll hide so well that no one will ever be able to find us."

"You are wrong. The law may not be able to find you . . . but *Mara Salvatrucha* will *always* know where you are. You double-cross us, and we'll get you. Your kids, too. They'll scream for a day or two before they die, and you'll be right there to hear every minute of it."

Carla closed her eyes and shuddered. "I'll do what you say."

He prodded her again with the gun. "You'll never know where we are, never know when we're gonna get you. Only way to be safe is to play along with what we want."

"I will, I will," she said. How many times did she have to promise before he believed her?

Suddenly, the painful weight on her throat went away. She blinked her eyes open and saw that the man had stood up. She didn't move. She was afraid to move.

The man who had done the talking jerked his head toward the front door. "Be seein' you, lady," he said with a mocking smile. The three of them went out, closing the door carefully behind them.

As soon as the men were gone, Andy rushed over to the sofa, bringing Emily with him. They piled down on top of Carla, hugging her frantically. She tried to comfort them, but she was almost too scared and stunned to do so. Finally she managed to sit up and pull the remnants of her shirt together over her breasts. Doris was stirring around on the other side of the coffee table. After a moment, she grabbed hold of the table and pulled herself into a sitting position. Her mouth was covered with blood.

"Wha . . . wha' . . . happened?"

Carla ignored her mother for the moment. Her pulse was still racing, but it had begun to slow a little as she regained more control over herself. "Andy," she said quietly, "go to your room and pack for a long trip."

He sniffled, wiped his eyes, wiped his nose. "Where are we goin', Mama?"

"Far from here."

"Are . . . are we gonna go see Daddy?"

Carla shook her head. "I've told you before, Daddy doesn't want us anymore. And now those men don't want us to stay here, so we're moving. Okay?" She would explain the details of it to him later, how they would all have new names and how they could never, ever trust anybody again or tell anybody the truth.

"Wha' the hell?" Doris muttered.

"Go and pack now," Carla told Andy. "Pack for your little sister, too. Can you do that?"

"We're goin' tonight?" he asked.

She nodded. "Yes. Tonight."

Andy headed for the room he shared with Emily, holding his little sister's hand as he led her out of the living room. Doris put her hands on the coffee table and said, "Damn it, Carla May, if you don't tell me what's goin' on—"

"You want to know what's going on?" Carla cut in sharply. "We're going on the run so those men won't come back and torture us all to death. Simple enough for you, Mama?"

Doris just gaped at her.

"And whether you like it or not, you're part of this now," Carla went on as she stood up, trying to gather the tattered shreds of her dignity about her as she was doing with her torn shirt. "I hope you said good-bye to that trailer of yours, because you're never going to see it again."

"Damn it, girl, have you lost your mind? I can't go nowhere! I got a job—"

"I think they can find another waitress at the truck stop. Now get up. You haven't unpacked yet, so that'll make things easier."

"You're crazy!" Doris said as she stumbled to her feet. "I never heard of such foolishness!"

"Mama . . ." Carla took a deep breath. "Shut the hell up."

That did the trick. Doris fell silent and just stared at her again, mouth open.

Carla wished she had known all along it was that easy.

10

Tom Brannon was in bed reading when Bonnie came out of the bathroom brushing her hair. It was a pretty good book, a Western novel by one of his favorite authors, but it would have had to be a damn sight more interesting than it was to keep his attention while his wife was standing there only a few feet away, wearing a pair of semi-transparent babydoll pajamas and brushing her long, thick brown hair so that her still-firm breasts rose and fell against the sheer material. The pajama top was short enough to leave her long, sleek, tanned legs bare.

"I didn't think they made babydoll pajamas anymore," he said as he laid the book aside on the little table next to the bed.

"They still make everything," Bonnie said. "You just have to order it on the Internet now." She turned and moved over to her dressing table, bending slightly to set down the brush. That gave him one hell of a nice view—as she knew perfectly well. As she turned back to him, she went on, "I didn't buy these on the Internet, though."

"Where'd you get them? You look really nice."

Bonnie glanced down at herself and smiled slightly. "Not bad for fifty years old, eh? That's half a century, Tom."

"Good Lord, you know you don't look a day over thirty-five. I'm the one who's getting decrepit."

"I wouldn't say that," she replied, looking pointedly at the erection tenting the sheet over his groin.

Tom laughed. "Well, the important things still work, anyway."

Bonnie came over to the bed and sat down, swinging a leg over so that she straddled him. The sheet and her panties were still between them, so she just snuggled against his chest, resting her head on his shoulder while he put his arms around her.

"You don't remember these pajamas, do you, Tom?"

"You'd think that I would, but . . . no, I'm afraid not."

"They're the ones I wore after Lisa was born, after enough time had passed . . . the first time that we, you know . . ."

"Ohhhh," he said. "Yes, I *do* remember now. That was quite some night, if I recall correctly."

"You recall very correctly." Her hips began to move so that she pressed intimately against him.

Tom Brannon felt a lot of things in that moment, primarily love for his wife, a love that was mixed with a strong, healthy lust. But there was also a sense of relief. He had worried that she would want to talk about everything that had happened today. She might get upset again, angry at the way he had risked his life to help Carla May. He could understand that, he really could. Bonnie didn't want to

lose him. He was glad she felt that way about him.
But sometimes there were troubles that a man just
couldn't avoid, things that he couldn't turn his back
and walk away from—not and still be a man.

She kissed him, parting her lips eagerly as he slid
his tongue into her mouth. Her arms went around
his neck. His hands slid down her back to pull up
the pajama top and delve under the tight panties.

When Bonnie broke the kiss, she said breath-
lessly, "I want you in me now, Tom."

She lifted her hips a little, and while he pushed
the sheet down, she worked some sort of feminine
magic that got rid of the panties and pajama top.
They fit together so well after all this time that when
she lowered herself onto him, neither of them had
to guide him into her. It seemed to sheath itself in
her heated clasp.

They both knew how to pace themselves, taking
it slow and easy until their passion was just too
strong to tolerate any more delay. Then Tom began
thrusting harder and faster, and Bonnie met each
of his thrusts with one of her own. She reached
orgasm first, throwing her head back and gasping,
but he was right behind her. Spasms shuddered
through him, matching hers.

When it was over, she sagged against him, breathing hard. He rubbed her back and shoulders and
stroked her hair while they whispered that they
loved each other.

It was easy to forget, at a moment like this, that
there was anyone else in the world except the two
of them. Tom wanted to shut all the rest of it out,
and for a while, he was able to do just that.

"Those pajamas must really inspire you," Bonnie said.

"Yeah . . . That was as good as that other night . . ."

She laughed softly. "Only back then, you were good for two or three times in one night."

He gave a mock groan and said, "Good Lord, woman, give a man a chance to recuperate! If I had known you were such a wanton, I . . . I . . ."

"You would have what?" she asked.

"I would have married you sooner," Tom said, and kissed her again.

They would have stayed there like that, cuddled together, if Max hadn't begun to bark somewhere outside. The sound had an angry, almost frantic urgency to it.

Bonnie pushed herself upright and frowned. "What's he carrying on about?"

"Probably got another snake cornered. Where there's one, there's usually another."

Bonnie shuddered. "I hate snakes."

"Me, too. I'd better go have a look."

"You're saying you want me to get off of you?"

"It's not necessarily what I want . . . but Max is liable to get bitten."

Bonnie slid off to the side. "Be careful."

"I'll just call him in if he'll come," Tom said as he got out of bed. "If there's a snake out there, it can go on somewhere else as far as I'm concerned."

He pulled on some jeans and slid his feet into a pair of sandals beside the bed. A fella didn't tramp around barefoot in the middle of the night. There were too many varmints in this part of Arizona that stung or bit.

There were other kinds of varmints, too, that were

even bigger threats. He hadn't said anything to Bonnie and she hadn't seemed to think of it, but he couldn't forget the warning Buddy Gorman had given them earlier in the day about *Mara Salvatrucha* seeking vengeance. That danger hadn't gone away.

The shotgun was in the kitchen, still loaded. He picked it up as he went to the door and snapped on the garage light. If Max was barking at a coyote or something like that, the light might be enough to scare it away.

Max kept carrying on, though, so Tom opened the door and called, "Max! Max, get in here!"

The barking stopped abruptly. Tom didn't like the sound of that. He stepped into the garage, poking the barrel of the shotgun out in front of him. The light spilled through the open garage doors, illuminating a stretch of the gravel driveway that led around to the side of the house where the garage was located. Tom moved closer to the doors, sliding quietly along beside Bonnie's SUV.

As the shotgun barrel moved past the back of the Blazer, a strong dark hand suddenly shot up and clamped around it, wrenching the weapon forward. Tom yelled in alarm and stumbled ahead as he tried to maintain his grip on the gun, but whoever had hold of it managed to jerk it out of his hands. Tom knew then what a bad mistake he had made by coming out here. It was an idiot move, just as surely as teenagers splitting up in a horror movie.

He could still fight back, though. Earlier that afternoon, he hadn't hung the hoe back on its hooks. He had just set it on the workbench. It was close at hand, just to his left. He snatched up the hoe and whirled it over his head as the man came out from behind the SUV, still holding the shotgun he had taken away from Tom. The guy hadn't turned the weapon around, though; he still had hold of the barrel. Tom swung the hoe and the wooden handle of the implement cracked across the man's forearm. He cried out in pain and dropped the shotgun.

It struck butt-first on the concrete floor and discharged, the heavy boom deafening in the close confines of the garage. The charge of buckshot went almost straight up, blowing a huge hole in the raised garage door. A few of the pellets tore through the arm of the intruder. He staggered back, clutching his bloody arm.

Tom didn't hesitate. He pressed the attack, swinging the hoe in a backhanded stroke at the man's head. The blade struck him on the cheek and opened up a gash from which more blood spurted. Tom lowered the hoe and rammed it into the guy's belly, making him double over and stumble back against the Blazer. Quickly, Tom twirled the hoe so that he could strike with the handle and brought it down as hard as he could on the back of the man's neck. The blow landed solidly and knocked the man face-down on the garage floor.

The bastard was out cold, and for a second Tom considered using the hoe to chop his head off, just as he had with the rattlesnake. But he didn't have time to think about that, because inside the house, Bonnie screamed.

It made sense that more than one of the gang members came out here to his house. He never should have left Bonnie alone in there. Still clutching the now bloodstained hoe, Tom lunged through the door into the kitchen.

He was halfway to the bedroom before he realized he should have grabbed the shotgun off the garage floor before he ran in.

Too late to do anything about that now. He skidded around a corner in the hall and sprinted into the bedroom, where he saw by the light of the bedside lamp that Bonnie was struggling furiously with a strange man. She had pulled a robe on over her nudity after Tom left the room, but it hung open as she pulled a hand free from the man's grip and clawed at his face while they stumbled around beside the bed.

Tom didn't warn the man by yelling, even though he was filled with rage that wanted to burst out of him in an incoherent shout. Instead he just lifted the hoe and swung it with all his might at the bastard's head.

If the blow had landed as Tom intended, it would have smashed the intruder's skull and the hoe would have wound up lodged in his brain. That was no more than he deserved. Instead the guy moved at the last second through pure bad luck, rather than intentionally dodging the blow, and the hoe struck him on top of the left shoulder. He screamed as the blade penetrated flesh and scraped on bone and then came free. Bonnie shoved him away. He stumbled against the wall.

Tom was a little off-balance from putting all his strength into the blow that had partially missed. The intruder recovered first, snatching a switchblade from his pocket, flicking it open, and coming at Tom. The long, wicked-looking blade slashed back and forth. Tom tried to ward it off with the hoe, but a couple of the strokes got through and left bloody cuts on his forearms. His anger enabled him to ignore the fiery pain for the moment. The slashes weren't deep enough to keep his muscles from working as he tried to defend himself against the knife-wielder.

He had the advantage in reach, but the switchblade was the deadlier weapon. From the corner of his eye Tom saw Bonnie scrambling into the closet. He hoped she would stay there, out of harm's way, until he had time to dispose of the intruder.

Bonnie had no intention of staying out of the fight. She emerged from the closet with the robe flying out behind her like a Valkyrie's cloak. Instead of a sword she had in her hands the Little League baseball bat their son Brian had left behind when he moved out. Tom had never been able to bring himself to get rid of it.

With her face contorted by fear and anger, Bonnie swung the bat, chopping down savagely at the back of the man's head. He never saw it coming. The hard wooden cylinder smashed into his skull. His eyes widened in shock and pain. His fingers opened involuntarily. The switchblade fell to the floor, hitting point first so that it penetrated the carpet and the wood underneath and stuck straight up.

Bonnie jerked the bat back and hit him again. The man fell to his knees. Bonnie swung the bat like a flail, this time striking him on the side of the head just above the right ear. He went down like a felled tree and lay there twitching slightly as blood leaked from his ears and nose and eyes.

Bonnie lifted the bat again and would have continued smashing it into the intruder's head until he was dead if Tom hadn't stepped over to her and grabbed it. "Bonnie!" he said sharply. "Bonnie, take it easy! It's over! He can't hurt us!"

Her bare breasts heaved as she stood there dragging breath into her lungs. For a second she glared down at the man she had just beaten to the floor, but then her face crumpled into tears and she let Tom take the bat from her as she sagged into his arms.

"Damn!" a voice said from the door of the bedroom. "That one feisty woman you got there, Brannon."

Tom jerked around, shoving Bonnie behind him. A third stranger, Hispanic and tough-looking like the others, stood in the doorway holding the shotgun Tom had left behind in the garage. He pumped the weapon as Tom took half a step toward him. The threat forced Tom to stop.

"Looks like she damn near beat Lupe to death," the man went on. "I got the feelin' you two ain't gonna be reasonable."

"You're M-15, aren't you?" Tom asked, breathing raggedly. "You came to kill us."

"We came to warn you you better get out of Little Tucson and not even think about testifyin' against our amigo. I can see now, though, that won't work. You're a stubborn gringo. You don't scare easy."

"Get the hell out of my house," Tom said.

"I got the gun, hombre, not you. I gonna blow the two o' you away. Then everybody else around here will think twice about crossing *Mara Salvatrucha*. Too bad I can't have a little fun with your wifey first. She a little old and skinny for my taste, though."

The barrel of the shotgun came up. Tom tensed, ready to throw the baseball bat at the man and then lunge after it in an attempt to distract him and tackle him before he could pull the trigger. Tom knew he stood little real chance of succeeding, but he couldn't just stand there and let the son of a bitch shoot them.

Before either of the men could move, a fierce growl sounded behind the intruder. He ripped out a curse in Spanish and tried to swing around, but Max had already launched himself into the air. A little over a hundred pounds of furious dog slammed into the man and knocked him off his feet. The shotgun thundered, but the buckshot went harmlessly into the wall. Max's teeth slashed at the screaming man. He grabbed the guy's upper right arm and shook it viciously.

Tom stepped closer, brought the bat up, swept it down hard. The thud of wood against bone silenced the intruder's screams. Max continued savaging the man until Tom grabbed the thick fur at the dog's neck and pulled him off.

"Back!" Tom ordered. "Stay back, Max!"

Reluctantly, the big mutt retreated. Tom saw a bloody lump on Max's head and knew that the men must have knocked him out when he was barking at them. They might have even thought that they had killed him.

This one had paid for that mistake. He was covered with blood. Tom checked for a pulse and found one. The bastard was lucky to still be alive. Max could have easily torn out his throat.

Tom dropped the bat and picked up the shotgun. "Stay," he told Max as he pumped another round into the chamber. "Guard."

"Tom," Bonnie said, "where are you going?"

"To see if there are any more of these sons of bitches hanging around."

"Not without me, you're not." She jerked the robe's belt tight around her waist. "You're not leaving me in here with these two."

"Come on," he said.

Together, with Tom out in front by a step, carrying the shotgun, they went down the hall.

It took about ten minutes to check the house, inside and outside. No one else was around. The three men must not have had any companions, or the others had taken off when the shooting started.

Tom handed the shotgun to Bonnie and got some nylon rope from a drawer under the workbench. He cut a couple of lengths of it with a utility knife from the same drawer and used the rope to tie the hands and feet of the first man he had knocked out. The guy was still unconscious, but Tom wasn't going to take any chances on him coming to and being loose to cause more trouble.

"Let's get the others tied up," he said. "I don't think they're going to regain consciousness any time soon, but you never know."

Taking the rope and the knife, he headed for the bedroom. Bonnie followed with the shotgun, her eyes flicking around, still alert for any sign of danger.

As they reached the door of the bedroom, she said, "Shouldn't we go ahead and call nine-one-one? Or Buddy?"

Tom had been thinking about that very thing. He shook his head and said, "Not yet."

"But you need help. Those cuts on your arms—"

Tom glanced down at the injuries. "They'll be all right," he said. "We'll clean them up and bandage them later."

"You might need stitches."

"We'll see." He cut more lengths of rope and bent to his task, trussing up the intruders securely. Both of them were still alive, although he didn't like the way the one Bonnie had hit with the bat was breathing. When he was finished, he tossed the rest of the rope and the knife on the bed and said, "That's it."

"*Now* we call for help?"

Again, Tom shook his head. "I've got another idea."

"What are you talking about? We need an ambulance out here, and the sheriff—"

"I think the world of Buddy Gorman, you know that," Tom said. "But I'm not sure I want him involved with this."

"For God's sake, why not?"

Tom rubbed a hand over his head. "Think about it. M-15 sent these guys up here to scare us off or kill us, whatever they thought would work. But their bosses across the border don't know what happened here. If these three turn up with the hell beaten out of them, the rest of the gang won't know where or how it happened. They can't blame it on us. But if the law gets involved, they'll *know*."

"It seems to me like you'd want them to know," Bonnie said. "You'd be sending a message to them that way."

"Yeah, I thought of that. But I don't know if challenging them is something I want to do right now."

"You think they won't just send somebody else after us?"

Tom shrugged. "Maybe. But I think they'll lay off for a while, anyway, and try to figure out what happened."

Bonnie looked skeptical, but she said, "I'll do whatever you think is best, Tom. You know that."

"You mean you'll go stay with Lisa and her family in Houston until everything calms down around here?"

"Nice try. I'll do whatever you want—except for running out on you."

Tom wasn't surprised by her answer. He said, "Keep an eye on these two while I get dressed. I don't think they're going anywhere, but be ready to use that shotgun if you have to."

She nodded. "Of course."

Once he had pulled on a shirt and boots to go with his jeans, he dragged the unconscious men one by one out to the garage. Bonnie and Max followed him. Tom lowered the tailgate on his F-150.

"What are you going to do?"

"These men need medical attention. I'd let them die if it was up to me, but I'm not in the habit of playing God."

Bonnie rubbed her hand in the thick fur at the dog's neck. "Max will need to go to the vet tomorrow. You can be stubborn about your injuries, but he saved our lives."

"I know he did. He's a good dog." Tom opened the passenger side door of the pickup. "Get in, both of you. I'm not leaving you here alone."

Bonnie looked down at the robe. "I'm not dressed."

"Don't worry."

She thought it over and nodded. At her command, Max jumped up into the truck and sat down in the middle of the bench seat. Bonnie climbed in after him while Tom locked the door into the house.

"I'm a little surprised some deputies didn't show up anyway," Bonnie commented as they pulled away and headed for the highway. "Some of the neighbors must have heard those shotgun blasts."

"Yeah, but a shotgun going off a couple of times isn't that unusual out here. Could have been somebody shooting at a snake or a coyote. That's what people will think."

Tom rolled both windows down part of the way as he drove toward Little Tucson with the three men in the back of the pickup. As usual in this dry climate, the night air had cooled off quickly once the sun went down. Bonnie pulled the robe a little tighter around her against the chill.

"I feel positively indecent, driving around at night with only a thin robe on."

"Well, if there are any truckers out on the highway, you can flash them."

She laughed. "You wish!"

Tom smiled wearily. The fact that Bonnie was able to banter with him was a good sign. A lot of women would still be crying and shaking with terror after everything that had gone on tonight. He knew she was scared and upset—hell, *he* was scared and upset—but she had the reaction under control.

He drove straight to the Sierrita County Hospital and turned in at the entrance to the emergency room parking lot. He stopped before he got to the door, although his headlights had already flashed across the entrance and probably alerted whoever was on duty inside. With the pickup's engine still running, Tom got out and went to the back to lower the tailgate. Quickly, he grabbed hold of the three men and pulled them out, letting them drop none too gently to the asphalt of the parking lot. Then he slammed the tailgate and hurried back to the cab. A backing turn, and then he gunned the truck toward the street. In the rearview mirror, he saw the door of the emergency room open and a couple of people came running out to see what was going on. They would find the injured men and take care of them.

"I hope we're doing the right thing," Bonnie said as they left the hospital behind them.

"So do I," Tom said.

But even though he didn't want to admit it, he had an uneasy suspicion that in a situation like this, there wasn't any right thing to do. No matter what path they took, the worst was yet to come.

11

Neither of them slept much that night. When they got home, they spent quite a while cleaning up and taking stock of the damage. The first thing they did was to make sure none of the blood from the three men had gotten onto them. There was always the threat of AIDS when dealing with men such as the ones who had invaded their home. Satisfied that they didn't have to worry on that score, Bonnie cleaned and bandaged the cuts on Tom's arms. She conceded that they didn't really need stitches, although they were certainly painful for him. Then they both donned rubber gloves, broke out the bleach, and began scrubbing up the blood in the garage.

When they were done there, they moved to the bedroom. "This carpet's going to have to be replaced," Bonnie commented with a sorrowful shake of her head.

"We'll pull it out of here tomorrow, cut it up, and burn it."

"Let's do it now," she said. "I don't want it in my house."

Tom shrugged and went to work. It took a couple

of hours and quite a bit of furniture moving, but at the end of that time the bloodstained carpet was rolled up and they carried it out of the house, Tom at one end of the roll, Bonnie at the other.

They found the torn screen and the broken window latch in the utility room where the two men who had gotten inside had gained entrance to the house. "I need to get better locks for all the windows and doors," Tom said.

"No bars, though," Bonnie said. "I won't live behind bars. No honest American should have to do that."

Tom nodded in agreement, although he knew that in some cases reality intruded on that ideal. An ugly fact, but true.

There was nothing they could do tonight about the holes in the garage door and the wall of the hallway that were caused by the shotgun blasts. Repairing them would have to wait until the next day.

"While we're at it, I think I want to repaint the bedroom," Bonnie said. Tom didn't argue with her. This was one case where whatever she wanted was all right with him.

Long after midnight, they finally settled down on the big sofa in the den. Bonnie didn't want to stay in the bedroom until they had finished the work in there, and she didn't want to spend what was left of the night in either of the guest rooms that had once belonged to their children. So she spread a blanket over the sofa, and Tom was more than happy to stretch out on it with her. They lay in each other's arms, savoring the closeness and the knowledge that they still had each other, despite the close call. They were comforted as well by the fact that there was a loaded shotgun on the floor next to the sofa for each of them, within easy reach.

Finally they dozed off and got a few hours of sleep, not waking until well after the sun was up the next morning. It would have been nice if all their troubles had gone away with the night . . .

Of course, that wasn't the case.

Buddy Gorman rubbed a hand wearily over his face and tried to concentrate on the road ahead of him. His mind's eye, though, was back in the emergency room of the Sierrita County Hospital, some six or seven hours earlier, when he had looked down at the bruised and battered faces of the three unconscious men who were being treated there.

The men didn't have any identification on them, of course. They were all in bad shape, although only the one with the fractured skull had a life-threatening injury. The doctors gave him a fifty-fifty chance of surviving—just like Fred Kelso, who was still hanging in there despite not having awakened from his coma. One of the other men had an ugly gash on his face, but that wound had been cleaned and stitched up by the time Buddy got there. The one who appeared to have been mauled by an animal was in worse shape and was still being worked on when Buddy arrived in response to the urgent call. The nurses and the doctor on duty in the ER had called the sheriff's department as soon as they found the unconscious men sprawled in the hospital parking lot.

That left Buddy with the problem of figuring out who they were and what had happened to them. He had a pretty good idea why they were in Little

Tucson. Lauren Henderson had the most finger-print experience in his department, so he had called her in to take the prints of the three men and e-mail them off to be compared with the state and national databases. Buddy hoped to have a response fairly early the next morning. At the same time, Lauren had sent the prints to the authorities in Mexico, Guatemala, and El Salvador. Buddy didn't expect to get lucky again and receive quick responses from those countries, but it didn't hurt to try.

From the hospital he drove to Carla May Willard's home, which he was disturbed to find empty. At least he assumed it was empty, since the place was locked up and dark and no one answered his knocks. Buddy had thought seriously about bust-ing down the door, but that would compromise any evidence he might find inside. He would be able to get a search warrant first thing in the morning, and by now that was a matter of just a few hours anyway. Feeling uneasy about it and hoping that he wasn't making the wrong decision, he drove home and got a little restless sleep before getting up and at it again.

County Judge Consuelo Ramos hadn't been happy about being interrupted while she was eating breakfast with her family, but once Buddy ex-plained the circumstances to her, she signed the search warrant right away. Taking Lauren with him, since she had been inside the Willard house the day before, he headed back there and used a pry bar to open the front door when there was still no response to his knocks.

The house was empty, which was both a relief and a mystery to Buddy. He had been afraid that they would find the bodies of Carla, her children, and her mother. Instead, although the furniture was still there, the people were gone.

Lauren checked the closets and reported that most of the clothes were gone. "It looks like they packed everything they could take with them and just left," she had told Buddy after the search.

He had looked the place over for any signs of violence or trouble and hadn't found any. As he and Lauren stood in the living room, though, she had noticed a couple of spots on the carpet.

"This might be blood. I can go back to the office and get a forensics kit to check it out."

"You do that," Buddy had told her. "Call me when you know for sure one way or the other."

"Sure. What are you going to do?"

"Go see Tom Brannon," he had replied. "I've seen places where people ran out before, and this looks like one of them to me. The only reason I can think of for Ms. Willard to take off like this would be if somebody from M-15 paid her a visit."

"Maybe they took her and the kids with them," Lauren had suggested.

"If M-15 kidnapped them, they wouldn't have had a chance to pack up all their stuff like that."

Lauren had nodded in acknowledgement of that point, then asked, "You think they went after the Brannons, too?"

"That's what I'm going to find out. I know one thing, though—Tom Brannon wouldn't cut and run just because somebody tried to throw a scare into him."

No, Buddy thought now as he neared the Brannon house, Tom wouldn't run. He would fight.

And those damn gang members wouldn't hesitate to kill him and Bonnie both.

Buddy saw smoke rising into the air behind the house as he drove up. He parked the cruiser in front of the garage, got out, and slammed the door. The sound brought Bonnie from inside the house. She was moving rather quickly, but she stopped short when she saw who the visitor was. "Oh, hello, Buddy," she said with a smile. He thought she looked nervous, despite the friendly greeting.

"Mornin', Bonnie," he said pleasantly. "Where's Tom? Around back burning trash?"

"That's right. Do you have any news, Buddy?"

"What? Oh, no, no news. Just visiting."

She didn't believe that, and he didn't blame her. He started around the house as she fell in step beside him.

Tom must have seen them coming, but he continued using a hoe to stuff something into the big trash barrel where the fire was burning. Then he turned and lifted a hand in greeting. He wore a long-sleeved shirt, which was a little unusual. "Good to see you, Buddy," he called. "What's up?"

Buddy stopped and looked at the thick black smoke coming from the barrel. An odd smell hung in the air, as if whatever was burning in there wasn't the usual household trash. "Sendin' smoke signals to the Navajos over in New Mexico, Tom?"

"You mean this? No, we've just been cleaning up. We're a little late on our spring cleaning this year, I reckon you could say."

"I see." Buddy thumbed his Cubs cap farther back on his head. "There wasn't any . . . trouble out here last night, was there?"

"Trouble?" Bonnie repeated quickly before Tom could reply. "Why should there be any trouble?"

"Just curious," Buddy said. "I've got a mystery on my hands this morning. Two of them, in fact."

"What sort of mysteries would those be?" Tom asked in apparently innocent curiosity.

"One of them is what happened to Carla Willard and her kids and her mother."

"Carla May?" Bonnie said, a worried frown appearing on her face. "Something happened to her and her family?"

"I don't know. They're gone. Just up and vanished. No signs of a struggle or any other trouble at their house, but they're sure enough gone."

"Maybe they just went on a trip," Tom suggested.

Buddy nodded slowly. "It did look like they had packed quite a few clothes to take with them. If they're on a trip, they're planning for it to be a mighty long one. That's not good."

"Why not?" Bonnie asked. "After what happened to Carla May, I don't blame her for wanting to get away from Little Tucson for a while."

Buddy scratched his chin. "Yeah, but we're gonna need her to testify for the grand jury when Porfirio Mendez's case comes up. I have to see if I can find her before then."

"I don't see why you have to bother with that," Tom said. "I can testify against Mendez."

"You didn't actually witness anything except the end of that rape, and Mendez wasn't even the one attacking Ms. Willard."

"But he robbed the bank," Bonnie said. "He and his friends shot poor Al Trejo and Deputy Kelso."

"I went over all the statements from the folks in the

bank yesterday. It all happened so fast, and they were so scared, a good defense attorney wouldn't have any trouble shaking their identifications. Besides, some of those people are going to be too scared to testify against a member of M-15—especially after everything that's happened lately."

"What about the video cameras in the bank?"

Buddy shook his head. "Not working. Just bad luck."

"You've got Carla May's statement," Tom pointed out. "Won't that be enough for the grand jury?"

"Enough for an indictment, maybe, but without her testimony I don't know if we can get a conviction at trial."

Tom glared at Buddy. "You can't mean there's even the remotest possibility that that animal could go free!"

"Anything's possible where the law's concerned."

Tom shook his head. "This just doesn't seem right. Anyway, by God, he was an accessory to that rape. He was standing right there watching!"

"You seem to be the only one who can testify to that," Buddy pointed out. "So I'll ask you again, Tom . . . any trouble out here last night?"

Tom didn't answer the question. He looked narrow-eyed at Buddy and said, "You mentioned having two mysteries to clear up this morning. What's the second one?"

"Who dumped the bodies of three badly beaten men on the hospital parking lot in front of the emergency room entrance last night?"

Tom shook his head and said, "I wouldn't have the slightest idea."

"I talked to the staff at the ER," Buddy said. "They

all told me they didn't get a good enough look at the vehicle that dumped those men to identify it, but they were all sure it was a big pickup." He turned his head and looked pointedly at the garage where Tom's F-150 was parked.

"There are a lot of big pickups in Arizona."

"Yeah, but I'm wondering what would happen if I got a real forensics team down here from Tucson and had them go over the bed of *your* pickup, Tom. I'm wondering what they'd find inside your house."

Tom and Bonnie both stiffened. Buddy didn't miss the reaction. Tom's eyes narrowed even more as he said, "I don't think I like what you're implyin', Buddy."

"Why don't you let me go in there and take a look around?"

Tom shook his head. "I don't think so."

"I can get a search warrant, you know."

"You'd do that, after all the years we've been friends?"

Buddy's temper finally got away from him. He snatched his cap off his head and said, "Goddamn it, Tom, I'm the sheriff of this county, and you're puttin' me in a hell of a bad position! One of those men is in such bad shape he's liable to die, and if he does that means there's likely to be a manslaughter charge against whoever walloped him!"

"That's crazy!" Tom blazed back at him. "Men like that—"

He stopped short, but Buddy hadn't missed it. "Men like what?" he asked. "I haven't said anything about who they were."

Tom didn't say anything for a moment, just stood

there with his face taut and angry. Then he said, "Do you even know who they are?"

"Not yet," Buddy admitted, "but I hope I will soon. I've got my office working on it. Now, how about letting me look around inside?"

Tom shook his head and gave him a flat, "No." After a second he added, "And for the record, Bonnie and I were home last night, and nothing happened."

"That's right," Bonnie said. "It was just a quiet evening at home."

Buddy just grunted. He didn't believe them for a second. He had a pretty good idea of how the night had played out. Those M-15 bastards had gone to Carla Willard's house first and thrown such a scare into her that she had packed up her kids and her mama and taken off for the tall and uncut. Then they had come out here, only to find that Tom and Bonnie Brannon didn't scare as easily. He figured that Tom was responsible for beating the hell out of those goons, but he wouldn't put it beyond Bonnie for her to have had a hand in the fracas, too. She would fight like a wildcat if she had to.

So he was left with the option of getting a search warrant and serving it on his oldest friend—or letting it go for now and waiting to see what else happened. Neither of those courses of action appealed to him, but he didn't see what else he could do.

"All right," he said at last. "If that's what you two say happened, then that's what happened."

"Thanks, Buddy," Tom said.

"But don't think this is over," Buddy went on. "I'll have to keep investigating, especially if that fella in the hospital dies. I won't have an unsolved homicide in my county if I can do anything about it."

"I thought you said there might be a manslaughter charge. You didn't say anything about homicide."

Buddy shrugged. "If I don't know the circumstances of a death, I have to regard it as a possible homicide. That's just standard procedure."

They didn't say anything to that, but he thought he saw worry lurking in their eyes. They knew the trouble was far from over. He put his cap back on and started toward his car.

"Buddy . . ." Tom said.

He looked back. "Yeah?"

"Thanks for checking on us."

"I plan to have a car out here more often from now on," Buddy said.

"Watching out for us . . . or watching us?"

Buddy just shrugged and went on to his car. There was a bitter taste in his mouth, and he didn't like it a bit. It wasn't bad enough that those M-15 bastards had killed and terrorized some of the citizens of Sierrita County. Now the situation had driven a wedge between two old friends, so that things between them might never be the same again.

The radio crackled as Buddy drove away from the Brannon house. He picked up the microphone and said, "Go ahead."

Lauren Henderson's voice came back, which meant she had information she wanted to deliver herself, rather than entrusting it to Dusty Rhodes.

"I got a response back from NCIC, Sheriff, on those fingerprints I sent them a while ago."

That meant at least one of the three men had been in the U.S. criminal justice system at one time, or the National Crime Information Center wouldn't have had their fingerprints on file. "Go ahead," Buddy told Lauren again.

"The subject with the fractured skull is Guadalupe Laurenco Almovodar, an El Salvadoran national with suspected strong ties to *Mara Salvatrucha*. He was convicted of drug smuggling charges in California three years ago and sentenced to twenty-five years in prison."

"What was he doing in Little Tucson, then, if he's supposed to be in prison in California?"

"He escaped nine months ago. There's one report of him being spotted in Tijuana not long after that, but he hasn't been in custody since then."

So he had busted out of jail and gone running back to his masters in M-15. Not surprising. "What about the others?"

"Nothing on them yet. It's a pretty safe bet they're the same sort as Almovodar, though."

Buddy couldn't argue with that. He keyed the mike and said, "Stay on it, Lauren. You get that bulletin out on the Willard family?"

"Yes, but I don't know if it'll do any good. If they're on the run from M-15, they're going to be lying really low."

"I know. Gorman out."

He hung up the mike, took his cap off, and sleeved sweat from his forehead, sweat that had formed despite the air conditioning in the cruiser. Even though it had been the only logical conclusion, he now had proof that the three men in the hospital were connected to M-15. Those lunatics wouldn't stop just because somebody—Tom Brannon, whether Buddy could prove it or not—had beaten the shit out of their men. On the contrary, that would probably just make them more eager to have their revenge on Little Tucson and everybody in it.

The sky was clear this morning, but Buddy felt like a storm was brewing. And when it finally broke, all hell would be busting loose.

12

Two days passed in relative quiet, although several members of the media from Tucson and Phoenix showed up in town, drawn by the outbreak of violence that had seen four deaths, five men badly injured, a kidnapping and rape, and an attractive young woman and her family missing. Buddy Gorman figured it was only a matter of time until the national media picked up on the story. Once that happened, the circus would come to Little Tucson. Buddy wasn't looking forward to that.

Nobody had seen hide nor hair of Carla Willard, her children, or her mother since the day of the bank robbery. Every police and sheriff's department in the state had been notified to keep an eye out for them, along with law enforcement agencies from Texas to California. Really, though, they could be anywhere in the country by now, especially if Carla had had enough money on hand to pay cash for some airplane tickets. Buddy had a feeling he might never see the Willards again.

Fred Kelso remained in his coma, as did Guadalupe

Almovodar. The two men who had been dumped at the hospital with Almovodar had regained consciousness but they weren't talking. Sullenly, they refused to identify themselves, and when Buddy had threatened to arrest them for vagrancy, they just sneered at him. He knew what would happen if he arrested them—they would make a phone call, and a short time later some high-powered lawyer would show up to get the charges thrown out. Even though Buddy was sure the men had threatened and perhaps even assaulted Carla Willard and attacked Tom and Bonnie Brannon, he couldn't prove it.

The spots on the carpet in Carla's living room were indeed blood, as Lauren thought. That didn't prove anything, either. Lauren had sent samples of the blood off to the crime lab in Phoenix for DNA testing; if it matched the blood of any of the men in the hospital, that would be a start. It would at least place them on the scene. But the results of those tests would take a week or maybe two, and in the meantime Buddy's hands were tied. All he could do was place a guard on duty at the hospital. Having a deputy there around the clock was going to put a strain on his manpower resources, as were his efforts to keep a closer eye on the Brannon place.

All through that breathing spell, Buddy continued to have the feeling that something was about to happen. He worried about it to the point that his wife Jean scolded him and told him he was going to have to relax. Buddy knew that was a lost cause. Something big was about to hit his town, none of it good.

* * *

Bonnie Brannon pulled into the parking lot at SavMart and looked for a place to park. The sprawling discount store was busy, as usual. While it was true that everybody in the county was nervous about the M-15 gang, they still had to do their shopping, and these days that meant a trip to SavMart.

Bonnie had to park quite a distance from the entrance, but at least the place was right next to a buggy corral, so she wouldn't have to go far to return her buggy once she finished unloading it into the back of the Blazer. It was late afternoon, and heat blazed up from the asphalt of the parking lot. Bonnie felt it through the soles of her canvas shoes as she walked toward the entrance. She wore a sleeveless blouse and a pair of blue jeans. The denim purse slung over her shoulder was heavy from the .38 inside it, but she found the weight of the gun reassuring. Not that she expected anything to happen in SavMart, for goodness' sake.

The past couple of days had been tense. Tom was upset because Buddy Gorman suspected him of being involved with what happened to those three men. Of course, Tom *had* been involved, and so had she. But Buddy's suspicion was like a festering sore, and it got on Tom's nerves. Bonnie knew that he wanted to tell the truth to his old friend, but that would just complicate matters.

Tom had patched the hole in the hallway and nailed some plywood over the damaged section of the garage door. Bonnie had gotten started on repainting their bedroom. Together they had driven into Tucson and picked out some new carpet at the big home improvement warehouse there. Carpet was one of the few things they couldn't buy at

SavMart. The roll was in their garage now, just waiting to be put down when they finished with the painting.

Those chores had occupied Bonnie's mind for the most part, keeping her from dwelling on the danger that still loomed over them. But at unexpected times, the sheer terror she had experienced that night came back to her and made her stop what she was doing. At those moments, she had to close her eyes and clench her hands tightly into fists, so tight that the nails dug into her palms, and wait for the trembling to pass. The first time Tom had caught her at one of those moments, he had tried to take her into his arms and comfort her, only to have her pull away. He had to understand that she needed to fight this thing herself. She didn't want him holding her, not then.

In time this would pass, she told herself. But only if there was no more trouble from M-15. If the gang came after them again, which seemed likely, she didn't know what she would do.

But until that happened, they had to carry on with their life in as normal a fashion as possible. This afternoon, for example, she had come to SavMart to buy groceries, while Tom was at the auto parts store, checking to see how Louly was minding the store.

Bonnie walked past an armored truck parked in the fire lane near the entrance. The automatic doors opened, and blessedly cool air washed over Bonnie as she entered the store. Carlos Flores, a retired physics teacher wearing the standard green SavMart vest with the "S" embroidered on it, gave her a big grin and said, "Hola, Señora Brannon. How are you today?"

"Just fine, Señor Flores," Bonnie answered with a smile of her own. The elderly man had taught both of Bonnie's kids in high school.

"Need a buggy?"

"Yes, please. Gracias." She took the buggy he pulled out from a long row of them next to the wall and pushed it on toward the seemingly endless aisles of the store. Sarah Jeffers stood behind the little podium near the check-out stands, a walkie-talkie clipped to her belt next to a big ring of keys. She was the supervisor of the cashiers and was ready to perform any voids or overrides and provide extra change for any register that ran short. She was Bonnie's age, and the two women had been friends for years. Sarah's husband Millard was the manager of this SavMart, as well as the mayor of Little Tucson. He always liked to say that it was really Sarah who ran both the store and the town. He claimed he was just a figurehead.

Sarah stopped Bonnie as she went by the podium. "Have you heard any news about that gang?" she asked.

Bonnie frowned. "Why would I know anything about them?" The words came out a little sharper than she intended.

"Oh, heavens, I didn't mean anything," Sarah said quickly. "I thought Buddy might have said something to Tom that's all."

Bonnie touched her friend's arm. "I'm sorry, Sarah. I didn't mean to snap at you. I guess I'm just a little on edge these days."

"I think we all are, so don't worry about it."

"Anyway, Tom hasn't talked to Buddy for two or three days, as far as I know. So I haven't heard anything about M-15." Her voice was vehement as she added, "It would be all right with me if I never heard anything about them again."

"Amen to that," Sarah said.

Bonnie summoned up a smile and pushed her buggy past the podium. From the corner of her eye, she saw Millard Jeffers emerge from the office behind the customer service counter. Two armed, uniformed men were with him, one of them wheeling a cart with a couple of plastic crates stacked on it. The men were from the armored truck outside, Bonnie realized, and were probably picking up the store's receipts to take them to the bank.

She was only about ten feet beyond the podium when she heard the screams from the store's entrance.

Her head whipped around. A couple of female customers were running away from the entrance doors, back into the store. They must have been on their way out when they saw the four men coming in. The men wore baggy sweatshirts despite the heat, and as they charged into the store, they drew machine guns from under the shirts. One of the weapons erupted in a burst of fire that sounded like thick cloth being ripped. Both of the fleeing women were struck in the back and flung forward by the impact of the bullets tearing through their bodies. Blood splashed in the air.

Carlos Flores tried instinctively to get in front of the men and block their way into the store. Another burst of automatic fire stitched into him and threw him back against the carts. He flipped over and landed in one of them, his blood spurting from the dozens of bullet holes in his body.

There were thirty or forty people around the check-out stands and the customer service counter, and most of them just stood there gaping at the results of the unexpected violence. The first ones to react were the two guards from the armored truck, both of whom reached for their holstered revolvers. But before they could draw the weapons, the four gunners opened up on them, spraying them with lead that made them dance a macabre, jittery jig as blood exploded from them. Millard Jeffers darted toward the office, trying to get out of the line of fire, but a slug caught him in the leg and sent him spinning off his feet. More bullets thudded into him, rolling him over and over. His body left a thick smear of crimson on the tile floor.

Even as that happened, his wife Sarah was in motion, lunging toward Bonnie and crying, "Get down!" She reached out and shoved hard against Bonnie's shoulder. Bonnie went down, unprepared for the push. Her hip hit the buggy and sent it rolling away. As she sprawled on the floor, she looked up and saw Sarah drop as three bullets slammed into her head, killing her instantly. She fell, landing on top of Bonnie, who couldn't contain a scream of horror as she saw what was left of her friend's shattered skull only inches from her face.

Bonnie twisted her head and looked toward the buggy, which had come to a stop about ten feet away. Her purse was where she had left it, in the fold-out child seat. The gun was useless if she couldn't get to it. She flinched as she put her hands against Sarah's body and started trying to shove the weight off of her.

The machine gun fire and the screaming continued, blending into a hideous melody of death. Fear welled up inside Bonnie. Even if she could get her hands on the .38, she realized, she wouldn't have any chance against four killers armed with machine guns. But if she lay there under Sarah's body, covered in Sarah's blood, the monsters who had invaded SavMart might take her for dead, too. Sickness roiled her belly, but she forced it down. Terror and rage warred inside her. If she could just kill even one of the bastards. . . .

She had to try.

She was about to summon up her strength for another attempt at getting Sarah off of her, when a man hit the floor beside her, a little girl in his arms. The girl was about three and was shrieking and writhing around. Bonnie wasn't sure if she was hit or not, but the man with her, probably her father, surely was. He had a black, red-rimmed hole in the center of his forehead where a bullet had entered, and the back of his head was a bloody mess where the slug had blown its way out. He was dead.

But his little girl was alive, and Bonnie knew she had to do everything she could to keep her that way. As the girl wriggled out of her father's limp arms, Bonnie reached out and grabbed her, pulling her down to the floor before she could stand up and run in terror, which would just make her a target. Bonnie held on to the girl with all her strength and rolled toward her, dislodging some of Sarah's weight that had been pinning her down. She hissed, "Hush! Hush now and be still! You have to stay down here and be quiet!"

Sure enough, a moment later the gunfire began to die away. The screaming and moaning of wounded people continued, however, until a man's voice bellowed, "Shut up! Shut up and listen, or we'll kill the rest of you!"

Some of the sounds subsided. Bonnie heard hurrying footsteps. She raised her head enough to see that a couple of the gunners were herding survivors into the front part of the store. Were they getting everybody together just so they could mow them down easier?

The little girl in her arms whimpered, and Bonnie said, "Be quiet now." The girl sniffled and, thank God, lay still.

The man who had yelled the orders before, climbed up onto one of the check-out stands so that everyone could see him. He swung the barrel of his machine gun menacingly back and forth. "Listen to me," he shouted, "and listen good! This is what you get for crossing *Mara Salvatrucha*! You get in our way, we kill you! You got what we want, we kill you and take it!" He took one hand off his gun and gestured to one of his companions, who started rolling out the cart that contained the store's receipts. "You kill one of us, we kill a hundred of you! You can't stop us! You can't even slow us down! The border is ours!"

No one still alive dared argue. They huddled there in terror, praying that this nightmare would soon be over and that they would live through it.

For dozens of people, though, an afternoon of shopping had proven to be deadly. Bonnie saw bodies sprawled everywhere she looked, motionless and covered with blood.

"You tell everybody what happened here!" the

gang spokesman continued. "You spread the word, you damn gringos! You piss off M-15—you *die!*"

With that, he fired again, aiming at the heads of the small crowd of survivors. Most of them screamed and dived for the floor, but a few were too slow and went down with bullets in their heads.

Bonnie stayed where she was, clinging tightly to the little girl. There was nothing she could do now, nothing except keep this one young life safe if possible. Shudders went through her as she fought off the creeping hysteria.

The leader jumped down from the check-out stand and sauntered arrogantly toward the blood-swamped entrance. The killer with the money was already gone. The other two flanked their leader, backing away with their guns covering the living and the dead, just in case anybody decided to stop them.

Bonnie waited about a minute after the men disappeared through the entrance. Then she slid the rest of the way out from under Sarah and got awkwardly to her feet, still holding the little girl. She tried to keep the child turned away from the awful sight of her dead father.

"Lady!" somebody called to her. "Lady, get down! They might come back!"

"I don't think so," Bonnie said as she walked unsteadily toward the buggy she had been pushing before all hell broke loose. She wanted the cell phone in her purse. Somebody had to call for help . . .

The sudden wail of sirens outside told her that calling was unnecessary. Someone had reported the atrocity already. The frantic calls must have flooded in to the sheriff's department.

The survivors began to climb tentatively to their

feet as Sheriff Buddy Gorman charged into the store, gun drawn, followed by Lauren Henderson, Wayne Rushing, and a reserve deputy Bonnie didn't recognize. Buddy's feet slipped a little in the blood on the floor as he came to a stop and looked around at the horrible scene.

"Good Lord," Bonnie heard him say, and it sounded like a prayer. He turned his head and said to Lauren, "Get every ambulance and paramedic you can down here, right away. And call Tucson and tell 'em we need help! Some of these people will probably have to be choppered to hospitals there."

Lauren nodded as she holstered her gun. She looked pale and sick, as if she might throw up at any second.

Bonnie could relate.

Buddy spotted her and hurried toward her. "Bonnie!" he said. "My God, Bonnie, is that you?"

She could understand how he might not be sure about her identity, splattered with gore as she was. She nodded and said, "It's me, Buddy. I'm all right. I'm not hit."

"The men who did this—"

"They're gone." Bonnie took a deep breath and steeled herself to be calm and helpful. "There were four of them. Hispanic, in their twenties, height ranging from five-six to five-ten, wearing jeans and sweatshirts. They were after the cash. A couple of guards from the armored truck parked outside were picking it up."

Buddy reached out and squeezed her arm. "You're doin' fine, Bonnie. Did you see their vehicle?"

She shook her head. "I was already in the store

when they came in. I don't have any idea what they were driving."

"We ought to be able to find somebody else who can tell us that."

"It won't do any good," Bonnie said grimly. "They're probably halfway to the border by now. You won't catch them."

"We'll sure as hell try." Buddy turned away to snap orders at his other deputies. They spread out to check on the survivors, performing crude first aid until the paramedics and ambulances arrived. When Buddy turned back to Bonnie, he said, "All this for a lousy robbery?"

"They took the money," she said, "but that wasn't their real objective."

He frowned. "What do you mean?"

"One of the men said this was what Little Tucson gets for crossing *Mara Salvatrucha.* They didn't make any secret of who they were, Buddy. They wanted us to know. That's why they left some of us alive."

"Good Lord," Buddy said again. "You make it sound like he was saying . . ."

Bonnie nodded. "Yes. He was saying that *Mara Salvatrucha* has declared war on America. But Little Tucson is where they're gonna start."

13

Tom was in the office at Brannon Auto Parts, going over the sales for the past couple of days, when he heard the sirens screaming past outside on Main Street. He got up from the desk and went into the store's main room, where Louly stood at the front window looking out.

"What's going on?" he asked her.

She glanced back at him and shook her head. "I don't know. A couple of sheriff's cars went by with their sirens on and their lights flashing, and it looks like the ambulances and fire trucks are headed the same way."

"Which way?"

"West."

Tom rubbed his jaw. "Must've been a bad wreck out on the highway."

He turned back toward the office, but before he got there the bell over the front door jangled as someone hurried in. "Tom, Louly," Ben Hanratty from the drugstore said excitedly, "have you heard what happened?"

"No, what?" Louly said.

Ben was wide-eyed. "I heard it on my police scanner. Some of those M-15s just went into the SavMart with machine guns and shot it up! Killed a bunch of people!"

Tom stiffened as every drop of blood in his veins seemed to turn to ice.

Bonnie had gone to SavMart to do some shopping this afternoon.

Without a word, he turned and ran out the back of the store. Louly called after him, but he ignored her. He flung himself into the pickup and cursed as he fumbled getting the key in the ignition. Finally it went in. He twisted it, and even though the F-150 started up right away, everything seemed to be taking twice as long as it should. Tom jerked the truck into gear and fed it gas. The tires slung gravel as he fishtailed down the alley and then careened out into the side street. Barely slowing to look for oncoming traffic, he swung onto Main and floored the accelerator.

He could see flashing lights far ahead of him and knew the emergency vehicles were headed for the same destination. He drove like a madman, weaving in and out of traffic and running red lights. The still-rational part of his brain tried to tell him that he couldn't do Bonnie any good if he got himself killed in a wreck before he even reached SavMart, but the terror gibbering in the front of his brain drowned out those more reasonable thoughts.

Luck was with him, though, and he hadn't plowed into anybody by the time he got to the parking lot entrance. He skidded the pickup off the road. The fire lane in front of the store was jammed with sheriff's-department cars, ambulances, and fire trucks. Tom brought the F-150 to a halt far out in the parking lot, not paying any attention to the fact that it was slanted across a couple of spaces. He ran toward the store entrance, his heart slugging heavily in his chest.

A large group of civilians stood near the entrance, shouting questions and being kept back by several firefighters and one of Buddy Gorman's reserve deputies. Some of these people were just curious bystanders, but many were relatives of folks who had been inside the store when the shooting started. They wanted to know what had happened to their loved ones. Fear lay heavy in the air like a bad taste on the tongue.

Tom managed to push through the crowd, ignoring the angry reactions he got, but when he reached the front of the mob and started toward the store entrance, one of the firefighters put a hand on his chest and pushed him back. "That's a crime scene, mister!" the guy yelled over the commotion. "You can't go in there!"

"My wife—" Tom began.

"I'm sorry, but the sheriff said to keep everybody out."

Tom's hands clenched into fists. He was about to shove the firefighter out of the way, but before he could do that, movement at the store entrance caught his eye. He looked past the firefighter and saw his wife emerging from SavMart, covered with drying blood. Buddy Gorman walked next to her, and Bonnie had a small child cradled in her arms.

Tom didn't have time to wonder who the little girl was. He just bellowed, "Bonnie!" and lunged past the firefighter before the man could stop him. The guy turned and started to lumber after him, but Buddy held up a hand and called, "No, it's okay!"

Tom rushed up to Bonnie and grabbed her, pulling her desperately into his arms. That jostled the little girl, and she began to cry. Bonnie got an arm around her husband's neck and hugged him hard, then said, "Take it easy, Tom. You're scaring her."

Tom stepped back a little so that he could look Bonnie over from head to toe. She had blood on her face and in her hair. Her jeans were splattered with it, but not as heavily. "Are . . . are you all right?" he managed to say. "Were you hit?"

Bonnie shook her head. "I'm fine, just shaken up a little. This isn't my blood, Tom." A catch came into her voice as she went on, "It's Sarah Jeffers'. She . . . she saved my life. She pushed me down when the shooting started, but she got hit. She's dead."

Tom hugged her again, more carefully this time. Relief at finding Bonnie okay was mixed with a growing horror at how close he had come to losing her forever.

Lauren Henderson came up behind Bonnie and said, "I'll take the little girl, Mrs. Brannon."

Bonnie turned to hand the sobbing child to the deputy. "What'll happen to her?"

"We'll take good care of her, don't worry," Lauren said. "Child Protective Services will take custody of her until we can find her mother or some other relative."

The little girl wailed, "I want my daddy!"

Lauren cradled the child against her shoulder and patted her on the back. "Come on, honey," she said. "Don't worry, you'll be fine."

As Lauren walked away, the little girl continued

crying for her daddy. Tom looked grimly at Bonnie and asked quietly, "The kid's father . . . ?"

"Killed in the shooting," Bonnie said. "I grabbed her and held her down, out of the line of fire."

"And probably saved her life," Buddy Gorman put in. "Tom, you'd better take Bonnie on over to the hospital and get her checked out. It'll free up an ambulance if you take her."

"I told you, I don't need to go to the hospital," Bonnie said. "I banged my hip a little on the buggy when I fell down, but that's all that's wrong with me. The doctors will have their hands full already without wasting time on someone who doesn't really need their help."

Buddy said, "You married a stubborn woman, Tom."

"Yeah." Tom glanced toward the store. "I heard it was M-15 that did this."

"There were four of them," Bonnie said without giving Buddy a chance to respond. "They held up the store, but it was an act of terrorism more than a robbery. They mowed people down with machine guns and then said it was because Little Tucson had stood up to them."

Quickly, Buddy said, "I'd appreciate it if you wouldn't go around talking like that, Bonnie. We don't want to throw folks into a panic. The sheriff's department will issue an official statement about what happened later."

"So you can put some spin on it and make it sound not as bad as it really is?" Tom snapped. "Damn it, Buddy, this was an . . . an invasion! It's just like when Pancho Villa crossed the border over in New Mexico and raided Columbus, only those M-15 bastards don't even have the excuse of being revolutionaries. They're just killers!"

Buddy's eyes narrowed. "This is a legal matter, Tom. Like I said, the sheriff's department is in charge."

"Then maybe you'd better ask for some help. Get the army down here or something."

"Why don't you just take Bonnie home, if she's bound and determined not to go to the hospital?"

"I am," Bonnie said.

"Fine," Tom grated out. "But this is too big for you, Buddy. You know it and I know it."

Buddy didn't say anything, and after a moment Tom slipped his arm around Bonnie's shoulders and led her away. Buddy called after them, "Somebody will be out to take an official statement from you, Bonnie."

Tom ignored his old friend and didn't look around. He was torn by anger and frustration, but mostly he was overwhelmed with relief that Bonnie was all right.

They were almost at Tom's pickup when Bonnie said, "My Blazer—"

"We'll come back for it after things calm down. Right now let's get you home and into the shower, so you can wash off all that blood."

Bonnie nodded. Her shoulders slumped with weariness, and there was an odd look in her eyes, as if she had gone numb inside. She was strong, though; she would get over it, Tom told himself.

But only if the horrors stopped—and if *Mara Salvatrucha* had anything to say about it, that might not happen any time soon . . .

* * *

Cipriano and Leobardo ushered the four men into the presence of Ernesto Luis Montoya. This meeting, like all of Montoya's meetings, took place in the surprisingly opulent room on the second floor of the otherwise seedy cantina in Nogales. Two of the men carried plastic crates. In response to a silent gesture from Cipriano, they placed the boxes on the floor near Señor Montoya's desk.

The leader of the gunners, whose name was Danilberto Santos, stood in front of the desk and said to the man who sat back in the shadows, "Everything went well, Señor Montoya. There is the money."

Montoya nodded, the motion barely visible in the gloom. "And the message I wanted delivered . . . ?"

"It was delivered, señor . . . in blood."

"How many did you kill?" Montoya voiced the question in a hoarse whisper.

"Hard to say for certain. More than a dozen, though, surely. Perhaps as many as two dozen."

One of the other gunners put in proudly, "The floors ran red with gringo blood, señor."

In point of fact, quite a few of those who had been killed in the Little Tucson SavMart had been Hispanics—Mexican-Americans, as they were once called. But it was the "American" part of that former designation that was important. To Montoya, anybody who lived north of the border was a gringo, and therefore to be scorned in his eyes.

"You made sure they knew who was responsible?" he asked coldly.

"Of course, señor," Santos said. "Those were your orders, and we carried them out precisely."

Because, who would willingly disobey the Eater

of Babies? One who did might as well go ahead and cut his own throat.

Montoya grunted. "*Bueno.* You and your men have done well, Danilberto. Tonight, any of the women here are yours for the taking, as well as all the food and drink you want."

Santos licked his lips. "*Gracias,* Señor Montoya."

Lazily, Montoya inclined his head toward the door. Cipriano and Leobardo moved in without saying anything, and herded the four assassins out of the room.

When they were gone and the two *segundos* had left the room as well, Montoya came out from behind the desk, crossed to the bar, and poured himself a drink. He picked up a remote control and switched on the giant-screen television. As he settled down on the lushly upholstered sofa in front of the TV, the anchorman on CNN intoned solemnly, "—reports of a shooting rampage today in Little Tucson, Arizona, where an unknown number of people lost their lives as gunmen entered a SavMart store there and opened fire with automatic weapons. Details are still sketchy, but from what we've been able to gather, this incident began as an armed robbery before it turned deadly. We have crews en route to the scene and will bring you a more complete report later. Repeating this story, a shooting rampage—"

Montoya pressed a button on the remote, changing the channel to Fox News.

"—massacre in Arizona," the gray-haired anchorman was saying. "At this time, we have few details, but in the town of Little Tucson this afternoon four armed gunmen opened fire in a SavMart store. The White House issued a statement expressing sympathy and concern for the citizens of Little Tucson and promised whatever federal aid is necessary, but a spokesman for the President declined to comment on charges from several opposition party senators that her lax immigration policies are partially to blame for this outrage."

Montoya chuckled and pressed the remote button again, switching the TV to yet another news broadcast.

"Perhaps as many as twenty-five people are reported dead in Little Tucson, Arizona, where bandits armed with automatic weapons robbed a SavMart store and opened fire on customers and employees. From what we've been able to learn, there are many injuries, and the death toll could rise even higher. We have reporters and camera crews on their way to Little Tucson—"

Montoya changed channels again, going from one broadcast to another. Most of them were talking about what had happened in Little Tucson, but the words he wanted to hear didn't come from the speakers. He scowled at the TV. Why didn't they say anything about *Mara Salvatrucha*? He glanced at the two crates full of money that sat beside his desk. He didn't care about the money. He had more money than he could spend for the rest of his life. What he wanted was to hear the Americans speak of M-15 with fear in their voices. He wanted to see them tremble and sweat when the name was mentioned. Power was everything, and without publicity there could be no real power. He suppressed the urge to throw his empty glass at the screen. Why were the American news people not saying who was really responsible for the outrage in Little Tucson? Why didn't they speak the name of *Mara Salvatrucha*?

But they would. Soon.

14

Tom was watching television in the bedroom when Bonnie came out of the bathroom wrapped in her robe, a towel in her hands which she vigorously used to dry her hair. "It's all over the news," Tom told her. "They're already calling it the Sav-Mart Massacre."

Bonnie stopped drying her hair and perched on the edge of the bed beside him. Together, they watched the newscast from one of the Tucson stations. Being fairly close, the station had gotten a reporter and a camera crew on the scene already. The national networks were relying on their affiliates in Arizona for immediate coverage, but this was a big enough story so that reporters from New York and California would be coming in soon.

The female reporter doing the stand-up was at the edge of the SavMart parking lot, with the sprawling building visible behind her. From the looks of things, the entire parking lot was blocked off. Several large, boxy vehicles were parked near the store entrance. The reporter identified them as belonging to the forensics department of the state police.

"We've confirmed that agents of the FBI and the Border Patrol are also on the scene," the reporter said. "A few minutes ago, we spoke with Sheriff Buddy Gorman."

The scene switched from live to videotape, but the background and the angle were almost identical. Buddy Gorman, looking tired and harassed and impatient, said to the microphone stuck in his face, "Yes, federal authorities have arrived, but they're here to assist us, that's all. The Sierrita County Sheriff's Department is in charge of the investigation."

From off-camera, the reporter's voice asked, "Is there any truth to the rumor, Sheriff, that the army or the National Guard will be called in? Will Little Tucson be placed under martial law?"

"Absolutely not. What happened here today was robbery and murder, not an invasion, and we're not going to treat it as such."

"But, Sheriff, some people are saying that the criminal gang known as M-15 has declared war on Little Tucson."

Buddy shook his head. "I don't have any comment on that except to say that the investigation into this tragic incident will continue until the people responsible for it have been identified and brought to justice."

He turned away, ignoring shouted questions from several reporters, and the coverage cut back to a live shot. The female reporter, looking remarkably cool considering the fact that it was late afternoon and the temperature had to be hovering around 110 degrees, said, "Those were Sheriff Gorman's comments just a few minutes ago. The sheriff declined to tell us how many people have been killed, saying that an official statement on the death toll would be issued later, but a source at the Sierrita County Hospital tells us that so far there are twenty-two fatalities and at least thirty other people were injured, many of them seriously. No names of the dead and wounded have been released. Reporting live from Little Tucson, this is—"

Tom pushed a button on the remote and turned the TV off. "Twenty-two people dead," he said in a hollow voice. "If you count the ones M-15 killed before, we're talking about more than two dozen murders. In less than a week!"

Bonnie put a hand on his shoulder and rubbed the stiff muscles in the back of his neck.

"I don't care what Buddy says," Tom went on. "This *is* a war, an invasion. It started small . . . more drug running, more smuggling of illegal immigrants . . . and people just said how awful it was and talked about how somebody ought to do something about it. Then more robberies, and a killing here and there, and then a bank robbery in broad daylight . . . and now this! What the hell is next? M-15 comes in and tries to take over the whole town?"

"That won't ever happen," Bonnie said.

Tom snorted. "Buddy can't stop it with just him and a handful of deputies."

"The FBI and the Border Patrol are here, the lady on TV said—"

"This may be more than the FBI and the Border Patrol can handle, too. Who knows how many of those M-15 bastards there are? Hundreds, anyway, maybe thousands."

"Take it easy, Tom. It's not your responsibility."

He turned toward her. "Damn it, I almost lost you today! You could have been killed!"

She met his angry gaze squarely and said, "Now you know how I felt when I heard about you tackling those men who kidnapped Carla May."

Tom couldn't argue with that. He was saved from the necessity of trying to do so by the ringing of the telephone. He turned to the bedside table and picked up the cordless unit from its base.

"Hello?"

"Tom, this is Pete Benitez."

Tom frowned in surprise. Pete Benitez was the editor and publisher of the Little Tucson *Eagle*, a weekly newspaper devoted to local news. Tom knew him fairly well, having run ads in the *Eagle* on a regular basis for years.

"What can I do for you, Pete?"

"I heard that Bonnie was at SavMart when those bastards shot the place up this afternoon."

Tom's hand tightened on the phone. "You're calling for an interview?" His voice was edged with anger.

"What? Lord, no! The *Eagle* can't compete with the dailies and TV, and I don't have any interest in trying to. I just wanted to make sure Bonnie was all right."

"Oh." Tom felt a little sheepish now. "Sorry I snapped at you, Pete. Bonnie's okay. Pretty shaken up, of course, but she wasn't wounded."

"That's good." Pete hesitated for a second, then went on, "You know, you *will* be getting requests for interviews, once the big news outlets know Bonnie was there. You'd better get an answering machine, if you don't already have one."

"We do, but thanks for the advice, Pete—"

"There's something else," the newspaperman cut in. "The little girl Bonnie saved . . . Deputy Henderson told me about what happened . . . the little girl is my cousin Hector's daughter Felicia."

"Well, I'm glad that Bonnie was able to—" Tom stopped short as the realization hit him. "That means . . ."

"Yeah. Hector was killed."

"Oh, Lord. I'm sorry, Pete."

"We all are." Tom heard the man take a deep breath, probably to get his grief under control, and then Pete went on, "That's still not all I've got to tell you. The town . . . hell, the whole county . . . is pretty well up in arms about this, and there's been a meeting called for tonight at the high school."

"A meeting?" Tom repeated. "What sort of meeting?"

"People want to get together to talk about what happened."

That might help some folks to feel better, but other than that it didn't sound too productive to Tom. He said, "I don't know—"

"They plan to talk as well about what we can do to keep anything like this from happening again."

That was more intriguing. "What are you getting at, Pete?"

"Most people like Buddy Gorman just fine," Pete said bluntly, "but not everybody believes that he's equipped to deal with a threat like this. Hell, we *know* he's not."

Tom nodded, even though he knew the man on

the other end of the phone line couldn't see him. "I've been thinking the same thing. Who organized this meeting?"

"I'm not sure. The word just started going around. I think you ought to be there, Tom. You're the only one who's taken on M-15 and won."

"There were only two of them—" he began.

"Plus the three who broke into your house, all of whom you put in the hospital."

"I don't know anything about that," Tom said flatly.

"Hell, I don't care whether you admit it or not. I told you I'm not fishing for a story. I just think you need to be at the meeting."

Tom thought it over, but only for a few seconds. "All right. I'll be there." Bonnie looked at him curiously, obviously wondering what he was talking about. He held up a finger to indicate that he would explain.

"Good," Pete said, sounding relieved. "Seven-thirty at the high school gym."

"Okay. Thanks."

Tom hung up, and Bonnie asked, "What meeting? What's this all about, Tom? Was that Pete Benitez?"

"Yeah," Tom said, answering the last question first. "That little girl you helped this afternoon was his cousin Hector's daughter."

Bonnie put a hand to her mouth. "Oh, dear Lord. That poor man who was shot was Pete's cousin?"

"Yeah."

"I feel so sorry for the families . . . for *all* the families." She shook her head, then went on, "What about the meeting?"

"People are getting together at the high school gym this evening."

"To talk about what happened?"

"To talk about how to keep it from happening again."

A frown creased Bonnie's forehead. "That sounds a little like you're talking about vigilantes."

"More likely people just want to put some pressure on Buddy Gorman to bring in help from the federal government."

"Are you going?"

"Pete said I ought to be there."

Bonnie nodded. "Then I'm going with you."

Tom wasn't going to argue with her. In fact, he was glad he hadn't been forced to try to persuade her to come along.

He wasn't sure if he was ever going to go anywhere without her—or even let her out of his sight—again.

Pete Benitez had certainly been right about one thing—the phone rang at least a dozen times in the next hour, as reporters began to get hold of the names of some of the people who had lived through the already notorious SavMart Massacre. Tom answered the first few times and told the persistent questioners on the other end that his wife wasn't giving any interviews just yet. After that, he ignored the ringing and let the machine pick up.

When it came time to leave for the meeting at the high school, Bonnie was dressed in a simple, tasteful dress, and Tom wore jeans and a sports shirt. As they got into the F-150 and left the house, they spotted several TV station vans parked on the road that circled through the residential area.

"They'll probably be camped on our doorstep by the time we get back," Tom said glumly.

"You can sic Max on them," Bonnie said.

"Damn high-tech vultures," Tom muttered as he drove past the vans with their satellite uplink equipment.

At this time of year, the sun was still fairly high in the sky at seven-thirty, and the heat was brutal. That didn't seem to have affected the turnout for the meeting. The high school parking lot was nearly full, and Tom saw quite a few people filing into the gym.

The bleachers were almost full, too, but Tom and Bonnie didn't have to hunt for a place to sit. Pete Benitez hurried up to them, a short, energetic man with red hair courtesy of his Irish mother. He pumped Tom's hand and said, "Glad you made it. Come on out onto the floor, both of you."

Tom frowned as he saw that several long tables had been set up on the gym floor, with folding chairs behind them. He was a little surprised to see Buddy Gorman sitting at one of the tables. Several members of the city council and some of the county commissioners were out there on the floor, too, along with some men and women in city clothes who he didn't recognize.

"What's going on here, Pete?" he asked, suddenly suspicious.

"You'll see." Pete tugged on his arm. "Come on."

Tom thought about jerking free from the newspaperman's grip and walking out, taking Bonnie with him, but his curiosity got the best of him.

Something was up, and Tom wanted to know what it was, even though he had an instinctive feeling that he wouldn't like it.

He allowed Pete to steer him and Bonnie behind one of the tables, where they sat down next to one of the men Tom didn't know. The man wore a dark, sober suit, had thinning brown hair and a neatly trimmed mustache. Tom couldn't decide if he looked more like an insurance salesman or an undertaker. On the other side of the stranger sat a woman who was also dressed very conservatively. She wore a pair of gold-framed glasses, and her blond hair was pulled back severely.

Pete Benitez went to a lectern that had been set up between a couple of the tables. The school's public address system, which was used at pep rallies and consisted of an amplifier and a couple of speakers, sat on the floor in front of the lectern. Pete picked up the microphone, which was attached to the amplifier by an electrical cord, switched it on, and tapped it, causing a couple of loud pops. He lifted the mike to his mouth and asked, "Can you folks hear me all right?"

An affirmative rumble came back from the crowd assembled in the bleachers, which fell silent as Pete continued, "Thank you for coming this evening. I don't have to tell you what happened this afternoon, or how shocked and horrified we all are about it. Some of you lost loved ones in this tragedy. Many of you have friends or relatives in the hospital right now, fighting for their lives. Sheriff Gorman has agreed to come here tonight and give us a statement on the most up-to-the-minute developments."

A little lukewarm applause sounded from the

bleachers as Buddy stood up and came to the lectern to take the mike from Pete Benitez. He brought it a little too close to his mouth, causing a brief squeal of feedback before he lowered it and said without preamble, "The death toll from this horrible incident stands at twenty-three."

Someone else died since that newscast he and Bonnie had seen earlier, Tom thought.

"The investigation is continuing," Buddy went on, "but at present we don't have any suspects in custody. I've requested assistance from the state police, and the FBI and the Border Patrol have also agreed to consult with us."

Somebody in the bleachers called out, "What about the army?"

Tom saw Buddy's face tighten. "There's no need for the army to come in at this point. No one wants to have Little Tucson placed under martial law."

From elsewhere in the bleachers came the shout, "You can't stop M-15, Sheriff! There's too many of 'em!"

Somewhat agitated, Buddy again made the microphone squeal for a second. "We haven't conclusively established the identity of the gunmen—"

"Hell, dozens of people heard them admit they were M-15!"

Pete took the microphone back from Buddy and said, "Folks, please take it easy. If we all start shouting, we won't be able to accomplish anything here tonight."

The man sitting next to Tom stood up and moved to the lectern, holding out his hand for the microphone. Pete hesitated for a second, then gave it to him. The man raised it and said in a controlled, attention-getting voice, "My name is Eugene Berry. I'm the special agent in charge of the Federal Bureau of Investigation office in Tucson." He gestured toward the blond woman. "My colleague, Special Agent Ruth Ford, has flown out from Washington to be with us tonight. The President has asked us to convey her deepest sympathy to the people of Little Tucson and Sierrita County."

One of the city councilmen, Walt Deavers, slapped a palm on the table in front of him and in a voice that carried clearly despite being unamplified demanded angrily, "Sympathy's all well and good, but when's the President gonna *do* something to put a stop to this?"

The blunt question brought an outburst of cheering and applause from the crowd. Unruffled, Agent Berry waited for things to calm down and then said, "While the federal government stands ready to assist, this is primarily a state and local matter—"

"Sure," the bald, irascible Deavers broke in. "When the Feds want to duck something, they say it's up to the states. But when the states do somethin' the Feds don't like, you boys don't waste any time comin' in and bullyin' everybody until you get your way!"

The audience whooped in agreement this time.

Agent Ruth Ford stood up and took the microphone from Berry. She didn't ask for it; she just took it, and although he looked like he wasn't happy about what she was doing, he gave it up.

"Perhaps I can clarify matters," she said crisply. "Acting under orders from the President and the Attorney General, the FBI will provide logistical and technical support for local authorities, but that is all, unless and until it can be proven conclusively that federal laws were broken."

Tom couldn't stay silent any longer in the face of this runaround. "What about those automatic weapons?" he asked. "Aren't those illegal under federal laws?"

Agent Ford turned her head and gave him a small, condescending smile. "Since we don't know exactly what sort of weapons the perpetrators used—"

"Yes, we do," Bonnie said quietly.

Ford frowned at her. "Ma'am, you are . . . ?"

"Bonnie Brannon. I was there." Bonnie's voice hardened. "Some of those bullets went a foot or two over my head. They killed one of my best friends and knocked her body right on top of me. I got a good look at those guns. They were Newcomb & Scheafer SST-25s, modified to fire in a fully automatic mode and accept hundred-round clips." Agent Ford stared at her in silence for a long moment, and Bonnie finally shrugged her shoulders. "I read a gun magazine every now and then. My subscription to *the Ladies' Home Journal* ran out."

Tom looked down at the table to keep from laughing out loud. Despite the grimness of the situation, some of the people in the audience couldn't help but be amused by the FBI agent's obvious discomfort. When Tom glanced at Buddy Gorman, he saw that even the sheriff had a faint smile on his lips.

Agents Ford and Berry weren't amused, though. Ford snapped, "Perhaps I should talk to you later and get your testimony, ma'am."

"Perhaps you should," Bonnie said.

Ford gave the microphone back to Pete Benitez, and then she and Berry sat down, neither of them looking happy now. Pete said, "We also have a representative of the U.S. Border Patrol with us this evening."

A bulky, middle-aged man with a graying crew cut stood up and accepted the mike. He said, "My name is Jerry Prescott. I know what you people are thinking. You think the Border Patrol ought to stop these illegals from coming over and raising hell on American soil. I wish I could give you people better news, but the Border Patrol is understaffed and underfunded. We just don't have the money or manpower to stop more than a fraction of the illegal immigration that's been going on in this part of the country for years. That's the unvarnished truth of it."

The blunt statement took the audience by surprise. In the relative quiet that followed it, Ford said sternly, "Agent Prescott . . ."

Prescott turned to look at her, and his face was set in resolute lines. He said, "I don't know about you, ma'am, but I'm damned sick and tired of shining people on and trying to spin everything like it's going to be all right. If the government would give us the tools, we might be able to help the situation down here. That's not going to happen, though, until they stop spending so much of the taxpayers' money on social engineering and raising the self-esteem of people who wouldn't have self-esteem problems if they weren't such goddamn lazy bums to start with!"

Thunderous cheers rolled out from the bleachers. The locals who were sitting at the tables got to their feet and joined the applause. Ford and Berry were both on their feet now, too, but they were in Prescott's face, jawing furiously at him, and although

Tom couldn't hear the words, he had a pretty good idea what they were saying. They were telling Prescott that he was through as a government agent. Even though they were FBI and he was Border Patrol, they could probably pull enough strings to get him fired.

Prescott saved them the trouble and confirmed Tom's guess at the same time, by taking out the leather wallet that contained his badge and identification papers. He threw it at Ford's sensibly-shod feet and then turned back toward the crowd, lifting the microphone to his mouth again. Berry made a grab for it, but Prescott was considerably larger and shrugged him off.

"I'll tell you people the truth, and this may be the only time you'll ever hear it from the government . . . You people are on your own! You got a sheriff here who seems like a good man, but he's no match for M-15! And all of you know they're behind all this trouble. If you want to stop what's going on . . . if you want protection . . . you're gonna have to do it yourself!"

Buddy Gorman closed in on Prescott, and the whole thing seemed to be on the verge of turning into a melee. Tom wished he hadn't brought Bonnie out here. Buddy succeeded in wrenching the microphone away from the Border Patrol agent—the *ex*-Border Patrol agent—and said loudly, "Nobody's taking the law into their own hands in Sierrita County!"

An idea sprang into Tom's head, and he shouted, "Then let's stop M-15 legally!"

Buddy turned to stare at him. Tom's words were loud enough, and unexpected enough, to have caused a momentary hush. Pete Benitez spoke quickly, while he had the chance, asking, "What do you mean, Tom?"

"I mean the people of this country have a right to stand up for themselves." Even without the microphone, Tom was making himself heard. "We have a right to do the things that need done when the government can't—or won't—do them! There's nothing illegal about people defending themselves, and citizens have a right to enforce the laws of the land! They've done it before, and they can do it again. *We* can do it!"

"You're talking about becoming vigilantes," Buddy accused.

Tom shook his head. "Vigilantes break laws. Patriots enforce them."

The words, simple as they were, struck a chord in those who heard them. Someone began chanting, "Patriots . . . patriots," and others took up the chant. The words echoed in the high-ceilinged gymnasium until the windows at the top of the bleachers were rattling just like they did when the crowd bellowed, "Dee-fense!" during a basketball game. Tom stood there as the sound washed over him, a little shocked at the reaction, even more shocked that he had stood up and made a speech. That really wasn't like him. He looked over at Bonnie, who smiled in encouragement and pride but looked worried at the same time. Buddy just shook his head, and the two FBI agents both glared at Tom. Prescott gave him a thumbs-up, then turned and walked toward the exit, clearly done with this.

Pete got the microphone back and after a while succeeded in quieting the crowd. Tom and Bonnie, along with the others at the tables, sat down again.

Pete said, "As you know, our mayor Millard Jeffers was one of those who was brutally murdered this afternoon. Mayor Jeffers was a fine man and a good mayor . . . but now we need someone to take his place. We need someone to lead Little Tucson in this time of danger. And I can't think of anybody better for the job than Tom Brannon!"

Tom's head snapped up at those unexpected words. He started to shake his head, but even as he did, he realized it was too late. Cheers and applause swept down from the bleachers and washed over him like a strong wave. He knew when something was barreling right at him like a freight train.

And on this hot summer evening, fate was doing just that.

15

Figuring he ought to nip this in the bud while he still possibly had a chance to, Tom held up his hands for quiet, and when the crowd settled down, he addressed Pete, Walt Deavers and the other city councilmen, and the county commissioners. "I'm honored by the offer, but I can't be mayor of Little Tucson. I don't live in the city limits, and I reckon that's a requirement for holding a city office."

Pete still held the microphone. He said into it, "Actually, it's not. I looked it up in the city charter. In order to hold a city office, you have to either be a resident . . . or own property in the city. You own the building your auto parts store is in, Tom. That makes you eligible."

That cut the legs right out from under his argument. He glanced at Bonnie as if asking her what the hell he should do next, but all she could do was shrug. He knew she meant that the decision was up to him.

Walt Deavers lumbered to his feet. "I looked up some things in the city charter, too," he said. "Turns out that in the event the mayor dies while in office, the secretary of the city council is the mayor pro tem and can take over the mayor's job."

Tom felt relief start to go through him.

But then Deavers went on, "However, the city charter also provides that the council can, at its discretion, appoint someone else to serve out the mayor's term. We've talked it over, Tom, and we appoint you."

Another burst of applause came from the bleachers. Tom felt a sense of futility creeping into him. He sensed that this whole thing had been a setup. Pete and the city council had decided before the meeting ever began that they were going to try to railroad him into taking the job of mayor.

He turned to Bonnie again and this time asked the question bluntly. "What do you think?"

"It's up to you," she said. "I can't make up your mind for you, Tom."

Her answer didn't surprise him. They had always regarded each other as equals when it came to family and business decisions, talking things through until they reached a conclusion that was satisfactory to both of them. But this was a personal matter, so she was going to leave it up to him.

Unfortunately, whatever he decided would have an impact on her, too. By accepting the job, he would be putting her at risk.

Hell, she was already at risk, he told himself. They all were, as long as the members of M-15 believed that they could carry out their atrocities any time they wanted, without fear of repercussions.

Maybe some repercussions were exactly what was needed.

His head jerked in an abrupt nod. "All right," he said. "I'm not sure any of us are doing the right thing, but . . . I'll take the job."

Thunderous applause and loud cheers came from the bleachers. Excitement was growing inside him. Maybe he could actually do some good. An idea had begun to percolate in his brain, an idea that might just work . . .

"Anybody have anything else to say?" Pete Benitez asked when the commotion finally died down again.

Someone in the bleachers cupped his hands around his mouth and yelled, "Give 'em hell, Tom!"

Tom just smiled and nodded.

Giving M-15 hell was exactly what he intended to do.

After the meeting broke up and the crowd left the gymnasium, Tom and Bonnie walked along the line of tables to the one where the city council members sat, along with Sheriff Buddy Gorman. With a faint smile on his face, Tom asked, "Are you boys sure you know what you're gettin' into?"

Before Deavers or any of the others could respond, Buddy said, "Tom, don't take this the wrong way, but I'm not sure this is a good idea."

"I'm not surprised you feel that way, Buddy."

Deavers asked, "Just what *are* you thinkin' about doin', Tom?" Then he held up a hand and went on, "Hold on a minute. Maybe we better swear you in first, before you answer that question."

Tom nodded. "However you want to do it is fine with me."

Deavers reached to his shirt pocket and took out a small, black book. "I got a New Testament here. Reckon that'll do to swear on."

The impromptu ceremony took only a moment. Tom put his hand on the New Testament and swore to uphold the laws of the city of Little Tucson and the State of Arizona. Once that was done, Deavers told him to pull up a chair and fill them in on his plans.

They all gathered around the table, including the county commissioners, except for Buddy, who got up and went over to talk to Special Agents Ford and Berry, who waited by the concession stand.

Pete Benitez asked, "What are we gonna do about M-15, Tom?"

"I don't see where we have much choice," Tom said, "but to form a group of armed citizens to patrol the border. The way I see it, no one is protecting us—not the state of Arizona. And not Washington, that's for danged sure. What happened at the Sav-Mart will be forgotten in a week and the rest of America will go back to sleep. Nope, we're on our own. Never thought it would come to this, but it's time to round up every able-bodied citizen of Little Tucson who has a weapon and form our own militia. I don't like the sound of that word anymore than you guys do, but dammit, a hell of a lot of our friends and neighbors were slaughtered here today and it's up to us and us alone to see it don't happen again. And if that means forming a militia, so be it.

"Ain't that taking the law into our own hands?" Deavers asked. "That's stickin' your nose in one big hornet's nest, Tom. And Buddy ain't gonna like that too much."

"Buddy means well," Tom said, "but we all know he's in over his head."

"What do we call our group?" Deavers asked. "I mean, we should have a name, right?"

"You could call it the Patriot Project," Pete suggested. "The way the people were chanting earlier, I think they'd take to it."

Tom thought about it and nodded. "That's fine with me. I don't really care what we call it, as long as it does the job."

"What is the job?" Deavers asked. "Stopping M-15?"

"Stopping all illegal aliens. From what I hear, some of the M-15 members pretend to be farm workers or some other sort of illegal immigrants. When they get caught by the Border Patrol, they claim to be innocent of everything except wanting a better life. That plays right into the hands of the folks who claim our borders ought to be even more open."

"Like the lady sittin' in the White House," one of the other councilmen said.

Tom shrugged in acknowledgment of the point. He wasn't interested in political arguments. As far as he was concerned they were a waste of time and energy, because politics was so mired down in inertia that anything substantive rarely if ever got done through that process. Things that really made a difference nearly always happened at the local level, at the grass roots.

Like the Patriot Project.

"I think we're looking at a small group . . . probably no more than a couple dozen . . . will patrol the border between Sierrita County and Mexico. From what that Prescott told us, it sounds like we can't depend on much, if any, help from the Border

Patrol, so we'll have to turn back the illegals ourselves. That means everyone will have to be armed,
just in case of trouble."

"But we won't start it," one of the men said.

"Exactly," Tom agreed. "We'll go out of our way
to avoid trouble, in fact. But if somebody starts
shooting at us . . . well, nobody can expect us not to
shoot back."

"Nobody but the damn ACLU!"

That brought a laugh from those assembled
around the table.

"What about turning the illegals back?" someone
asked. "Seems to me like we wouldn't have any au-
thority to do that."

"What they're doing is against the law," Tom
pointed out. "That's why they're called illegals. And
as citizens of the United States, we *do* have the right
to enforce the law. You've all heard of a citizen's
arrest, haven't you? They stand up in a court of law,
so I reckon what we're setting out to do would
stand up as well."

"But you don't know that," Pete pointed out. "We
won't really know unless one of the cases comes to
trial."

Tom shrugged again. "You never know what a
judge will say or do. A lot of them are power-crazy,
too. But I'm willing to take my chances."

"So am I," Deavers said. "Count me in, Tom."

The others all chimed in, pledging their support.
Tom leaned back in his chair and nodded, satisfied
that they should go forward with the plan. He
glanced around. Freedom and justice and liberty
had a habit of sprouting up in strange places.
There probably weren't many places stranger for

such a thing to happen than inside a sweltering high school gymnasium that smelled vaguely of sweat socks.

"We'll meet at City Hall tomorrow and start working out all the details," he said as he got to his feet. The others nodded in agreement and stood up to leave. Tom took hold of Bonnie's arm and would have turned toward the exit himself, but Buddy Gorman called from behind him, "Hold on a minute, Tom."

He turned to look behind him and saw Buddy stalking toward him, trailed by the two FBI agents. "What is it, Buddy?" Tom asked as his old friend came up to him.

"I heard what you're planning. You can't go through with it."

"Why not?"

"Well . . . you just can't! It's against the law. I'd have to arrest you. And believe me, Tom, I don't want to do that."

"Against what law?" Tom challenged. "What would you charge me with? Anyone who joins the Patriot Project will be legally licensed to carry a gun. There's no law against driving around or hiking through the countryside. And you know as well as I do that a citizen's arrest is legal, and so is self-defense."

"Damn it!" Buddy burst out. "You *want* somebody to shoot at you, so you can shoot back!"

Tom shook his head. "That's just not true. If there's no shooting at all, that's fine with me." He paused. "But think about this, Buddy. If somebody *does* shoot at us, chances are it's gonna be a member of M-15. Some poor migrant worker who just wants to make some money for his family isn't going to be armed and looking for trouble. If he's stopped, he'll just turn around, go back across the border, and try again some other day. The only ones who'll fight are the criminals, the same sort of lowlife scum who shot Burt Minnow and Madison Wheeler, the same kind of animals who murdered Al Trejo and put Fred Kelso in a coma and mowed down a couple of dozen people in SavMart this afternoon! Why are you worried about bastards like that?"

Buddy's face was pale and tight with strain. "I worry about the law," he said. "That's all." He paused and then added, "That's not completely true. I worry about *you*, too, Tom."

Tom didn't know what to say to that. He felt the pain of the wedge that had been driven between him and his oldest friend. That was one more mark against *Mara Salvatrucha* as far as he was concerned.

Agent Ford stepped forward and said coolly, "You asked what charges could be brought against you if you go through with this, Mr. Brannon. What about conspiracy and federal civil rights violations?"

Tom met her icy gaze squarely. "Doesn't there have to be a crime in order for there to be a conspiracy? I've said it over and over. The Patriot Project isn't going to break any laws. We won't deprive anybody of their civil rights, either. We'll just tell the illegal immigrants to go back across the border. Most of them will do it. The ones who won't will be brought back here and turned over to Sheriff Gorman or the Border Patrol, in accordance with the law. What happens to them after that is out of our hands."

"But if you're attacked—"

"We'll fight back, which we have every legal right to do."

Agent Berry said, "You're going to regret this, Brannon. You'll have the federal government on your back for the rest of your life. You'll never file a tax return again that won't be gone through with a fine-tooth comb. You'll be paying penalties to the IRS from now on. And you and your wife will never see a penny of your Social Security benefits, damn you!"

The man had gotten so worked up during his threats that spittle was flying from his mouth by the time he was finished. Agent Ford turned to look at him, and so did Buddy Gorman. Ford said quietly but firmly, "Agent Berry, there's no need to be so upset."

From behind them, a voice asked, "Agent Berry, do you mind if I quote you on that?"

They all turned to see that Pete Benitez had come back into the gym. He smiled at the two federal agents.

"No comment," Ford snapped. "And anything said in here just now was off the record."

"I didn't agree to that," Pete pointed out. "I've been saying that my little paper can't compete with the big boys, but you know, maybe with a good enough scoop, it could. Like, say, a federal agent threatening a law-abiding American citizen with the IRS. Threatening to take away his Social Security benefits for no good reason. Sounds pretty newsworthy to me."

"You little prick," Berry growled as he took a step toward Pete.

Ford's hand closed on his arm and prevented

him from going any farther. "Agent Berry!" she growled.

"What was that you called me?" Pete asked. "A spic? Just because my last name is Benitez? Now we've got a federal agent threatening U.S. citizens *and* using racial slurs?"

"You know what I said!" Berry shouted at him. "I called you a goddamn prick!"

"Ohhhh. Well, never mind, then."

"Come on, Agent Berry," Ford said as she tugged on Berry's arm. "Let's get out of here."

Muttering under his breath, Berry allowed her to steer him out of the gym. Tom, Bonnie, Buddy, and Pete watched the two federal agents walk out.

Buddy sighed. "Man, I really don't like bein' on the same side as those two."

"Then don't be," Tom said. "They're wrong, and you know it."

"The law doesn't choose sides."

"That's *exactly* what it does," Tom said. "The good guys are on one side, and the bad guys are on the other."

"I wish the world were still that simple," Buddy said.

16

They went by SavMart to pick up Bonnie's Blazer on their way home. She drove the SUV while Tom followed in the pickup. When they reached the road they lived on, Tom saw that his prediction had been accurate—there were even more cars and news-trucks parked along the road now. Well-dressed men and women stood around waiting, obviously reporters. Much less dapper cameramen lounged nearby. All of them came to attention as Tom and Bonnie drove up.

It took some careful maneuvering not to run over any of the media. Tom wondered how celebrities put up with it all the time. No wonder some of them hauled off and punched the paparazzi. He figured he wouldn't be able to tolerate it for more than a day or two.

But he might have to get used to it, he reminded himself. If the Patriot Project got off the ground, it would attract a lot of media attention.

As the garage doors went up in response to the signal from the control unit in Bonnie's Blazer, she drove in quickly, followed by Tom who took the second space in the two-car garage. Tom stepped out of the pickup and heard shouted questions coming from the horde of reporters running toward the house. Quickly, he jabbed the button on the wall that lowered the garage doors. They began to come down, but he was worried that they wouldn't close in time. Then he began to worry that some of the reporters would try to stick their arms under the descending doors so they could wave microphones at him and demand answers to their inane questions. That would be all he needed, for a couple of those parasites to get their arms stuck and broken under the doors. The lawsuits would never cease.

Luckily, the doors thumped down on the concrete floor of the garage before any of the reporters could get there. Tom saw them through the windows in the doors, clustering in the driveway, and he could hear their persistent shouts. He ignored them as best he could and followed Bonnie into the house, making sure the door was locked securely behind them.

One thing you could say for all this media attention, he thought—M-15 wouldn't try any more revenge raids on his house while the reporters were around. Nobody could sneak up on the place with that pack of hungry jackals right outside.

Bonnie fixed a snack for them and they tried to watch some TV, but it was hard to concentrate. Besides, neither of them wanted to relive the afternoon's events through the newscasts that were on almost every channel. After a while, as they sat together on the sofa, Tom said to his wife, "You seem unusually quiet tonight."

"I'm tired. It's been a horrible day."

He nodded. "Just about the worst one I can remember."

Without warning, she burst out, "And tonight you went and made it worse!"

He drew back a little, his eyes widening in surprise. "What are you talking about?" he asked. "What did I do?"

"The Patriot Project, remember?"

"I thought you were all right with me taking the mayor's job!"

"I didn't know you planned to paint a big target right on your back!"

Tom stared at her. "You think that's what's going to happen? You think M-15 will come after me again?"

"They already have a grudge against you," she pointed out. "One of their own is in the hospital under guard, and when he gets out he'll be going to jail because of you. But that's nothing compared to what it'll be like when they hear about what you've started tonight." She trembled so hard she had to clasp her hands together to keep them from shaking. "I was there, Tom. I was there in SavMart and saw what they did and heard what that awful man said. The Patriot Project will be a slap in their faces, and they won't stand for it. They'll have to stop you."

A frown creased his forehead as he said, "This isn't like you, Bonnie. You're a fighter. Always have been. You brained that bastard with the bat when they broke in here and never hesitated to take him out. Hell, you spoke up at the meeting tonight when that Agent Ford was trying to give everybody the runaround. I've never been prouder of you."

"That woman got on my nerves," Bonnie acknowledged. "And I'll fight if I'm backed into a corner, Tom, you know I will. But this is different. You're just asking for trouble."

"What would you rather we do?" he asked stiffly.

"We could pack up and leave. We could go stay with Brian or Lisa. We could even move for good."

Her answer shocked Tom. He stared at her for a moment before he was able to say, "I couldn't do that. This is my home. I've lived here all my life. My folks, and their folks, are from these parts. Our kids grew up here, I've got a business here. Those roots go too deep to pull up."

"It's just land," Bonnie said, her voice dull and touched with hopelessness now. She knew she was fighting a losing battle. "We could live anywhere else and be just fine, as long as we're together."

"I don't think so. I think I'd leave too big a part of myself here." Tom couldn't stay sitting down. He got to his feet and began to pace back and forth between the sofa and the TV. "And it's not just land. It's our home. Some people want to come in here and either force us out of our home or kill us. I'm surprised you want to cooperate with them."

Bonnie shot up from the sofa and moved in front of him, making him stop abruptly. "You think I'm a coward?" she blazed at him. "You think I want to give up?"

"I know you're not a coward," he said. "But it sure sounds like you're thinking about giving up."

"I just . . . I just don't want to see you hurt." Her

voice broke. "I don't want to see anybody else hurt. I saw too many people die . . ."

Her hands came up and covered her face as sobs began to wrack her. Of course she was upset, Tom told himself, thinking that he deserved a swift kick in the butt for arguing with her at a time like this. After all, it had only been a matter of hours since she had been trapped in the middle of a terrifying bloodbath and had barely escaped with her life. She'd been forced to witness the atrocity at close range, and he was sure that some of those awful images would plague her for the rest of her life.

He stepped closer to her and put his arms around her, relieved that she didn't draw away. He held her tightly and murmured softly to her as he patted her on the back with one hand. She sobbed against his shoulder. He couldn't change anything, couldn't make it better, but at least he could hold her.

Finally, after drawing in several deep, shuddery breaths, she calmed down enough to straighten and look into his eyes. "You're going through with it, aren't you?"

"I don't have any choice," he told her softly.

She wiped at her eyes with the back of a hand. "Well, then, I'm part of it, too."

"Now, wait a minute . . ." Tom began.

"Are you saying I'm not a patriot?"

"No, not at all—"

"Then I'm going on patrol with you." She smiled weakly. "Hell, I'm a better shot than you."

He didn't like the idea, but he decided it would be better to wait until later to argue with her. Let the trauma of today's events fade a little first.

"We'll see," he said.

"No, we won't," she insisted. "I'm not a kid, Tom. I know perfectly well what that means. And I'm telling you, I'm part of this."

"All right," he said, frustrated because she knew him too well for him to put anything past her. "I guess I can use somebody to watch my back, anyway."

"And you'll watch mine."

"Of course."

"We'll be a team." She laughed. "M-15 won't stand a chance against us."

Tom smiled back at her and wished that was true.

The word got around fast. When Tom and Bonnie drove up to the City Hall in Little Tucson the next day, there must have been two hundred people milling around in front of the building—and that didn't include the dozens of media members carrying on with their feeding frenzy.

That frenzy got worse when the reporters spotted the F-150 and recognized it. Instead of parking in front of the building as the crowd surged toward the pickup, Tom gave the vehicle some gas and wheeled quickly around to the back. He and Bonnie barely made it through City Hall's rear door before the shouting reporters got there.

The city council was waiting for them inside the meeting room. Buddy Gorman and Pete Benitez were there, too, along with a man Tom didn't know. Obviously, though, the man recognized Tom. He stood up and extended his hand, saying, "Mr. Brannon?"

Tom hesitated but took the man's hand, casting a curious glance at Buddy as he did so. Buddy's face was impassive, not giving away any information.

Tom shook hands with the man and said, "I'm Tom Brannon. This is my wife Bonnie."

"Ralph Vandiver," the stranger introduced himself. "I work for the U.S. Border Patrol."

Tom's eyes narrowed. "I reckon you're taking the place of the agent who quit yesterday."

"That's right." Vandiver didn't look uncomfortable as he admitted that fact. "Jerry Prescott's a good man, but he got carried away."

"Sounded to me more like he got fed up."

"I don't know of a single Border Patrolman who's not frustrated by the situation," Vandiver said bluntly. "Everything Jerry said was true. We don't have enough money, enough manpower, enough equipment . . . you name it, and we don't have enough of it. Except for miles and miles of border and thousands and thousands of people who want to get across it. Those things, we have plenty of."

Tom found himself instinctively liking the lanky, brown-haired Border Patrolman. He wasn't going to let his guard down just yet, though. "Why have you been sent here to Little Tucson?" he asked. "What is it you're supposed to do?"

"Are you asking as the mayor of Little Tucson?"

Tom shrugged. "If you want it that way, sure."

"All right, then. Officially, my orders are to monitor the situation and make sure that all federal laws and regulations concerning immigration are followed to the letter."

"And unofficially . . . ?"

Vandiver grinned. "Unofficially, I'm here to catch you doing something wrong and nail your ass to the wall, Mayor."

Tom grunted in surprise and said, "At least

you're honest about it. Why don't you have a seat, and we'll get this meeting underway."

Walt Deavers asked, "Are you sure you want this gov'ment man here, Tom?" He waved a big, gnarled hand at Vandiver.

"I don't mind," Tom said as he pulled out a chair for Bonnie and then sat down himself. "Mr. Vandiver can see for himself that the Patriot Project is going to be perfectly legal." He took a notebook out of his pocket. He had jotted down a few thoughts before coming to the meeting. "First of all, we have to set up some criteria for volunteers. I think they should be at least eighteen years old. We can't have any minors running around out there."

There were nods of agreement from the others.

"They'll have to furnish their own weapons and be legally licensed and qualified to carry them," Tom went on. "I don't want any troublemakers, either. Nobody who's been in trouble with the law for anything worse than a parking ticket."

Deavers grinned. "Goin' back to the age limit thing . . . I'm seventy-five. Is that too old?"

Tom smiled back at him. "I wouldn't turn away anybody who's still as spry as you, Walt. We'll judge that on a case-by-case basis."

"What about women?" Vandiver said.

Tom looked at him in surprise. "What about them?"

"Will you accept female volunteers? Because this Patriot Project of yours is a public organization, correct? If you don't accept women, you'll be guilty of sexual discrimination."

"I plan to be part of the patrol, Mr. Vandiver,"

Bonnie spoke up. "I don't think anybody will be turned away simply because she's a woman."

"That's right," Tom agreed. "And before you bring up the question of racial discrimination, you'd better look around the room. There are several Americans of Hispanic descent here."

"And I'm one of 'em," Pete put in. "Don't let this red hair fool you."

Warren Miller said, "I'm part Apache, and I've already had several members of the tribe ask me about joining up. So I reckon we've got the Indian angle covered, too."

"I don't see any blacks here," Vandiver pointed out.

"Check your census records," Pete said. "There aren't any blacks living in Sierrita County at the moment. That's not because they're not welcome, though. Several black families have lived here in Little Tucson in the past, and there's never been any racial trouble. Black, Hispanic, Native American, we don't care. We all get along."

"You can call us Indians," Warren said. "We don't particularly care about that political-correctness crap."

Vandiver leaned forward, rested his hands on the table, and said, "You're telling me you don't have any rednecks in this county?"

"Now who's prejudging people?" Tom asked quietly.

Vandiver grimaced and sat back in his chair, but he didn't say anything.

"Sure, we've got some bigots in the county," Tom went on. "No matter how hard the government tries, you can't legislate away somebody's dislike for somebody else. But we don't have any trouble from them because we've got a damn fine sheriff. If some skinhead or white supremacist wants to raise hell, he goes up to Tucson or Phoenix to do it, because he knows if he tries anything around here, he'll wind up in jail."

There was a moment of silence after Tom's forceful statement, a moment that was broken by Buddy Gorman's quiet, "Thanks, Tom."

"Just tellin' the truth, Buddy," Tom said with a shrug. "We may not see eye to eye on everything, but that doesn't mean I don't appreciate what a good lawman you are." He turned back to Vandiver. "So you can't get us on any sort of discrimination charges, and we carry our guns legally. What's left?"

Vandiver shook his head. "Don't get me wrong, Mr. Brannon. I'm not unsympathetic to what you're doing here. I'll follow my orders, to the letter. But I'm not the FBI."

"Fair enough," Tom said with a nod. He looked around at the others. "Let's get back to it."

The discussion continued as they hashed out how the Patriot Project would be organized and would carry out its work. Buddy and Vandiver remained but didn't participate. Tom didn't mind them being there. Everything about the Project had to be open and above-board, or it would defeat its purpose.

After a while, the doors of the meeting room opened, and Bonnie looked around and then touched Tom's arm when she saw who was coming in. He glanced at her and saw her cut her eyes toward the door. He looked over his shoulder, then looked again as he recognized the newcomers. As he came to his feet, he said, "Mom, Dad, what are you doing here?"

Herbert Brannon shuffled forward, his gnarled hands tightly gripping the aluminum walker he used to support himself. His wife Mildred, Tom's mother, trailed behind him, one hand lifted anxiously, ready to reach out and grab her husband to steady him if need be.

Herb wore stiffly pressed jeans and a shirt with silver snaps on it instead of buttons, as he had every day of his life for as far back as Tom could remember. His cream-colored Stetson was perfectly creased and his boots shone with polish. In a voice that was still firm despite his advanced age, he said, "I come to sign up."

"Sign up for what?" Tom asked.

"Why, the Patriot Project, o' course!"

"As soon as he heard about it, nothing would satisfy him except that I drive him into town," Mildred put in. "You know how your father gets, Tom."

"I know how I get when the world starts goin' to hell in a hay wagon!" Herb snapped. "I don't intend to stand by and let my boy rassle with the devil all by his own self, neither."

Tom said, "I appreciate that, Dad, but I'm not sure it would be a good idea for you to be involved with this."

"It was a good idea when I drove a Sherman tank all the way from Normandy across France and Germany into Hitler's livin' room with ol' Blood 'n' Guts George Patton, wasn't it? By God, if we had a few o' them tanks patrollin' up and down the border, none o' them Mexican gangsters would get in, that's for damn sure!"

"You might have a point there, but we don't have any tanks." Tom shot a glance of appeal toward his mother. "Mom, maybe you could—"

"Don't look at me," she broke in. "I've long since given up trying to talk any sense into your father's head."

Herb took one hand off his walker. He dug in the pocket of his jeans and brought out a heavy pocketknife. The knife's grip was black and silver and decorated with a fancy silver insignia consisting of two lightning bolts. Slapping the knife down on the table, he said, "I took that off'n a dead SS officer in Berlin after him an' me got in a tussle. If the SS didn't scare me, no bunch o' Mexican thugs is goin' to."

"That was more than sixty years ago, Dad," Tom pointed out. "If you were the same man now you were then, I'd be glad to have you help out. But you're not."

He hated to be so blunt with his father, but he knew how stubborn Herb was. The old man glared at Tom and drew in a deep breath. "That's a fine way to talk to your own daddy," he accused.

"I'm sorry," Tom said, and meant it. "But you just can't get mixed up in this, Dad. You fought your war already. This battle is ours to win or lose."

Muttering under his breath, Herb picked up the pocketknife, stuffed it back in his jeans, and gripped the walker tightly as he turned to shuffle away. Tom stepped closer to his mother and said quietly, "I'm sorry, Mom. But he'll understand when he gets over being mad and stops to think about it."

"I wouldn't count on that, Tommy."

She started to follow her husband, but Tom

stopped her by saying, "There's something else I need to talk to the two of you about. I'd like for you to come and stay with Bonnie and me until this is all over. Or it would be even better if you spent some time with Helen or Jessie." Those were Tom's sisters, neither of whom lived in the area anymore.

"You mean we should leave the ranch?" Mildred asked with a frown.

"Just temporarily. Until all the trouble blows over."

Slowly, she shook her head. "Your father will never agree to that. I'll talk to him, but it won't do any good."

"Try anyway," Tom urged her.

At the door of the meeting room, Herb turned back and called, "Are you comin', old woman?"

"Keep your shirt on," she told him. She reached out and squeezed Tom's arm, then went to join her husband. She helped him out of the meeting room, holding the door for him.

Tom turned back to the group gathered there and began, "Sorry for the interruption—"

"Don't be," Walt Deavers said. "Your dad's not the only old vet who's gonna want to be part of this. Hell, I'm no spring chicken myself. I missed out on the Big One, but I carried a rifle in Korea. You were in Vietnam, Tom. It'd be a good idea to get as many volunteers with military experience as we can."

Tom nodded. "That's true."

"Because no matter what you want to call it," Pete Benitez spoke up, "this is liable to turn into a war before it's over, Tom."

Tom hoped Pete was wrong about that . . . but in his heart, he feared the little newspaperman was just as right as he could be.

17

The next few days were a whirlwind of activity for Tom Brannon. With Bonnie at his side nearly all the time, he coordinated the formation and organization of the Patriot Project. The first thing that needed to be done was to interview the volunteers who wanted to be part of the project. There were more than Tom had ever expected, close to a thousand, in fact. He had started out by saying that the group should consist of around two dozen people. The sheer numbers of the turnout forced him to revise that estimate upward. He was determined, though, not to accept more than a hundred or so volunteers. If the group got any larger than that, it could become unwieldy and hard to control.

The interviews took place at the City Hall and were conducted by a committee consisting of Tom and Bonnie, Walt Deavers, Warren Miller, and Ray Torres, one of the county commissioners. Some of the volunteers were too young while others were old and in poor health. Those were the easy ones to send home with the sincere thanks of the city of

Little Tucson, Sierrita County, and the Patriot Project. Some didn't own any guns, and the committee thanked them and sent them home, too. A few openly admitted they had been in trouble with the law. Some of them had cleaned up their act and seemed to genuinely want to make amends for their unsavory past by helping out now, and Tom hated to turn them away. In the end, though, he had to, knowing that the project and its members had to be as squeaky-clean as possible to stand up to the scrutiny of the liberal media, not to mention the Border Patrol and the FBI.

Some of the potential troublemakers were easy to pick out. One group of men came in together, carrying beer bottles and wanting to know if this was where they came to sign up to shoot "Meskins". Another bunch had shaved heads, black leather vests, wristbands studded with silver spikes, and belt buckles emblazoned with swastikas. Tom suspected that both groups had shown up knowing that they would be turned down. The way they headed straight for the media after he told them that the Patriot Project couldn't use their services confirmed his theory. They were there just hoping to get their fifteen minutes of fame. A little face time on TV, a sound bite or two, that was all that mattered.

The soft-spoken, mild-looking ones were harder to pick out. Tom had to look for some indefinable something in their eyes that warned him they were trouble just waiting to happen. When he turned them down, they just shrugged and went away, their eyes still cold and dead.

No one had forgotten about the SavMart Massacre. Several men who had lost wives or children in the tragedy showed up to volunteer, their faces haunted by grief. Tom turned them down as gently as possible. He understood that most of them just wanted to do something to help, so that no one else would have to suffer as they had suffered. But it was possible that some of them were looking for revenge, and they could easily turn into the sort of loose cannons that could bring the whole operation crashing down.

In the end, he had his hundred volunteers, all of them upstanding, law-abiding, patriotic American citizens who were fed up with the floodtide of illegal immigration and the violence it brought with it. They were fed up as well with the government turning a blind eye to the dangerous situation and keeping the Border Patrol weak and ineffective. Their ages ranged from eighteen to seventy-five, with Walt Deavers being the oldest member and Billy Garza, who had been an all-state running back on the Little Tucson High School football team the previous autumn, being the youngest. In the fall, Billy would be going off to the University of Arizona on an athletic scholarship, but in the meantime he wanted to do something to help the town where he had grown up. That desire to help was a sentiment shared by all the volunteers, whether they were lifelong residents of the area or had only moved there in recent years.

Once the volunteers had been selected, the next step was to break up the border into areas and figure out how many Patriots would patrol each one. While that was being done, patrol leaders were being picked out from the volunteers, because each group had to have someone in charge. Tom hadn't realized that there would be so much planning involved. Nothing could be left to chance, though. If the operation was too haphazard, it ran the risk of falling apart quickly. He couldn't let that happen.

And all through the hard work, he also had the distraction of the media to deal with. His phones at home rang so much he finally unplugged them and relied on his cell phone for staying in touch with people, since that number wasn't as easy to get. Somehow the reporters managed, though, and now the cell phone buzzed almost constantly. He only answered when he recognized the number that came up on the display. He couldn't walk the streets of Little Tucson without being accosted by a bunch of well-dressed, hair-sprayed people with microphones. He talked to Louly on the phone, but he didn't go to the auto parts store anymore.

She reported that business hadn't been very good, probably because of all the reporters practically camped out on the sidewalk, hoping to corner the store's owner, the man who was the architect of the Patriot Project. Tom just chuckled wryly and told her to do the best she could. If it got too bad, she could close the store and go home until all this fuss blew over, he said. She told him not to worry about that.

Not surprisingly, nothing had been seen or heard of *Mara Salvatrucha* since the SavMart Massacre. The members of M-15 were lying low, unwilling to venture out into the blizzard of news coverage.

Like a snake curled up in the shade of some rocks, they could afford to wait a while. Sooner or later, though, their very nature would force them to slither out into the open again, their fangs full of venom . . .

* * *

The man stood at the window of the office in a glittering Mexico City high-rise and gazed out at filth and squalor. These buildings, these towers of steel and glass and wealth, rose from poverty, from the dung heaps of the great unwashed masses. It was that way everywhere the man had been—his native Riyadh, London, New York, now Mexico City. Always the same. The rich rising to the heavens while the poor clamored about their feet.

Allah must have loved the poor. He had made so very many of them.

The man's reflection peered back at him from the window glass. Around thirty years old, with sleek dark hair and a thin mustache, a slightly round face with olive skin, a slender body clothed in a suit that cost enough to have fed a Saudi Arabian village for a month. Whenever he left these rooms that served as both his office and his living quarters, he wore the traditional Arabian head covering known as the kaffiyeh. He missed the robes that he had worn in his homeland, but the expensive suit served a purpose. He dealt with infidels, and they were shallow, soulless creatures, easily impressed by a blatant display of wealth. His years of trafficking with Westerners had taught him how to turn their own weaknesses against them, and he did it gladly, knowing that Allah understood. Anything that served the holy cause could be justified, especially if it served to bring about the destruction of Allah's enemies.

The phone on the massive glass-topped desk rang. Sami Al-Khan turned away from the window and his musings. He crossed the room to the desk, his footsteps quiet on the deep carpet. Picking up the phone, he said hello and listened to the voice of the man on the other end. A smile lit up his face and made it appear even more cherubic. "Señor Garcia-Lopez," he said in faintly British-accented English, a product of his years at Oxford. "How good it is to hear from you."

The smile disappeared from Al-Khan's face as he listened to the angry words coming from the phone. He didn't try to break in. It was better to let Señor Hector Garcia-Lopez vent his fury. Garcia-Lopez was a billionaire, one of the richest men in Mexico, although of course his wealth paled beside that of the Saudi royal family, of which Sami Al-Khan was a member. For more than fifty years, since Garcia-Lopez was a small boy, in fact, he had been selling heroin and cocaine, and on that platform he had built his considerable fortune. He was accustomed to being listened to. He was accustomed to being feared—and rightly so.

"I understand, señor," Al-Khan said when Garcia-Lopez finally paused to draw a breath, "and I share your concern. I, too, was surprised when I heard about what happened in Arizona. This SavMart Massacre, as the American media call it, draws much unwelcome attention to our subordinates. Señor Montoya acted rashly when he ordered such a high-profile raid . . . Of course he was angry at being defied by the Americans. I understand that. But now the attention of the world is focused on this little town in the middle of nowhere. There are too many eyes watching. I prefer discretion."

What he preferred was working behind the scenes

toward the destruction of the Great Satan. He had done that by funneling money to Al-Qaeda and other groups; he had even funded freelance terrorists who belonged to no particular organization. He let others sit around in their seedy furnished apartments and plan their great strikes against the infidels. They knew how to get in touch with him when they needed money or some other assistance. Those little men were fond of planning and strategizing and coming up with outlandish schemes that had little or no chance of working. The actual carrying out of any plan more complicated than packing a car full of explosives and blowing themselves up along with a few dozen people was usually beyond them. But all it took was for one of those far-fetched notions, one out of a thousand—like flying airplanes into American skyscrapers—to work, and then the infidels truly suffered.

What everyone lost sight of was the fact that it would take scores of such attacks to equal the death toll exacted each year by the partnership formed between Sami Al-Khan and Hector Garcia-Lopez. Every time one of the hated Americans died of an overdose or was shot down while trying to commit a robbery to finance another purchase of drugs, it was a victory for Allah. Garcia-Lopez cared only for the money that the drugs put in his pocket. Al-Khan's motives were much more noble. He was going to destroy the Great Satan from within. He was going to spread his corruption until America's soul rotted and the most evil nation in the world collapsed on itself. Just thinking about it made a warm feeling spread through him. Already he had known great luxuries and the ardor of many beautiful women here on Earth. If he succeeded in his goal, what sort of wonderful reward would Allah have waiting for him when he entered heaven? It was almost beyond his comprehension.

"Yes, of course," he said as he dragged his attention away from his heavenly reward and back to Garcia-Lopez's ranting. "I will summon Montoya and speak with him. I agree, something must be done. Perhaps things should have been handled differently to start with, but since they were not, the threat must be dealt with as it is . . . Yes, of course, señor."

Al-Khan said his good-byes and hung up the phone. As he turned back to the vast window, he saw that evening was settling over the sprawling city. The lights were beautiful as they began to come on, spread out at his feet like a field of diamonds.

Dealing with that animal Montoya should have been Garcia-Lopez's responsibility. After all, M-15 was part of the Mexican's sprawling drug empire. The members of *Mara Salvatrucha* came out of the jungles of Guatemala and El Salvador and thought *they* were running things, but those at the top of the pyramid, like Montoya, knew who was really pulling the strings. He would come to Mexico City if Al-Khan ordered him to. He wouldn't like it, but he would come. And to keep the peace with Garcia-Lopez, Al-Khan would speak to Montoya and explain that something must be done about the problem they faced across the border in Arizona.

Something must be done about Thomas Brannon and his so-called Patriot Project.

* * *

Dusk was coming on, making it harder to see. Tom lowered the binoculars from his eyes and wondered if they ought to try to get some night-vision goggles. That would sure help. The Border Patrol had them, just not enough agents down here to use them. Somehow, though, Tom didn't think Ralph Vandiver would turn over any unused goggles to the Patriot Project.

"Anything?" Bonnie asked from the ground.

Tom shook his head and dropped down from the tailgate of the F-150 where he had been standing as he slowly surveyed the countryside around them with the binoculars. "Nope. It's pretty quiet this evening."

The border was about half a mile to the south. The pickup was parked on a slight rise. The terrain wasn't really as flat as it appeared on first glance. There were little hills and shallow valleys, brush-choked gullies, and dry creek beds lined with stubby paloverde trees. Off to the east a short distance from where Tom and Bonnie waited, a wide draw ran north and south, extending over the border into Mexico. It was like a highway for illegal immigrants, because it gave them some cover as they tried to sneak into the country. Some of them even tried to get across in the daytime, feeling confident in their ability to avoid the Border Patrol.

Border Patrol agents weren't the only ones out here now, though. Now anybody trying to get across the border illegally had to worry about the Patriots, too.

The walkie-talkie sitting on the tailgate crackled. "Somebody coming up the draw, Tom," Warren's voice said. The Apache and one of his friends were parked on the other side of the draw, keeping an eye on it.

Tom picked up the walkie-talkie and pressed the button. "We're on our way." He and Bonnie hurriedly got into the pickup.

Enough reddish light remained in the western sky so that Tom could drive without lights as he headed quickly toward the draw, which was only a few hundred yards away. The illegals probably heard the pickup's engine as it approached, but there was nothing he could do about that. The F-150 rocked to a stop near the edge of the draw, and he and Bonnie piled out, each of them carrying a rifle.

Across the draw, headlights flicked on, washing out over the low, brushy area. Warren's voice called loudly, "Hold it! *Alto! Alto!*"

In the glow of the headlights, Tom spotted three men in jeans and ragged shirts and battered hats running through the brush. The illegals veered toward the side of the draw where he and Bonnie were stationed. They were trying to get away from the lights and the shouting and didn't take the time to think that they might be running right into more trouble. Tom slid down the bank, saying over his shoulder, "Cover me from up there!"

"Not hardly!" Bonnie said as she came down after him.

He bit back a curse. *Stubborn woman. Stubborn, stubborn woman.*

They cut quickly through the brush, homing in on the thudding of footsteps and the crackling of branches. Tom told himself that Bonnie would be all right. She could take care of herself. They had been out on patrol together before, had, in fact, stopped several groups of illegals and turned them back to Mexico. The Patriot Project had been in full operation for a week now. In that time, not one shot had been fired, despite all the hand-wringing and predictions of disaster from the media and the left-wing politicians. There hadn't been any violence at all, not even a scuffle.

But in that week, close to a hundred would-be illegal immigrants had been stopped and sent back across the border. Just as Tom had thought would happen, once the men and women were caught, they departed peacefully.

Of course, they tried to get away first, and he didn't mind admitting that a few of them had done just that. The patrols couldn't be everywhere, and they couldn't stop all the illegals they spotted. If they'd had any help at all from the Border Patrol, it might have been a different story.

But unlike what had happened with the earlier Minuteman Project, when Border Patrol forces in the area had been increased, this time the government had pulled back, putting fewer of its agents in the field. When Tom had asked Ralph Vandiver about that, the man had shrugged and said that he was just following orders.

Tom suspected that the FBI, in the form of Agents Ford and Berry, had something to do with those orders. But the pressure came from higher up, too, all the way from Washington, in fact. Although the President couched her words very carefully when she answered questions about the Patriot Project, it was obvious to anyone who could read between the lines that she wanted this grass-roots movement to fail. If this little bunch of local men and women succeeded at something when the government couldn't, it would represent a direct threat to the centralized power of the federal bureaucracy. The President couldn't stand for that. That was why she had ordered that the Patriot Project be left on its own. She hoped that given enough rope, they would hang themselves.

So far, it hadn't worked out that way, and that had to be a pretty bitter pill for certain folks in Washington to swallow.

Tom forced his mind back to what he was doing. The crashing in the brush was close now and coming right at them. He motioned for Bonnie to stop at the edge of a little clearing and did likewise himself, planting his feet. He held the rifle slanted across his chest, ready to use but not pointing at anything or anybody—yet.

The three illegals broke out of the brush on the far side of the clearing, about twenty feet away. "*Alto!*" Tom shouted, and the three men frantically skidded to a stop. Their heads jerked from side to side as they desperately searched for a way out. More noises came from the brush behind them as Warren and his partner closed in. The headlights from Warren's pickup didn't shine directly on this spot, but the beams of illumination were close enough so that their glow lit up the scene.

"Stand where you are," Tom firmly told the men in Spanish. He was fluent in the language, as most people who lived in this area were. "We're not going to hurt you. We just want you to go back to Mexico."

"*El . . . El Patriotas?*" one of the men gasped.

Tom nodded and said, "*Si.*"

He saw the resignation come into the faces of the men, and he was confident that in a minute they would turn around and trudge back toward the border. Some of the patrol members would follow them to make sure they went all the way back across into Mexico. That was all the Patriots could do, as long as the illegals cooperated.

But before that could happen, a powerful light suddenly flashed on, almost blinding Tom. He said, "What the hell!" and instinctively brought the rifle up. He wasn't sure where the light was coming from.

"Oh, my God!" a woman's voice said in a half-scream. "He's going to shoot us! Look out, Chet, he's going to shoot us!"

"Don't shoot!" a man shouted. "We're unarmed! Don't shoot!"

Tom heard a rush of footsteps and turned his head, squinting against the light that still assaulted his eyes. He saw that the three Mexican men had bolted back into the brush. "Comin' your way, Warren!" he shouted. Then he turned back and snarled, "Shut off that damn light!"

"You won't shoot us?" the man asked nervously.

"No, damn it, I'm not going to shoot anybody!" Tom said, even though at that moment the idea sounded mighty appealing.

The light clicked off. It took a few seconds for his eyes to adjust to the relative dimness. Bonnie was having trouble, too. She asked, "Can you see anything?"

"Not much," Tom told her. He hoped these strangers, whoever they were, didn't represent a threat. Maybe they were unofficial volunteers who had come out here to get in on the action. Their accents hadn't sounded like they were from these parts, but that didn't really mean anything. People moved in from all over the country, drawn by the clean air and the slower pace of life.

Still blinking, he saw two figures push through the brush and emerge into the clearing. The woman was in the lead. She was short, with long dark hair, and wore an expensive pair of slacks and a jacket that were totally out of place in these surroundings, as were her shoes. The man who followed her was almost twice her size, tall and broad-shouldered and probably a hundred pounds overweight. He wore an ill-fitting gray suit and a pair of thick glasses. His light brown hair was cut short. He carried a briefcase in one hand and a hand-held spotlight in the other.

The woman looked at Tom and said, "You're Tom Brannon." The accent was definitely east coast.

"That's right," Tom said, in no mood to be overly polite. "Who are you?"

She reached into the little bag she carried and took out, of all things, a business card. Tom was so surprised that he instinctively took the card when she held it out to him.

"Callista Spinelli," she said. "I'm an attorney with the American Civil Liberties Union. This is my partner, Chet Eggleston."

Tom looked down at the card in his hand. There wasn't enough light for him to really read it, but he didn't doubt what it said. "The ACLU." He shook his head. "Why am I not surprised? I've been waiting for some of you to show up."

"Some of what?" Spinelli challenged him with a toss of her head. "Decent people who have respect for the rights of others and don't want to see them trampled by a bunch of trigger-happy, reactionary, right-wing racist Neanderthals?"

"Oh, my goodness," Bonnie said quietly. "This is going to be fun, isn't it?"

That depends on your idea of fun, Tom thought.

18

"I thought you were going to shoot us, I really did," Chet Eggleston said as he mopped sweat off his forehead with a handkerchief. "My life flashed in front of my eyes . . . and it wasn't that pretty a picture."

"I don't go around shooting at people for no good reason," Tom said.

"No," Callista Spinelli put in. "You just shoot them because their skin is a different color than yours."

Tom's jaw tightened. As a matter of fact, everyone he had ever shot at in his life *had* been a different color than he. But that had been more than thirty years earlier in Vietnam, and it wasn't what Spinelli was talking about anyway.

"You're all wrong about that, ma'am," he said.

"Get him," she said to Eggleston. "He's a cowboy, calling me ma'am like that. What is it with you cowboys that you like to go around shooting people for no good reason?"

"You say cowboy like it's a dirty word."

"It is in my book," she said with a sneer.

Bonnie looked over at Tom. "Is she just dense, or is she trying to be obnoxious?"

"Hey, lady!" Spinelli said, her accent becoming more pronounced. "You got something to say to me, you just go ahead and say it. Bring it on, okay?"

Tom put a hand on Bonnie's arm, but Bonnie just smiled faintly and shook her head. She wasn't going to go after that crass little loudmouth, no matter how much she might want to.

They had gone back to Tom's pickup, where he saw that a rental car was parked nearby. Obviously, the two ACLU attorneys had been out driving around, hoping to find some members of the Patriot Project on patrol. They had spotted the headlights and come blundering in. The distraction had allowed the three illegals to get away. Warren had radioed a few minutes earlier that he and his partner hadn't been able to find the three men.

"Listen, because of you, three men illegally entered the United States a little while ago," Tom said now.

"Good," Spinelli shot back at him. "Then we've accomplished something worthwhile tonight. We'll accomplish even more tomorrow when we get an injunction shutting down this little Gestapo you've set up, Mr. Brannon."

Tom's eyes narrowed. "I don't appreciate the comparison, Ms. Spinelli. As my father would tell you if he was here, he and old Blood 'n' Guts Patton fought their way all across France and Germany to get rid of the Gestapo and everything else that had anything to do with the Nazis."

"Then it's too bad you have to dishonor your father by acting like a Nazi."

Tom rubbed his temples wearily. He had never

encountered people like Callista Spinelli in person before, but he had seen them on newscasts and read their comments in the newspapers. One of their favorite tactics was to call anyone they disagreed with a Nazi. They preached tolerance but had none of their own.

"Look, you can take a whole legion of lawyers into court if you want—"

"Oh, we will, I assure you."

"But it's not going to do you any good," Tom went on doggedly. "We're not breaking any laws."

"What about depriving people of their civil rights?"

"They're not American citizens. They don't *have* any civil rights. And even if they did, we haven't deprived anybody of anything. We just turn 'em around and send them back across the border."

"Barbarian," Spinelli said. "They have *human* rights, no matter where they're from."

"Nobody's saying they don't. That's why we haven't hurt anybody. We don't *want* to hurt anybody."

"Then why are you carrying guns? Huh? Tell me that, cowboy."

Tom gritted his teeth for a second and then said, "In case we have to protect ourselves from somebody who wants to hurt *us*."

"Which you wouldn't have to worry about if you weren't out here taking the law into your own hands—"

Shaking his head, Tom turned away from her and said to Bonnie, "Let's go. We're just wasting time here."

Spinelli quivered with rage as she said, "Hey, mister, don't turn away from me when I'm talking to you! Chet, this cowboy just insulted me! Aren't you going to do anything?"

"Take it easy, Callie," Eggleston said. "It won't do any good to get so worked up that you pop a blood vessel."

Spinelli threw her hands in the air. "Now you're turning on me, too?"

"No, no, of course not," Eggleston said quickly. "Why don't you just go sit in the car for a minute, and I'll talk to these people."

Spinelli didn't want to go, but Eggleston talked her into it. When she was in the front seat of the rental car and he had closed the door behind her, he came back over to the pickup and said, "Sorry about that, folks. Callie's just really passionate about what she believes in."

Bonnie said, "So are we, Mr. Eggleston."

"Yes, well . . . Do you mind if I set my briefcase on the tailgate of your pickup for a minute?"

Tom shrugged. "Go ahead."

Eggleston set the case on the tailgate and snapped the catches open. He pawed through a stack of papers and said after a few seconds, "Ah, here they are." He took out two documents and turned to hand them to Tom and Bonnie, who took them without thinking. With a friendly smile, Eggleston continued, "There you go. You've both been served. Those are subpoenas requiring you to appear tomorrow morning at a hearing in Tucson for the granting of a temporary restraining order prohibiting any further activities by the so-called Patriot Project."

Tom stiffened. "Why, you—"

"There's no need for name-calling, Mr. Brannon," Eggleston went on smoothly as he snapped the briefcase shut. He picked it up and added, "We'll see you in court."

"That slick son of a bitch," Tom said as he looked down at the paper in his hand, not caring if Eggleston heard him or not.

"We knew something like this had to be coming," Bonnie told him. "To tell you the truth, I'm surprised it took them a week to get around to it."

Tom sighed. "Yeah, I suppose I am, too."

"Look at it this way, Tom. Now you've got a chance to prove in court that you've been right all along. If the judge rules against their motion, they won't have any choice but to go away."

Slowly, Tom shook his head. "They're lawyers, honey. They may scurry out of sight like cockroaches when the light comes on . . . but they're still there."

Ernesto Luis Montoya struggled to keep the seething rage tamped down inside him. To be summoned here to Mexico City like a mere lackey was an insult. To have to answer the snapping fingers of this Arab was even worse. Montoya had come as a favor only to Señor Garcia-Lopez, who had been his silent partner in M-15 ever since Montoya had assumed command of the operation. There was a connection of some sort—financial, almost certainly—between Señor Garcia-Lopez and this Sami Al-Khan. Montoya had to respect that—but he didn't have to like it.

The two men had met on several previous occasions, in Al-Khan's office here in Mexico City and at Señor Garcia-Lopez's luxurious villa in Acapulco. Al-Khan did not offer to shake hands when Montoya was shown into the office, and for that Montoya was glad. Arabs were almost as bad as gringos.

"Please have a seat, my friend," Al-Khan said as he gestured toward a thickly upholstered chair in front of the massive desk. "Would you like a drink?" As a Muslim, Al-Khan did not use alcohol, of course, but there was a small, well-stocked bar for visitors and business associates on the other side of the office.

Montoya shook his head impatiently in response to the offer. "I would prefer to get on with it," he said. "Why did you ask me to come here?"

Al-Khan settled himself behind the desk and clasped his slightly pudgy hands together on its glass top. "Señor Garcia-Lopez asked me to discuss a certain situation with you."

"What situation?"

"The one in Little Tucson, Arizona, involving the Patriot Project and the man called Brannon."

Montoya made a sharp, slashing motion with his hand. "I have that under control."

"Oh? What have you done since ordering the massacre that resulted in a storm of media coverage, the increased attention of the American government, and the formation of the Patriot Project?"

Montoya's hands clutched the arms of the chair. He held on tightly, rather than giving in to the impulse to take this greasy little man's throat and squeeze it until the Arab was dead. "That was a lesson for the people of Little Tucson, to teach them not to defy me."

"It seems not to have worked," Al-Khan said. "As I said, what have you done since then?"

Montoya took a deep breath. "I have sent several

of my men across the border to test this Patriot Project."

"And?" Al-Khan asked as he raised neatly trimmed eyebrows.

Montoya didn't want to answer, but Al-Khan's gaze was unflinching. Finally, Montoya said, "They were stopped and turned back."

"Did they put up any resistance?"

"I ordered them not to . . . this time."

"So Brannon and his Patriots, they have the potential to form an effective barrier against the traffic you had established across the border?"

"Not at all! I can smash them any time I want!"

"Then I suggest you do so, Señor Montoya. I prefer discretion, but it appears to be too late for that. Now that the gauntlet has been thrown down, the challenge must be answered. *Mara Salvatrucha* must be restored to its former glory. The Americans along the border must live in fear of M-15, as they had been until this man Brannon came along." Al-Khan leaned forward, and suddenly he did not look so soft and ineffectual anymore. "Do what you must, Señor Montoya, but stop Tom Brannon and the Patriot Project . . . *now.*"

Word of the hearing on the TRO had gotten out, and the scene was bedlam around the federal courthouse in Tucson. Tom, Bonnie, and the lawyers for the city of Little Tucson and Sierrita County had to slip into the courthouse through a rear door to avoid the media mob. The courtroom itself was a haven of peace and quiet, because Judge Elgin Malone had banned cameras and allowed only a small contingent of reporters inside. Malone was a crusty old-timer. He was also extremely liberal, one of the lawyers informed Tom, and Tom felt his hopes sink. He *knew* the law was on his side—but if the ruling went against him here today, it sure as hell wouldn't be the first time some liberal judge had ignored the law and followed his personal biases.

The bailiff called, "All rise!" and everyone got to their feet as Judge Malone came in and took his place on the bench. He gaveled the court to order and told everyone to sit down. As Tom looked over from the defense table, he saw Callista Spinelli and Chet Eggleston sitting at the plaintiff's table along with several other expensively dressed attorneys. Spinelli smirked at him. She was enjoying this.

The next forty-five minutes were pretty much a blur to Tom. He had a layman's knowledge of the law, but he wasn't able to follow all the procedural gibberish that both sides in the case went through. Finally, though, he was called to the stand to explain what the Patriot Project was and his role in it.

When he was sworn in and seated, Spinelli stood up and said with a smile, "Good morning, Mr. Brannon. Thank you for being here."

Tom nodded to her and replied in his best cowboy drawl, "Mornin', ma'am." He was rewarded by a slight tightening of Spinelli's lips and a grin from Bonnie, who sat in the front row of the spectator seats.

Spinelli began to shoot questions at him, asking him to describe the activities of the Patriot Project. Tom answered them as honestly as possible. Every time Spinelli tried to make it sound as if the Patriots were doing something illegal, immoral, and downright racist, Tom had an answer for her, deftly turning aside the spurious allegations. Several times his attorneys objected, and for the most part Judge Malone sustained them, although it seemed to Tom that he did so grudgingly. Spinelli was growing more frustrated, and she finally snapped, "No further questions."

One of Tom's lawyers got to his feet and said, "Tell us, Mr. Brannon, about the events that led to the formation of the Patriot Project."

Spinelli shot up out of her chair. "Objection! Irrelevant!"

"How can it be irrelevant, Your Honor?" Tom's lawyer said. "The origins of an organization go right to the heart of its motives."

"The motives of those . . . people . . . aren't what's at issue," Spinelli argued. "All we're concerned with here are their actions, which are indefensible!"

Judge Malone picked up his gavel but didn't use it. He said, "That's what we're trying to determine, Ms. Spinelli, whether or not the actions of the Patriot Project are indeed defensible. The objection is overruled."

Spinelli sat down, obviously gritting her teeth. Eggleston leaned over to whisper to her, probably telling her to calm down before she started damaging their case with the judge. They had had an advantage going in because of Malone's liberal leanings, and they didn't want to squander that.

Tom's lawyer asked, "Why *did* you suggest starting up the Patriot Project, Mr. Brannon?"

Tom took a deep breath. "Because somebody had to protect the citizens of Little Tucson and Sierrita County from M-15."

"What's M-15?" They wanted to get this on the record.

"*Mara Salvatrucha.* A criminal gang composed primarily of Guatemalans and El Salvadorans who have taken over all the drug smuggling and the rest of the illegal activity along the border." Tom paused for a second. "They've also murdered more than two dozen American citizens in the past couple of weeks."

Spinelli was up again. "Objection! Again, this is irrelevant, and on top of that, no one has proven that this so-called M-15 gang even exists, let alone that it was responsible for any of the crimes that took place in Sierrita County."

"Counselor, you're not going to get anywhere insulting my intelligence by arguing that M-15 doesn't exist," Judge Malone said. He turned to Tom. "But you should confine your answers to matters of fact, Mr. Brannon, not speculation. How do you know M-15 is to blame for what's happened in your town?"

"My wife was there at the SavMart Massacre, Your Honor—"

"Objection! Use of the word massacre is inflammatory and prejudicial—"

"There's no jury here, Ms. Spinelli," Malone said, "and I'm neither inflamed nor prejudiced by the word. Both of your objections are overruled." He turned back to Tom. "What were you saying about your wife, Mr. Brannon?"

"Just that she was there, Your Honor. She heard the men who killed all those people in SavMart say that they were part of M-15."

Spinelli started to stand up, but Eggleston put a hand on her arm and held her down. He lumbered to his feet instead and said quietly, "Objection, Your Honor. That's hearsay."

Tom's lawyer said, "Mrs. Brannon is in the courtroom. I can put her on the stand if you'd like."

"That still wouldn't prove anything, Your Honor," Eggleston said. "Just because Mrs. Brannon heard one of the criminals claim to be from M-15 doesn't mean that they were. I could claim to be from the moon, but obviously I'm not."

"You're arguing in circles, counselor . . . but you're right about the hearsay. I'll sustain the objection. You may have reason to believe the perpetrators were members of M-15, Mr. Brannon, but you can't state it as a fact."

"Yes, sir, Your Honor . . . but folks act on what they believe to be true all the time, don't they? What else can they do?"

Malone's bushy eyebrows raised as he stared at Tom. After a few seconds he nodded to the lawyer and said, "Go ahead, counselor."

For the next few minutes, in response to his lawyer's questions, Tom laid out the tragic events of the past few weeks, including the deaths of Burton Minnow and Madison Wheeler, the robbery of the Little Tucson Savings Bank and the shooting of Deputy Fred Kelso, and the kidnapping and rape of Carla May Willard. The team of ACLU lawyers didn't waste their breath objecting. Judge Malone already knew about all of this, anyway. Everybody in the state did. It had been impossible to escape the news coverage.

"So we had a community meeting and decided to try to do something about it," Tom concluded.

"That's when and where the Patriot Project was born."

Malone asked a question of his own. "Was it your idea?"

"Yes, sir, Your Honor. I remembered reading about the Minuteman Project from several years ago, and I thought something like that might work again. I thought we ought to keep it on a smaller, more local level, though. We've succeeded in that. All of our volunteers are from Sierrita County, and they're good, solid citizens."

Tom's lawyer started to say something, but Judge Malone stopped him with an upraised hand. He looked squarely at Tom and said, "Mr. Brannon, tell me again exactly what you and your people have been doing out there, and how you go about it."

Tom nodded and launched into a detailed description of the patrol activities, this time without any leading questions from Spinelli. When he was finished, Malone asked, "You carry guns?"

"Yes, sir, but we haven't had to use them. They're strictly for self-defense."

"None of your people have fired a shot?"

"No, sir."

"What about other violence? You beat up these immigrants before you throw them back across the border?"

"We haven't thrown anybody anywhere, Your Honor. We walk or drive with them to the border and watch them go back across. That's all we do. Nobody's lifted a hand to them."

Spinelli couldn't restrain herself. She stood up and said, "That we know of, Your Honor. It's entirely possible that these vigilantes have killed and buried any number of immigrants. There could be a mass grave out there—"

Tom's lawyer started shouting an objection. Spinelli yelled back at him. Malone lifted his gavel and banged it on the bench until everyone fell silent. He looked at Tom and asked, "You want to answer that accusation, Mr. Brannon?"

"It's a lie, Your Honor," Tom said tightly as he struggled to keep his own temper under control. "I give you my word that there's been no violence involving our patrols. That's all I can do."

Malone nodded.

"And one more thing," Tom added. "The people we've been turning back . . . they're not just immigrants. They're *illegal* immigrants. They're breaking the laws of this country, laws that we're just trying to enforce."

Spinelli was still on her feet. "You just don't want any more Mexicans coming in!" she blazed at him. "You're nothing but a damned bigot!"

Malone's gavel slammed down. "Ms. Spinelli!" he thundered. "I know you feel strongly about this, but I'm very close to holding you in contempt of court!"

Eggleston grabbed Spinelli's arm and pulled her down into her chair as he got up. "We apologize, Your Honor," he said quickly. "We have nothing but the highest respect for the dignity of this court."

"Then sit down and shut up. And that goes double for you, Ms. Spinelli." Malone looked at Tom's lawyer. "Do you have anything further, counselor?"

"No, Your Honor."

Malone turned a baleful gaze on the ACLU table. "What about you?"

Eggleston shook his head and said, "Uh, no, Your Honor."

"Then I've heard enough. We'll take a ten minute recess to let things cool off, and then I'll make my ruling. Mr. Brannon, you can step down."

Tom was glad to get off the hot seat. After everyone had risen and the judge had left the courtroom, he sat down again at the defense table and took a deep breath. Bonnie leaned over the railing and put a hand on his shoulder. "You did fine, Tom, just fine," she said.

"I just told the truth."

"That's always the best defense, isn't it?"

Tom glanced at Spinelli and Eggleston and the other ACLU attorneys. With people like that infesting the legal system, he wasn't sure the truth had much real meaning anymore, as much as he would have liked to believe otherwise.

The ten-minute recess stretched out to more like fifteen. Finally, the judge returned, and when everyone was seated again, Malone began by saying, "I don't believe in vigilante justice. This is a nation of laws, and we have a system in place for enforcing those laws that doesn't include private citizens. That should be sufficient to deal with any problem."

Tom's heart sank.

"But sometimes it isn't," Malone went on. "Sometimes there are extraordinary circumstances that force private citizens to become involved in the justice system. That is the foundation of the concept known as the citizen's arrest."

That gave Tom a little hope. He leaned forward in his chair as Malone paused and cleared his throat.

The judge resumed, "If you had told me that a

group of private citizens could go out and enforce our immigration laws without breaking any laws themselves or depriving people of their civil rights, I wouldn't have believed it. And yet in the absence of any evidence to the contrary, I'm forced to conclude that the Patriot Project is doing just that. Therefore—and understand, I say this reluctantly—the motion for a temporary restraining order is denied." He smacked the gavel down. "This court is adjourned."

The uproar was immediate. Spinelli shouted, "But Your Honor, the potential for abuse here—"

"I can't rule on potential, counselor, only facts. And I said this court is adjourned!"

Bonnie, Tom's lawyers, and several friends gathered around him. Bonnie hugged him while the others slapped him on the back and congratulated him. "You won, Tom!" Bonnie said excitedly. "I knew you would."

Tom smiled tiredly. He had found the whole ordeal draining and hoped he would never have to set foot in a courtroom again. He glanced toward the doors, where the reporters who had been in the audience were rushing out to file their stories. Someone pushed past them, coming into the courtroom, and Tom was surprised to see that it was Buddy Gorman. Buddy looked at him . . .

And from the grief and horror that he saw in his old friend's eyes, Tom suddenly knew that he hadn't won at all. He hadn't won a damned thing.

19

The blood was everywhere. Even though he had believed he was too numb with shock to feel anything else, the sight of his parents' blood splashed around the living room of the house where he'd grown up sent Tom Brannon reeling like a fist to the gut. He staggered and might have fallen, but Buddy Gorman was right beside him, and the sheriff's strong right hand closed around Tom's arm and held him up.

At least the bodies were no longer here. They had already been removed by the coroner and taken to the morgue in the county hospital. The fact that Tom didn't have to see with his own eyes how his mother and father had been butchered was scant consolation, but at least it was something.

"Come on back outside, Tom," Buddy said quietly beside him. "I told you you didn't need to come in here."

"I . . . I had to see it for myself," Tom choked out. "I had to see *that!*"

He lifted a shaking hand and pointed to the words scrawled in blood on the living room wall.

STOP NOW BRANNON OR YOU ARE NEXT

Tom allowed Buddy to turn him around and steer him out of this chamber of horrors. They went out onto the porch, where a wooden swing hung from chains attached to the roof overhang. Tom's legs felt weak. He sank gratefully onto the swing. Buddy sat down beside him.

"We got an anonymous call telling us to come out here," Buddy said after a moment of silence. "I wasn't in the office, of course. I'd gone up to Tucson, to the courthouse. I got one of those damn subpoenas, too. Dusty took the call and sent Francisco out here. He radioed for an ambulance and back-up right away, but . . . it was too late."

"What happened?" Tom grated out. "You were here before they were taken away. What happened to them, Buddy?"

"I don't think there's any reason to go into detail—"

"Damn it, I have to know!"

Buddy took a deep breath. "Well . . . I reckon your mother answered the door. They bulled their way in—"

"How many?"

"Lauren found some footprints in . . . well, in the blood . . . and says she got five different right shoe prints. So we figure there were five of them."

"To handle a couple of people in their eighties." Disgust joined the grief in Tom's voice.

"Yeah, those M-15 boys are some brave sons o' bitches, that's for sure."

Tom wiped the back of his hand across his mouth. "Go on."

"From the looks of things, your dad tried to fight them, but they shot him. A shotgun blast right to the chest. Had to have killed him instantly. He went down fighting, Tom, but there probably wasn't much pain. Knowing Herb, he was probably cussin' 'em for all he was worth, too."

Tom nodded. "I expect so. And Mom . . . ?"

"Another shotgun blast," Buddy said. "They didn't . . . I mean . . . there was no sign that they tried to . . ."

"I know what you're trying to say."

"Yeah."

Tom turned his head, as if to look back over his shoulder and through the wall to the blood-splattered living room. "Two shotgun blasts wouldn't have caused that much blood," he said.

"No. They, uh . . . they used knives . . . machetes, maybe, from the looks of the wounds, Lauren said . . ."

"They chopped my folks to pieces."

"After they were dead, Tom," Buddy said. "You got to remember that. Your mom and dad were already gone when it happened."

"Then they used some of the blood to write that warning on the wall."

Buddy nodded. "That's the way we've got it figured."

Tom clasped his hands together and stared out at the small yard in front of the ranch house. He had played there as a kid. He had ridden his bicycle up and down the dirt road that led to the highway. He had sat in this very swing with his mother beside him, a book open in her lap as she read to him.

Over there on the porch steps, he had sat with his father and learned how to whittle and listened to the yarns that Herb had loved to spin . . .

Tears welled up in his eyes as he said, "This is my fault."

"What? Hell, no, Tom—"

"You told me more than a week ago that *Mara Salvatrucha* likes to strike back at their enemies through their families. I knew right from the start that I needed to get Mom and Dad out of here. I said something to them about it more than once."

"We all know how stubborn Herb was," Buddy said. "And your mom wouldn't go against his wishes."

"Yeah, well, I could have marched in here, picked him up, and carried him out. He couldn't have stopped me."

"Don't be too sure about that. He was a mighty tough old bird."

Tom gazed down at the porch. "Still my fault . . ."

Buddy suddenly shot to his feet, unable to contain his anger. "Goddamn it, Tom!" he shouted. "You know whose fault this really is?" He pointed toward the living room. "It's the fault of the bastards who *did* it, that's who! The same evil sons o' bitches who've been murdering our friends and neighbors and getting away with it! That's who's to blame!"

Tom didn't say anything. He kept staring at the porch floor for a long moment and then finally lifted his head to look at his old friend. He stood up and started down the steps.

"Where are you goin'?" Buddy asked.

"Home."

"That's a good idea. Bonnie's there, and that's

where you should've gone to start with. I told you it wouldn't do any good to come out here."

"Going to get my guns," Tom said without looking around.

Buddy frowned, gave a little shake of his head, and then hurried after him. He grabbed Tom's arm and pulled him around. "What did you say?"

"That I'm going to get my guns," Tom answered dully. "You're right, Buddy, at least part of the way. I still think I bear some of the blame for this, but most of it belongs to M-15. I'm going to Nogales to settle the score with them."

"Nogales!"

"That's where their headquarters is, from everything I've heard and read about them."

"So what're you gonna do?" Buddy asked. "Just march across the border loaded for bear and start asking everybody you see where to find M-15?"

"If I start asking questions, I'm willing to bet that they'll find me."

Buddy's eyes narrowed. "And it never occurred to you that that's exactly what they're hoping you'll do?"

Tom's jaw tightened. "You mean this wasn't really a warning? They killed my parents just to bait a trap for me?"

"It could be that way," Buddy said. "A warning, if that's the way you took it, and bait if it's not."

"I can't just—" Tom looked toward the house and shuddered. "—ignore this."

"Nobody's askin' you to. But you can't go charging into Nogales with guns blazing like the Lone Ranger, either."

"Then . . ." Tom's voice broke. "Then what can I do?"

"Go home," Buddy said gently. "Go home to your wife, and the two of you hold on to each other as tight as you can for a while. Forget about the Patriot Project and everything else. Get some rest. Let things sort themselves out for a day or two." He paused. "Let *me* sort some things out."

Tom's eyes narrowed. "You? What are you talking about, Buddy?"

"I'm still the sheriff of Sierrita County, you know. This is my jurisdiction, and it's my job to investigate this crime."

"What can you do? The bastards are long gone."

"As a law enforcement official, I just might have some resources available to me that you don't, Tom. Let me look into it, all right?"

Tom frowned and rubbed a hand over his close-cropped hair. "Bonnie would pitch a fit if I went down to Mexico right now."

"Damn right she would."

"I guess . . . I guess you're right, Buddy. I'll go home."

"You're not just telling me that so I'll leave you alone, are you? Got any plans to sneak off and head down there later?"

Tom grimaced and shook his head. "No, you've got my word on it."

Buddy nodded emphatically and said, "That's good enough for me. Come on, now. I'll give you a ride, get you through the mob of reporters."

"Lord, is this ever going to end?" Tom muttered under his breath.

"It'll end. We'll get through it, and one way or another, it'll end. Good people won't stand for this.

You'll see, Tom. This is the beginning of the end for M-15."

Tom wished with all his heart that he could believe that. But as he glanced back at the house where two good people had met an untimely and unholy end, he wasn't sure.

Maybe this was one time when the good guys weren't going to win.

Buddy Gorman was as weary as he'd ever been in his life when he walked into the sheriff's office after dropping off Tom at the Brannon's house. He could trust Bonnie to look after his old friend and keep him from doing anything foolish. At least, Buddy hoped that was the case.

He stopped just inside the door, a frown creasing his forehead as he saw who was waiting for him.

Agents Ford and Berry stood up from the straight-backed wooden chairs just inside the door, in front of the wooden railing that divided the public part of the office from the section for authorized personnel only. Both of the FBI agents wore sunglasses, even though they were inside a building. Buddy wondered if that was part of their training at Quantico.

"Sheriff Gorman," Ford said, "we heard about what happened to Brannon's parents. Is there anything we can do to assist you in the investigation?"

"Murder's a state crime, not a federal one," Buddy said tightly.

"That's true, but if there's an indication that the crime was committed by foreign nationals—"

"Nobody said there was."

Berry said, "There are rumors that M-15 was behind it, that a warning was left for Brannon to back off on what he's been doing."

"The sheriff's office isn't going to comment on any rumors."

"Come on, Sheriff," Ford said impatiently. "You know very well that this matter is too big for you to handle. You need to turn it over to us—"

"So you can bury it," Buddy cut in, "the way you've tried to bury everything else M-15 has done down here?"

"Why would we do that?" Berry asked angrily. "We're law enforcement officers, too, damn it. Why would we want a bunch of killers to get away with their crimes?"

"Because it makes your bosses in the Justice Department and *their* boss in the White House look bad to have the border so open that killers can go back and forth without any trouble. You'd rather sweep it all under the rug so that the rest of the country will forget about it, rather than doing the hard work of actually putting a stop to it."

"You can't be talking about closing the border," Ford said.

"No, that wouldn't work at all, would it?" Buddy said scathingly. "If the border were closed, then all the businesses in Texas and Arizona and California that rely on illegal immigrants for their work force would be out of luck, wouldn't they? Those businesses represent a lot of campaign contributions for politicians on both sides of the aisle, not to mention the one in the White House. She can talk all she wants to about feeling sorry for the illegals and wanting them to have a better life, but we know it's all bullshit. It's all about the money. It always is."

Both of the agents glared at Buddy as he concluded his angry remarks. But at the same time they looked uncomfortable, and he knew his words had hit home. He was right—the federal government didn't really care about the people of southern Arizona. The bureaucrats just wanted the whole thing to go away so it wouldn't be an embarrassment for them anymore.

That wasn't going to happen. Not while Buddy Gorman was the sheriff of Sierrita County.

He stepped past them, through the gate in the railing. "You'll have to excuse me," he said curtly. "I've got work to do."

"You'd better reconsider, Sheriff," Berry said.

"I don't think so."

Buddy stalked past the dispatcher's desk. Dusty gave him a big grin. Lauren was at her desk over in the corner, going over some reports, and she was smiling, too. They had enjoyed being on hand for Buddy's reaming-out of the FBI agents.

Buddy went into his office and shut the door. He sat down behind the desk, and a moment later a knock sounded on the door. "Come in," he said, knowing that it couldn't be Ford or Berry. The agents would have left by now, both of them steaming.

Lauren came in carrying a sheaf of papers. "Here are the preliminary forensics reports, Buddy. I picked up a few fingerprints, but nothing that matches so far."

"I'm not surprised. Most of those M-15s have never been arrested over here on this side of the border."

"We might get something back from Mexico or Guatemala or El Salvador in a few days."

"Or we might not."

Lauren shrugged and admitted, "We might not."

Buddy nodded toward the desk. "Just leave the reports. I'll look at 'em later." He added, "And thanks for all your hard work, Lauren."

"No problem, boss." She hesitated. "How's Mr. Brannon doing?"

Buddy shook his head. "Not good. He thinks it's his fault, and I had to talk him out of going down to Nogales to shoot up the place."

"He would have just gotten himself killed."

"Yeah."

Nogales . . . That was the key, Buddy thought as Lauren went back out, leaving the reports on his desk.

And he believed he had a key of his own that just might break things wide open.

Every law enforcement officer, even the most straight arrow, bent the rules a little every now and then, for the simple reason that no law could be truly universal and cover every case. Bad cops crossed that line for their own benefit, but good ones ventured over it only for a good reason, usually to help somebody else.

In Buddy's case, he had let Diego Vasquez off the hook on a possession rap because Diego was just a kid and because his father, Jaime Vasquez, had been one of the starting guards on the Little Tucson High School basketball team at the same time Buddy and Tom Brannon had been the starting forwards. Buddy had truly believed that Diego was a good kid who would get straightened out if he just had a chance.

He had been wrong, at least partially. Diego wasn't a good kid, and he hadn't straightened out. He had run off to Nogales and fallen in with an even worse crowd than the one that had given him the joint Buddy could have busted him for. But Diego hadn't completely forgotten the favor Buddy had done for him, and on several occasions during the past five years, Buddy had gotten a phone call from Diego, tipping him off to something bad that was about to go down in Sierrita County. It was kind of like having a deal with the devil and it made Buddy a little uncomfortable, but every cop had his sources and had to make use of them, even the unsavory ones.

Now Buddy used his cell phone to call the number he had written on a piece of paper he took from his wallet. A man's voice grunted in answer, "Flora's Café."

"Tell Diego his dry cleaning is done," Buddy said, feeling foolish as he always did when he got in touch with Diego this way. He understood that codes and passwords helped keep Diego safe, though.

The man on the other end of the phone grunted, and then a few moments of silence went by. The next voice Buddy heard belonged to Diego, who said, "What is it?"

"I'm coming to Nogales," Buddy said. "Tell me where to meet you."

"Oh, man," Diego responded quickly, "that ain't a good idea. You can't—"

"I can," Buddy said. "Come on, Diego, you owe me, and you know it."

Diego sighed. "All right. There's a place just this side of the border called Ochoa's, sells cigars and candy and magazines. Tell me when. But I don't like this, Buddy."

"Neither do I," Buddy said. "I'll be there tonight. Eight o'clock."

"Don't come dressed in your sheriff suit, okay?"

Buddy just grinned and said, "I'll see you then, Diego."

20

There were towns called Nogales on both sides of the border, or if you preferred to think of it that way, you could consider it one town split down the middle by the international boundary line. Either way, it was a dusty, ugly, heat-blasted place, a typical pair of bordertowns with plenty of cantinas and whorehouses and seedy little shops.

One of which Buddy Gorman found himself standing in that evening, leafing through a pornographic magazine that contained some of the filthiest pictures he had ever seen.

He didn't look like a sheriff now. He wore a gaudy shirt and light-colored trousers, and anyone glancing at him would take him for an American tourist out to wallow in the squalor found south of the border. He had seen plenty of guys who really fit that description, so it hadn't been much of a challenge to duplicate their appearance. His jaws worked as he chewed gum and flipped through the pages of the skin mag.

Diego sidled up beside him and said quietly, "Man, you are one fuckin' crazy gringo."

Buddy grinned sideways at him. "You don't know the half of it, amigo. Is there some place around here we can talk?"

"Talk right here," Diego said. He was a handsome young man, well-dressed without being gaudy about it. Buddy wasn't sure exactly what sort of things Diego was mixed up in down here—drugs almost surely, prostitution probably, maybe swindling a few lonely American women who came here on vacation, although there wouldn't be many of those—but his crimes were on a small scale, the sort that wouldn't bring him to the attention of the big-shots like *Mara Salvatrucha.* "Tell me what you want," Diego went on, "and then get back on the other side of the border where you belong."

Still holding the magazine, Buddy said without looking at the young man, "I want M-15."

Diego started to turn away. "You crazy, all right. Get outta here. I can't help you."

"Just give me a name or a place to go," Buddy said quickly. "A place to start."

Diego sighed. "This is about what happened up there in your town, that SavMart Massacre?"

"Some of it, yeah. And it's about a couple of old people who were slaughtered like animals in their own home. They were the parents of a good friend of mine. My best friend."

"Yeah, that sounds like somethin' M-15 would do. But I can't help you, Buddy. I don't have nothin' to do with those hombres. They're loco."

"I know that. But I want to get my hands on one of them, anyway. Somebody I can take back to Little Tucson to testify about what happened to Tom Brannon's folks."

Diego's eyes narrowed. "M-15 don't testify. You can't get 'em to talk, man. Especially not with all the rules you gringos got to follow."

"Maybe I'm getting tired of following all the rules," Buddy said softly.

For a long moment Diego studied him intently, and then the young man sighed again and nodded. "You gonna be stubborn about this, ain'tcha?"

"Oh, yeah."

"Gimme a minute. I'll make some calls, see what I can find out."

Diego took a cell phone out of the pocket of his expensive jacket and sauntered toward the rear of the store. Buddy glanced over at the elderly proprietor, who was the only other person in the place. The old man didn't look at him, just stared straight ahead as if Buddy and Diego weren't there. Buddy put the magazine back in the rack and started to pick up another one, then stopped when he saw the Great Dane and the girl on the cover. Maybe he would just wait without looking at any more magazines.

Diego rejoined him in a few minutes. "There's a guy named Ortiz," he said. "A real bad-ass hombre. He's been braggin' about how he and some other guys killed a couple of old gringos."

Buddy stiffened. "Then he's the guy I want to talk to."

"He's supposed to be payin' a visit to a girl I know in a little while. If you want . . ." Diego grimaced and shook his head. "Man, I don't know why I'm doin' this. You gonna wind up gettin' me killed. But if you want, you could be there when Ortiz comes in."

Buddy nodded. "That's exactly what I want. Thanks, Diego. *Muchas gracias.*"

"Save it," Diego snapped. "Tell me again in an hour . . . if we both ain't dead by then."

If the girl in the sleazy hotel room was a day over fifteen, Buddy would be surprised. She wore a thin slip that clung to the lines of her slender body, and her dark nipples showed through it. She sat at a dressing table running a brush through her long dark hair while Diego talked to her in Spanish, and when he finished she said, "Hokay."

Diego turned to Buddy and said, "When Ortiz comes in, you'll be in the closet. Wait until they start fuckin', then you can take him. Be quick about it, though. After you knock him out, bring him into the hall. I'll be waiting, and we can take him down the back stairs and into the alley where you left your car."

"The car will still be there, right?"

"My muchachos got strict orders not to touch it, man."

Buddy nodded. "All right, sounds good."

He took a deep breath. Yeah, assault and kidnapping sounded like good things for a lawman to do. Something inside him cringed at the very idea. But he reminded himself of why he was doing this and of the sort of man this Ortiz was. Even if this was a step over the line from which he could never fully return, he was prepared to go ahead with it. He owed that to Tom Brannon. Hell, he owed that to the citizens of Little Tucson who had elected him. If he could put together a solid case against a member of M-15, he might be able to force the government to step in and actually *do* something. That was his hope, anyway.

He glanced at the girl and added, "Uh, you think maybe I ought to jump him before they start . . . you know . . ."

Diego waved a hand and smiled. "Don't worry about that, man. It ain't like she's sacrificin' her virginity or anything like that. Is it, *chica?*"

The girl just laughed and shook her head.

"Well, all right," Buddy said. "I guess it would be better if Ortiz was, uh, distracted . . ."

"Now you're talkin'," Diego said.

He left the room. Buddy went to the tiny closet and opened the door. Before he could step inside, the girl said, "Jefe?"

He looked back and saw that she had taken a joint from a box on the dressing table. She held it up and smiled, offering it to him. Buddy shook his head and said, "No, thanks."

The girl shrugged, reached down, and pulled the slip most of the way up her sleek brown thighs. She looked at Buddy and raised her eyebrows quizzically. "No, *gracias,*" he said, refusing that offer as well.

"Plenny of time," the girl said.

Buddy put his hands up in front of him and moved them back and forth slightly. "No, but *muchas gracias.*"

The girl shrugged her bare shoulders, and Buddy retreated gratefully into the closet, pulling the door behind him until only a small gap remained. He blew out his breath, thinking about his wife and feeling very glad right now that he was a faithful husband.

It was hot in there. Sweat beaded on his forehead

and rolled down into his eyebrows. His shirt was damp. He reached down and touched the gun in his trousers pocket. The serial number was filed off it, and it had never been registered anyway. It was a flat little .32 automatic, deadly enough at close range. Nestled beside it in Buddy's pocket was an old-fashioned sap that had belonged to his uncle, who had carried it when he worked in the Cook County Jail back in Chicago, in the fifties. Buddy supposed that made the sap an antique, but it still worked just fine.

Long minutes dragged by. Buddy began to wonder if Ortiz was even going to show up. But then footsteps sounded in the hallway outside, and the door to the room creaked open. Buddy couldn't see the girl, but he heard her greeting the man who had stepped into the room.

Buddy could see their shadows through the narrow gap, but that was all. He heard moaning and figured that they were kissing. The girl was carrying on like she was aroused. Typical whore behavior. Then Buddy smelled marijuana smoke. Ortiz hadn't declined the offer of a joint.

A few minutes later Buddy heard the bedsprings squeak. The sound got louder and faster. He slipped the gun out of his pocket and put it in his left hand. Then he clutched the sap in his right hand. He pushed the door open with his foot.

The bed was only about five feet away. Two fast steps would bring him next to it. Ortiz was on top of the girl, still wearing his shirt, pumping away at her. Buddy took the first of those two steps and lifted the sap.

From the corner of his eye he saw movement and

jerked his head in that direction to see the door to
the hall opening. A man stepped through it, a big
grin on his face as he said something in Spanish
about Ortiz hurrying up so somebody else could
get some. Then he froze as he spotted Buddy.

Buddy had stopped in midstride. He pivoted as
the second man suddenly bellowed a warning to
Ortiz and clawed at the gun in his belt. Buddy
swung the sap and felt as much as heard the satis-
fying crunch as it landed on the man's nose. The
man went backward, blood spurting from the
crushed nose. Buddy hoped that enough shards of
bone had gone up into his brain to kill him.

He tried to turn back toward the bed, but as he
did Ortiz came up with a yell and slammed a fist
into Buddy's chest. The blow knocked Buddy back
a step. He slashed at Ortiz's head with the sap but
missed. The sap landed on Ortiz's right shoulder
instead, and that was almost as good because the
man's face contorted in agony and he fell to a
knee, clutching his right shoulder with his left
hand. Buddy figured the blow had numbed Ortiz's
whole right arm.

A gun roared behind him and Buddy's left ear
felt like somebody had pinched it. A part of his
brain knew that a bullet had just grazed him, but
for the most part he was operating purely on instinct now. He twisted around and saw that Ortiz's
friend wasn't dead after all. He had a busted nose
and blood all over his chest and the lower half of
his face, but he was definitely still alive and about to
take another shot at Buddy.

Buddy brought up the .32 in his left hand and
triggered three shots before the man looming in

the doorway could fire again with the old-fashioned revolver he held. The bullets caught the man in the chest and threw him backward. He hit the wall on the other side of the corridor with a crash and bounced off, pitching forward to land face-down on the threadbare carpet runner.

People started shouting. This was a cheap, squalid hotel used almost solely by prostitutes and their customers, and the patrons had to be accustomed to some trouble now and then. But a pitched gun battle would attract attention even in a place like this.

Everything was screwed, but Buddy thought he might still be able to salvage the situation if he acted fast enough. When he turned back toward the bed, he saw that Ortiz was struggling to get up from the floor. Buddy kicked him in the face and sent him sprawling. He leaned over the man and rapped him on the skull with the sap just for good measure.

Then he looked at the bed and almost threw up. The bullet that had clipped his ear had gone on past him and caught the girl in the head just as she jumped up from the stained mattress. Her nude body was sprawled across the foot of the bed now, her wide eyes staring sightlessly at the ceiling with its peeling paper. The black hole in the center of her forehead hadn't bled much, but there was a pool of crimson on the mattress under her head.

Buddy swallowed the bile that tried to well up his throat and jammed the sap back in his pocket. Still holding the gun, he bent to grab Ortiz. He hoisted the man's senseless form, grunting from the effort as he draped Ortiz over his shoulder. Then he staggered out in the hall, stepping over the body of the man he had killed. Where the hell was Diego?

The young man appeared at the top of the rear stairs, holding a bloody handkerchief to his head. "Buddy!" he called. "*Andale! Andale!*"

Buddy hurried, all right, stumbling toward the stairs with his limp burden. "What the hell happened?" he gasped as he and Diego started down.

"I saw Juan start to go up after Ortiz and tried to stop him. He hit me, knocked me half loco for a few minutes. Then I heard the shooting . . . You killed him?"

Buddy nodded as they continued to clatter down the stairs. "I'm pretty sure I did."

"He was with Ortiz, when those old people were killed."

Buddy felt a throb of fierce satisfaction go through him. At least one of the murderers of Herb and Mildred Brannon had received justice.

They reached the bottom of the stairs. Diego pushed out through the door that led to the alley. Buddy was right behind him. The way things had been going, Buddy was a little surprised that his car was there and seemingly untouched, just as Diego had promised. He supposed he had to have some good luck sometime.

Sirens wailed somewhere close by. The Nogales police responding to the shooting. They might actually investigate the matter, since the dead man was a member of M-15 and Buddy figured that the cops were probably in the gang's back pocket. But it was only a few blocks to the border, and he intended to be back across before anyone could stop him.

Balancing the unconscious Ortiz on his shoulder, Buddy fished his keys out of his pocket and handed them to Diego, who popped the trunk lid. Buddy lowered Ortiz into the trunk and slammed it closed.

"*Gracias*, amigo," he said to Diego as he took the keys back. "I can't thank you enough."

"You can thank me by not ever comin' down here again," Diego said. "Not only that, but don't expect to be hearin' from me again, either. We're square, man. I don't owe you nothin' no more."

Buddy nodded. "I'm sorry about the girl."

"The girl? What you talkin' about?"

"When the bastard you called Juan shot at me, he hit her instead. She's dead, Diego."

He looked stricken. "*Muerte?* Aaiiee . . ."

"If there's anything I can do—"

"Just get outta here, man. And like I said, don't come back."

Buddy could have been wrong—it was hard to tell in the shadowy alley—but he thought he saw tears shining in Diego's eyes. No pimp would cry over a dead whore, would he? Maybe sometimes . . .

With a shake of his head, Buddy got in the car and started it, relieved when the engine caught normally. He pulled away, leaving Diego in the alley. What a fine, upstanding cop he was, he thought bitterly. He'd shot a man and gotten a girl killed. Neither of them had been innocents, but the girl, surely, hadn't deserved such a fate.

But Herb and Mildred hadn't deserved their fate, either, he reminded himself, and neither had the dozens of other people *Mara Salvatrucha* had killed, most of them good friends of his.

The port of entry was in downtown Nogales. Most American tourists parked their cars in lots just north of the border and walked across, relying on cabs for getting around the Mexican city. But you could drive if you were brave enough or had a good enough reason, and there were a few cars waiting in line to go through customs either way. Buddy waited his turn patiently. He wasn't worried about the Mexican customs agents; they would barely glance at him on his way through the checkpoint. It was always possible that the American agents might decide to search his car, though. If that happened, he was up shit creek, because they would find Ortiz. Of course, he could claim ignorance and say that someone had dumped Ortiz in the trunk while the car was parked. That story *might* be believed. But there would still be a lot of questions that he didn't want to answer.

As expected, the Mexican customs agent on duty just waved him on through. The American took a look at his driver's license and the badge that was next to it in the wallet. "You're the sheriff of Sierrita County?" he asked.

"That's right," Buddy said, keeping his voice level and calm.

"Hear you've been having lots of trouble up there."

"More than our share."

"Why were you in Mexico?"

Buddy reached down to the seat and brought up a paper bag he had placed there earlier. He handed it to the agent, who opened it, looked inside, and handed it back.

"If you want to trust those Mexican antibiotics, Sheriff, that's your business, but I'm not sure I would."

Buddy smiled. "Yeah, I know, but my wife's sold

on 'em. She's got a sinus infection, and she says they work better than the American ones. Cheaper, too."

"Well, good luck to her." The customs agent stepped back and motioned for Buddy to drive ahead.

He didn't heave the huge sigh of relief he felt until he was several blocks away from the border crossing. The Mexican pharmacies just across the line did a huge business with American customers, and they were open twenty-four hours a day. Buddy had figured that stopping for a couple of bottles of antibiotics would give him just the excuse he needed to be in Nogales.

And now he was on his way home. When he got there, he would stash Ortiz somewhere and work on him until the man told him everything he wanted to know about M-15 and the gang's involvement with the murders of Herb and Mildred Brannon. Buddy had never beaten a confession out of a suspect in his life, but after everything else he had done tonight, that didn't seem so bad. As long as he didn't let the ACLU get even a whiff of what was going on . . .

He drove carefully until he was out of Nogales, veering northwest from Interstate 19 on the state highway that led to Little Tucson. As always on the desert, the night air cooled off quickly. Buddy turned off the air conditioning and rolled down the windows.

It must have been the rush of air that kept him from hearing the helicopter until it was right on top of him. Suddenly it swooped past him like a huge bird of prey and flew on down the otherwise empty desert highway. Buddy hit the brakes as the chopper turned.

What the hell! The damn thing was coming right at him now. In the glow of his headlights, he saw the man leaning out from the cabin, saw the flicker of orange as the machine gun in the man's hands opened up. Then the windshield shattered, splintering into a million razor-sharp shards. Buddy screamed as some of them lanced into his eyes and slashed his hands on the steering wheel. The car careened wildly back and forth.

A giant fist slammed into Buddy's left shoulder, driving him back against the seat. The car bounced madly as it left the road. Buddy came up in the seat, slamming his head against the roof. A thunderous hammering filled his ears, and somehow he knew it was caused by the high-powered machine gun rounds hitting the car. If one of them struck the gas tank . . .

Then the car began to roll, and that was exactly what happened. It came apart in a huge ball of orange flame that threw pieces of the destroyed vehicle hundreds of yards in every direction. Anyone inside it was instantly incinerated.

The helicopter swooped over the site of the explosion, hovered there for a moment, and then flew toward the south, back across the border. The men inside it had done the job they came to do. Diego hadn't lasted more than a few minutes under torture, and then he had told them exactly what kind of car to look for. Cipriano Asturias brought the machine gun back inside the cabin. Once he and his brother reported to Señor Montoya that Ortiz would never be able to testify against M-15, they could go ahead and kill Diego. Foolish young man, to think he could hide what he was doing from the eyes of *Mara Salvatrucha.*

The chopper disappeared into the distance, the eggbeater sound of its engine fading to nothingness, as behind it the wrecked car continued to burn fiercely.

And some yards away, the heat blistering his skin, the man who had been thrown clear bare seconds before the explosion, kept trying to crawl away. He was blind, his face covered with blood, and he felt the hot drops falling on his hands as he clawed at the desert sand . . .

21

Tom fought his way up out of sleep as the cell phone on the nightstand rang. Out of habit, he reached for the regular phone first, forgetting for the moment that he had unplugged all of them to keep the reporters from calling constantly. Then he realized it was the cell and picked it up instead. The screen was lit up, and the number it displayed belonged to the Sierrita County Sheriff's Office.

A chill shivered along Tom's spine. The bedside clock read 3:30 A.M. Buddy wouldn't be calling at this time of the morning with good news.

"Whosit?" Bonnie murmured sleepily from beside him.

"Buddy," Tom said as he pushed the button to take the call.

Only it wasn't. After Tom said hello, a woman's voice asked, "Mr. Brannon?"

"Yeah?"

"This is Lauren Henderson. From the sheriff's office."

Tom sat up straighter in the bed. He knew Lauren,

but not all that well. Well enough, though, to tell that she was really upset about something. "What is it?"

"Buddy . . . Sheriff Gorman . . . There's been an accident . . . It's terrible . . . I thought you'd want to know . . ."

"Is he alive?" Tom grated out. Even as he asked the question, he wondered if what had happened to Buddy had really been an accident—or if this was another strike by M-15.

"He's alive," Lauren said. "Barely, though. He was in really bad shape when he was brought in. The doctors at the hospital don't know if he'll make it or not. If a trucker hadn't come along the highway and seen the wrecked car . . ."

"It was a car accident?"

"Buddy's car went off the road and rolled over and then the gas tank exploded. If he hadn't been thrown clear when the car rolled, he would have died for sure."

"My God," Tom said softly.

"That's not all of it," Lauren went on. "Since you're the mayor now, as well as Buddy's friend, I suppose you have a right to know. He was shot, too. His whole car was shot up. And . . . there was what was left . . . of a dead man in the trunk."

Tom closed his eyes and rubbed his temples. What the hell had Buddy been doing? The only thing he was sure of was that M-15 had to be mixed up in this somehow.

"Has Buddy been able to talk?"

"No, he's unconscious. The ER doctor said he might never wake up."

"I'm coming down there to the hospital." Bonnie's hand tightened on Tom's shoulder as he spoke.

"There's really nothing you can do—"

"I can be there," Tom cut in. "That'll have to be enough for now."

Lauren was silent for a moment, then she went on, "I'm at the office right now, but I was thinking about going back to the hospital, too. I'll meet you there, Mr. Brannon."

"All right. Thanks for calling, Deputy."

Tom broke the connection, and Bonnie said, "Buddy's hurt, isn't he? Was it M-15?"

"Looks like it."

"Will he be all right?"

"I don't know," Tom said with a shake of his head. "I'm going down to the hospital to see about him."

"I know. I'm coming with you."

He turned toward her and hugged her hard for a moment. He had never doubted that she would want to come with him. In fact, he would have been surprised if she hadn't.

"I'm starting to think M-15 won't stop until they've killed everybody in the county," Bonnie said as they got dressed.

"Yeah, it seems like they've declared war on us, all right," Tom agreed. "But they've forgotten one thing."

"What's that?"

"We can make war right back at 'em."

The doctor said, "Sheriff Gorman has a broken shoulder, four broken ribs, a punctured lung from one of those rib fractures, numerous deep cuts and lacerations from being thrown through the windshield, head trauma, and severe damage to his eyes.

If he lives, I doubt if he'll ever have any vision to speak of. The broken shoulder was caused by a bullet wound, and of course he lost a great deal of blood. We don't know yet if there was any brain damage beyond a concussion."

"He can recover from all those things, though, right?" Tom asked.

The doctor shrugged. "He's been lucky to stay alive this long. Who knows how much longer his luck will last?"

Tom rubbed a hand over his head and frowned. The thought of Buddy, helpless and blind, made him sick. But the thought of Buddy being dead was worse.

"Deputy Henderson said something about there being another man in the car . . ."

The doctor nodded. "He's in the morgue, what's left of him. There's not much besides charred bones. That was quite an explosion."

"Any way of identifying him?"

"You'll have to ask the deputy about that. Dental records, maybe. Or DNA, but that seems like a long shot. It's not my area of expertise, though."

Tom looked over at Lauren, who was standing with Bonnie beside the door into the Intensive Care Unit. They were looking through the small window in the door, but Tom wasn't sure they could see anything except maybe Buddy's wife Jean, who sat in a wooden chair beside the bed.

He went over to them and said, "Deputy Henderson, we need to talk."

Lauren nodded. She wasn't in uniform but rather wore jeans and a University of Arizona T-shirt. She had her badge and her holstered revolver clipped to her belt. Her shoulder-length brown hair was loose instead of pulled back in the ponytail she usually wore on duty.

She followed him about twenty feet down the hall to a small waiting area with reasonably comfortable chairs. As they sat down, Tom said, "Tell me everything you know."

Lauren took a deep breath. "Like I told you on the phone, a trucker came along and spotted the wreck off to the side of the road. He stopped to take a look around and found Buddy . . . Sheriff Gorman."

"Buddy's fine," Tom said with a faint smile. "That's what I call him, too."

"Okay. The trucker called nine-one-one on his cell phone. The night dispatcher sent an ambulance out right away, along with Deputy Montero. Then he called me, even though I was off duty, because I'd asked him to let me know if anything happened."

Tom nodded. He could understand Lauren wanting to be kept abreast of the situation.

"I came here to the hospital first to check on Buddy, then went back to the office to make sure nothing else was going on in the county. That's when I called you. Then I came back over here." She shrugged. "That's all I know. You're up to date, Mayor Brannon."

"Make it Tom," he told her. "Have you seen the body of the other man, the one who was in the trunk?"

She nodded, a grim expression on her face. "Not much left. We'll be lucky to ever identify him."

"But he was definitely inside the trunk?"

"Yes. The lid was popped from the rollover, but the skeleton was relatively intact and still inside the trunk."

"So he was locked in there?"

"Unless someone came along and dumped a body inside the trunk while the car was still on fire. I suppose that's remotely possible, but I'd consider it highly unlikely. The heat would have been too bad for anybody to get close enough to do something like that."

Tom agreed—which left him with a question he wasn't sure he wanted answered.

Why had Buddy Gorman locked somebody inside the trunk of his car?

"Do you know what he was doing down there, or where he had been?"

Lauren's eyes narrowed as she looked at him. "Are you asking me as the mayor of Little Tucson, or as Buddy's friend?"

"For right now, as Buddy's friend. Did he tell you what he was planning to do, Lauren?"

She hesitated for a second longer, then shook her head. "No, I don't have any idea. But he must have gone to Nogales. There's nothing else in that direction."

Nogales . . . Tom remembered what he had said the previous afternoon about going to Nogales and how Buddy had talked him out of it. Buddy had promised to investigate the murders of his parents . . .

Had his investigation taken him to Nogales? That was the only answer that seemed to make any sense.

"I'm not trying to tell you how to do your job, but if I were you I think I'd check with the authorities on this side of the border in Nogales and see if they know whether Buddy was down there last night."

Lauren nodded. "I was thinking the same thing. And *I'm* not trying to tell you how to do *your* job, Tom, but somebody's going to have to take over running the sheriff's office for the time being."

"That'll be up to the county commissioners . . . but I intend to recommend to them that they make you the acting sheriff."

"What!" The exclamation was startled out of Lauren. "I assumed that Wayne would take over."

"Wayne Rushing is a good man, but he's never been any more than a small-town deputy. Same with Francisco. But you were a full-time officer on the Phoenix police force and were doing really well when you left there. You'd have been a detective soon, and who knows how far you might have gone."

"Buddy talked about me, I see," she said tightly.

"Buddy was frustrated that he couldn't get you to work more than part-time. He wanted to give you more responsibility. He said you could handle it better than anybody else in his department."

"I suppose he wondered why I left Phoenix, too."

Tom shrugged. "Maybe so, but he didn't say anything to me about it. I guess he figured it was your business."

"That's right, it is." She hesitated a moment, then went on, "I had a relationship that ended. A broken heart, as corny as that sounds."

"Why are you telling me now?" Tom asked.

"Because you want me to be the acting sheriff, and I'm telling you I'm not cut out for the job. I'm not strong enough, obviously, or I wouldn't have run off down here to get away from the hurt."

"Something hurts bad enough," Tom said, "anybody's gonna run to get away from it. And you haven't let it affect the way you do your job since you've been here. Like I said, Buddy was really pleased with your work."

"Well . . . I've been happier here than I expected to be."

Tom wondered if that was because she had found somebody here in Little Tucson to mend that broken heart of hers. He didn't ponder the matter for long, though.

"So can I tell the commissioners you'll take the job?"

Lauren thought for a moment longer and then nodded. "I guess I can give it a try."

"Good. Anything you need, just let me know and I'll do what I can to help."

She reached out and touched his arm for a second. "I'm sorry that you've had to go through so much, Mr. Brannon . . . Tom. My God, it hasn't even been twenty-four hours since you lost your parents, and now Buddy—"

"Buddy's going to make it," Tom said.

"If anybody's stubborn enough to do just that, it's him."

Tom put his hands on his knees and pushed himself to his feet. "There's nothing I can do here. Might as well go home and try to get some rest. I've got a busy day coming up. Funeral arrangements, you know."

Lauren nodded. "I'm so sorry. It's all so unfair. Right from the start, from the day of the bank robbery and Carla Willard's carjacking, all you've done is try to help people. And look what it's gotten you."

Tom rubbed the back of his neck. "I guess sometimes the price is high for doing the right thing."

"It should never be *that* high."

He nodded in agreement. Lauren was right. M-15 had gone too far, further almost than the human brain could comprehend. And they showed no sign of giving up or even backing off any. He had called it a war, and he wasn't the first one to use that word.

How could anybody fight a war that was impossible to win? Was there even any hope, any reason to keep trying? Little Tucson couldn't look to the federal government for help, that was obvious. The people had tried to help themselves with the Patriot Project, and that had led to even more tragedy. Tom was convinced that whatever had happened to Buddy had happened because of his investigation into the deaths of Tom's parents.

Maybe it was time to give up. Maybe Bonnie was right and they ought to leave. Hell, maybe everybody who lived in Sierrita County ought to pack up and leave the place to M-15. Let somebody else deal with it.

Sick at heart but trying not to show it, Tom walked back down the hall to join his wife and take her home.

No matter what else happened, one thing you could depend on was that it would be hot in the summertime in these parts. The sun was already scorching at ten o'clock the next morning when

Tom stepped out of Crabtree's Funeral Parlor. He
and Ed Crabtree had spent the past hour going
over the funeral arrangements for Tom's parents.
Ed looked worn out, and Tom could almost feel
sorry for the man. There had been so many funer-
als over the past couple of weeks that Ed had to be
exhausted, and on top of that, his father-in-law had
been one of the people killed in the SavMart Massacre. That tragedy had left almost no one in Little
Tucson untouched.

Tom paused on the sidewalk in front of the funeral
parlor and looked around. For once, downtown
Little Tucson looked almost normal again. All the
news crews were over at the hospital, reporting on
Sheriff Gorman's valiant fight for life. Tom thought
about walking down to the auto parts store to see how
Louly and Sal were doing. From his phone conversa-
tions with Louly, he knew that while business hadn't
been good, it hadn't dried up completely. Tom decided he could take a few minutes to do that. He had
left Bonnie at the hospital to sit with Jean Gorman.
She would be safe enough there for a while. Lauren
had assigned two deputies to the door of the ICU,
even before the county commissioners had met in
emergency session early this morning and appointed
her the acting sheriff.

Tom turned to walk along the sidewalk, but he
had gone only a couple of steps when a big black
car pulled up to the curb next to him. The front
and rear passenger doors swung open as Tom stiffened, wondering if this was going to be another
attack by M-15.

Two men got out of the car, but they weren't Hispanic gangsters. One was white, one black, and

both wore sober dark suits and sunglasses. The thought that immediately flashed into Tom's mind was *Secret Service*. They looked just like the sort of agents he had seen on TV protecting the President.

"Mr. Brannon?" the black man said. "Would you come with us, please?"

"Why?" Tom asked bluntly.

"Someone wants to talk to you."

"Well, what if I don't want to talk to *her*? She hasn't done anything to help matters down here. Hell, it's the sort of thinking that she and all her left-wing friends have done over the past thirty or forty years that's caused a lot of this problem!"

Both of the men frowned, and the white one said, "Sir, we don't know what you're talking about."

"You're not Secret Service?"

"No, sir," the black man said.

"Then who do you work for?"

"He'd prefer to introduce himself to you. But he said that if you were reluctant to accompany us, we should tell you . . . he can help with M-15."

That was surprising, and just intriguing enough to make Tom curious. He wasn't sure things could get much worse than they were, and besides, these guys—and the two dressed just like them he could see through the open doors of the car—sure didn't look like *Mara Salvatrucha*.

"Why the hell not?" Tom muttered. He stepped down off the sidewalk to get into the car.

It was cool inside, despite the fact that two of the doors had been standing open for several minutes. The car was as sleek and fancy as any Tom had ever ridden in. He sat in the backseat, between two of the men. He had no idea where they were taking him, but surprisingly, they didn't go very far, just a few blocks, before the driver pulled the car into the parking lot of the local Dairy Queen. He stopped next to an old red pickup that must have dated from around 1960.

"Inside," the black man said, nodding toward the Dairy Queen. "He's waiting for you."

He went inside the Dairy Queen, which wasn't busy this time of morning. The breakfast rush was over, and it wasn't time for lunch yet. Only a few people were in the place, and one of them was a silver-haired old man who sat in a booth at the back. He saw Tom come in and raised a hand to catch his eye. Tom walked toward him.

The old-timer was a stranger. Tom knew he'd never seen him before. The man wore a cowboy shirt with pearl snaps instead of buttons on it, and at the sight of it a pang of grief and loss went through Tom. That was the same sort of shirt his dad had always worn.

"Tom Brannon, ain't it?" the man greeted him. "Sit down. Get you somethin' to drink or some ice cream, maybe?" The man twirled a long red plastic spoon in a cup full of some thick ice cream concoction in front of him. "Goddamn, I love these Blizzards! I been thinkin' I ought to buy Dairy Queen, just so I could have 'em all the time."

"No, thanks," Tom said as he slid into the booth.

The man extended a knobby hand across the table. He said, "My name's Hiram Stackhouse."

It took Tom a couple of seconds to recognize the name as he shook hands with the old man. When it dawned on him, he couldn't stop himself from saying, "You own SavMart."

Hiram Stackhouse nodded. "Damn right I do. Ever' single one of 'em, includin' the one right here in Little Tucson. And I don't take kindly to havin' a bunch o' thugs come in and shoot up one o' my stores and slaughter a bunch o' my employees and customers. It's bad for business."

Stackhouse paused and took a bite of his ice cream, licking his lips as he savored the taste.

"What is it you want from me?" Tom asked.

"Don't want nothin' from you. I'm here to help you, son, give you anything you need to help you fight them M-15 bastards. Money, weapons . . . hell, you want it, I can provide your own private army of ex-Special Forces commandos."

Tom leaned back against the hard plastic seat. "You've got your own army?"

Stackhouse chuckled and said, "Well, it might be better to call 'em a security force. The gov'ment tends to get a mite antsy when a private citizen talks about havin' his own army. Not that I'm all that worried about the gov'ment. Fact is, another reason I'm here is to call off the dogs. I can get the FBI and the Border Patrol off your back. Hell, if I kick up enough of a fuss, I can prob'ly get the pain-in-the-ass ACLU to leave you alone."

"You can do that?" Tom said in disbelief. "You can call off the FBI and the Border Patrol?"

Stackhouse said, "Son, you have any idea how much money goes through SavMart in a year? You know how much hell it'd raise with the economy if folks got up in the mornin' and every single Sav-Mart store was shut down, even for a day? I could do that, you know. I'm the boss. I don't answer to no corporation or nothin'. I say shut 'em down, and they stay shut down until I say open 'em again. And if I wanted to, I could just leave 'em closed from now on, with all the merchandise still inside 'em. I got so damn much money already I couldn't spend it all if I lived to be five hunnerd years old!" He laughed again and went on, "So you damn well better believe folks in Washington sit up and take notice when I call and say I want somethin'."

Tom could believe it. And he had the feeling that this old man might be crazy enough to follow through on any such threat. He remembered reading about Hiram Stackhouse. He was either the richest or second-richest man in the country every time the financial magazines published such a list. And while he wasn't quite as eccentric and reclusive as Howard Hughes had been, he was right up there.

The hope that just about disappeared from Tom after what had happened to Buddy suddenly reignited. One man couldn't do much against *Mara Salvatrucha* . . . but one man with the backing of a billionaire who controlled an economy larger than that of many countries . . . well, anything might be possible there.

"You know," Stackhouse said when Tom hesitated, "killin' your ma and pa like that, ain't very Christian. If it was me, I'd open a can o' whoopass on them greasers."

Tom nodded slowly and said, "Yeah, I reckon it's time we did exactly that."

22

Ernesto Luis Montoya was followed by Cipriano and Leobardo Asturias when he stalked into the luxurious office on the fortieth floor of the Mexico City high-rise. Montoya carried a folded American newspaper in his hand and slapped it lightly against his thigh as he approached the desk where Sami Al-Khan sat. The Saudi wore an annoyed expression on his round, normally bland face. He had not summoned Montoya to Mexico City or called this meeting. It was Montoya's idea, and Al-Khan didn't like being told what to do. He was cooperating, though, because he did not wish to offend an associate of Señor Garcia-Lopez.

"Señor Montoya," Al-Khan said curtly. "What can I do for you?" Then, in an attempt to smooth over the situation somewhat, he added, "How was your flight from Nogales?"

Montoya ignored the second question and slapped the newspaper on Al-Khan's desk so that the headline faced up. It read PATRIOT PROJECT RALLY IN LITTLE TUCSON. In smaller type, a subhead read

VOLUNTEERS FROM ALL OVER COUNTRY TO CONVERGE ON ARIZONA TOWN.

Al-Khan glanced down at the newspaper, which came from Phoenix. "I saw it," he said with a shrug of his narrow shoulders. "Why should it concern you, Señor Montoya? You know nothing will come of it. In the end, the Americans will not be able to stop us. They have too great an appetite for drugs and cheap labor. Their own weakness will destroy them."

Montoya picked up the paper again and read from it. "Patriot Project organizer Tom Brannon said that with the new volunteers, the patrols will be able to stem the tide of illegal immigration across the border, especially by members of the notorious M-15 gang. Brannon said, 'No bunch of cheap thugs is going to invade this country and get away with it. We will stop the so-called *Mara Salvatrucha* from ever bothering honest people again.'" In a sudden burst of rage he ripped the paper in two. "Cheap thugs! He called us cheap thugs! Such disrespect cannot go unpunished!"

Al-Khan spread his hands. "It is annoying, yes. It sends a bad message to our men for such things to be said. But what can you do? You already killed this man's parents. Perhaps you should kill his wife next. Or perhaps his children, if you know where to find them."

Montoya threw the pieces of newspaper on the floor and said, "I intend to kill Brannon."

"Yes, yes, of course," Al-Khan said with a nod. "I suppose the time has come to do that. Once he is dead, this Patriot Project of his will fall apart."

"No," Montoya said. "If there is one thing my people know, it is the power of a martyr. If we simply kill Brannon, people will rally around his memory. They will still plague us like gnats."

Al-Khan was getting impatient now. "What else can you do?"

"Kill them all. Burn Little Tucson to the ground. Wipe it from the face of the earth so that no one will ever dare to disrespect or defy *Mara Salvatrucha* again."

Al-Khan stared at Montoya in obvious disbelief for a long, silent moment. Then he said, "You are insane! You cannot attack an entire American town like that!"

"I have three hundred men, all of whom will follow my every command. Little Tucson has only an acting sheriff and a handful of deputies—"

"And the Patriot Project!"

Montoya waved a hand. "A few dozen gringos, most of them ignorant rednecks. If we attack tomorrow, on the day of this rally, we can wipe them out, too."

"But there will be more volunteers there—"

"Tourists and news media," Montoya said with a sneer. "Not fighting men. They will stand no chance against us, especially with me leading our men personally."

Al-Khan stared down at his desk with his fingers pressed to his temples. "This is mad, utterly mad," he muttered. "We cannot do this. To attack so openly . . . An organization such as ours is best served by stealth. We operate in the shadows."

"No," Montoya declared flatly, "an organization such as ours is best served by fear. The fear our enemies feel when we drive them before us. The fear they feel when they hear the cries of their women.

And the fear their deaths will inspire in others who might someday dare to cross us."

Al-Khan shook his head. "It's too risky. It will draw too much attention. The American government turns a blind eye to us because it is easier to do so, and because they worry about offending the world community that doesn't give a damn about them to start with. But such an attack will bring them together, galvanize them . . ." He looked up in horror at Montoya. "In the name of Allah, we don't want to wake them up again, now that they've finally gone back to sleep! I forbid it! Do you hear me, Montoya? I forbid it!"

"I hear you," Montoya said. He made the slightest of motions to Cipriano and Leobardo, then went on to Al-Khan, "If it worries you so much, amigo, you must put it out of your mind."

The brothers did not appear to move hastily, but suddenly they were around the desk. Al-Khan let out a startled yelp as Cipriano pulled him up out of his chair. Then Cipriano's hand closed around his throat, cutting off any further outcry. Leobardo picked up the heavy chair in which Al-Khan had been sitting, and handling it as if it weighed very little, he slammed it against the wall of glass behind the desk. The glass was thick and sturdy and required several blows before it shattered. Pieces of broken glass plummeted forty stories to the street below. Car horns began to honk as the deadly missiles rained down. Cipriano forced Al-Khan toward the broken window. The Saudi struggled desperately, but he was no match for a man with the speed and strength of a jaguar.

Montoya walked leisurely around the desk and

reached the broken window just as Cipriano and Al-Khan did. He reached out and placed his hand on Al-Khan's chest, feeling the expensive fabric of the Saudi's jacket against his palm.

"Put it out of your mind," he said again as he pushed. At the same time, Cipriano let go of Al-Khan, and the man went backwards out the broken window, shrieking in terror. He kept screaming as he fell toward the ground so far below.

Forty stories up, the three men still in the office were too high to hear the impact when Al-Khan landed. But they heard the car horns begin to honk even more frantically, and Montoya smiled. He led the way out of the now-empty office, taking out his cell phone as he did so. He punched in the number of CNN's Mexico City bureau, which he had looked up earlier.

He had a news tip about what was *really* going to happen in Little Tucson tomorrow.

"—breaking news. A man identifying himself only as the leader of *Mara Salvatrucha*, the notorious gang also known as M-15, has contacted CNN and claimed that he and his men will be in Little Tucson tomorrow when the rally for the so-called Patriot Project takes place. We've just spoken with Tom Brannon, the organizer of the Patriot Project and the rally, and he insists that everything will go on as planned."

A videotaped image of Tom appeared on the TV screen. "We're not going to let ourselves be scared off by some punks," he said. "Besides, I don't think they'll really show up. They're just bragging."

Back to the news anchor, a woman with sleek blond hair. "According to Lauren Henderson, the acting sheriff of Sierrita County, there will be extra officers on duty tomorrow to provide security for the rally. Henderson said that law and order will prevail in Sierrita County.

"Meanwhile, as news of this development spread through the town of Little Tucson, many of the residents began to pack up and leave."

A shot of the highway to Tucson, clogged with slow-moving cars and pickups and SUVs.

"This looks like something we see when a hurricane approaches the coastline, something which these desert dwellers have never experienced. The exodus shows that while Brannon and Sheriff Henderson maintain a show of confidence, most of the citizens of Little Tucson fear the threat of M-15 and are getting out while they can. Meanwhile, many of the would-be volunteers for the Patriot Project who planned to arrive in the little town for the rally tomorrow have changed their plans and will be staying home instead, far away from the scene of potential violence.

"In Washington tonight, at the White House, the President downplayed the threat, stating that she had assurances from the Mexican government that there would be no attack on Little Tucson. Therefore, no National Guardsmen or other federal troops will be deployed to the area. 'We must learn to settle our differences through talking,' the President said. 'It is my hope this controversy will open up a healthy dialogue between people on both sides of the border.'

"A spokesperson for the American Civil Liberties

Union stated that while it was unlikely there would be any trouble in Little Tucson tomorrow, ACLU attorneys will be on hand to monitor the situation and ensure that due process is followed at all times and that no one's civil rights are violated by vigilantes."

As Tom chuckled, Bonnie said, "I thought all the lawyers had left."

"They have, as far as I know. They took off for the tall and uncut as soon as they heard that M-15 might show up tomorrow in full force. They're all afraid there may be shooting."

"There will be, won't there?"

Tom nodded slowly. "I'd say you can count on it."

"I'm not leaving. I'd be lying if I didn't admit that part of me wants to . . . but I'm not going."

"I'm not surprised. Part of me wishes it had never come to this, too. But a showdown is the only way. We could never root them out below the border, so we had to make them come to us."

"They'll be here, all right. After the things you said, they can't not come."

"Tomorrow," Tom said. "At high noon."

At first glance, Little Tucson looked like a ghost town. Nobody was moving on the street. All the businesses were closed. The windows in some of them had been boarded up, increasing the resemblance to a community waiting for a hurricane to hit.

That was a pretty apt comparison, Tom thought as he stood on the sidewalk in front of the auto parts store. A hurricane of evil and violence called *Mara Salvatrucha* was probably bearing down on Little Tucson at this very moment.

He glanced up at the sun, which was almost directly overhead. It wouldn't be much longer now. If M-15 was coming, they would be here soon.

A sheriff's cruiser turned the corner and came to a stop in front of the store. Lauren Henderson got out and came around the front of the car to step up onto the sidewalk, in uniform now, her service revolver on her hip and a pump shotgun in her hands.

"Buddy and Fred Kelso and all the other patients from the hospital are on their way to Tucson in Careflight helicopters," she told Tom. "Buddy's hanging in there."

He nodded. "I'm glad to hear it. That's one thing less we have to worry about. What about the rest of the citizens?"

"There's not more than thirty people left in town," she said, "and that counts me and my deputies. The others who stayed behind are all well-armed and ready. They'll converge on Main Street at the first sign of trouble." She shook her head. "It's hard to believe that an American town is about to come under attack by an outside force, and the government is standing by and doing nothing."

"They can't afford to do anything. It would make them look bad."

"How are they going to look after what happens here today?"

"Lord knows," Tom said softly. "I suppose that all depends on what we do. But I can tell you one thing . . . if we all get wiped out, the folks in Washington will wring their hands and cry crocodile tears, and in the end they won't do a damned thing except maybe send a strongly worded note to the

Mexican government. Putting on a show is all this administration knows how to do."

"What a damned shame it's come to that."

"Yeah," Tom agreed. "A damned shame."

They both took deep breaths and squared their shoulders, as everybody in America except the politicians did in times of trouble. "You're going to make your stand here?" Lauren asked.

He nodded. "Bonnie and Louly are inside the store. I tried to talk Louly into leaving town with the others, but it was a waste of time."

"Yes, I imagine it would be," Lauren said.

That brought a slight frown to Tom's face. He hadn't realized that Lauren even knew Louly. But he didn't have time to think about that now.

For one thing, he heard footsteps on the sidewalk and turned to see the last two people he thought he would see in Little Tucson this morning. Callista Spinelli strode toward him angrily, followed by the sweating Chet Eggleston. Tom had thought that all the ACLU lawyers were gone. Obviously, he'd been wrong.

"You're really going through with this?" Spinelli demanded angrily as she and Eggleston came up to Tom and Lauren.

"Going through with what?" Tom asked.

Spinelli gestured toward the red, white, and blue banner strung across Main Street from the auto parts store to the building across the street. The banner read in big letters WELCOME PATRIOT PROJECT.

"This stupid rally, that's what," Spinelli snapped. "I checked. You don't have a permit for it, and even though you're the mayor, you need a permit for a public assembly."

Tom just looked at the lawyer for a moment, then glanced over at Lauren. Both of them burst out laughing. The very idea of Spinelli getting in a snit over a permit was ludicrous. The fact that they were laughing at her just made Spinelli more furious.

"All right, tell you what," Tom said. "The rally's cancelled, how about that? Matter of fact, there was never going to be a rally. Now, why don't you and Mr. Eggleston get in your rental car and get out of Little Tucson while you still can?"

"Absolutely not," Spinelli said. "I've heard all the talk about how M-15 is going to attack the town, and I don't believe it. I'm still not sure this so-called M-15 really exists. I think it's just a boogeyman you and your friends invented to use as an excuse for oppressing poor immigrants who don't want anything except a chance at their rightful share of the wealth this country had hoarded illegally."

Lauren just stared at her for a moment before saying, "My God, are you really that stupid?"

"Careful, Sheriff. I'll slap you with an injunction so fast—"

Lauren took a step toward her. "How about if I just slap *you*?"

"Ladies, ladies," Tom said, moving to get between them.

"Don't patronize me like that!" Spinelli whirled on him. "You white, patriarchal oppressor! It's you and your kind who are to blame for everything that's wrong with this country!"

Eggleston mopped sweat off his forehead with a handkerchief and said quietly, "Callie."

She ignored him and continued her tirade directed at Tom. "Ever since your kind set foot in

America and started stealing from it and killing its rightful owners, you've tried to grind everyone who's different than you under your heel—"

"Callie," Eggleston said more forcefully.

"You make me ashamed to be an American—"

"Callie!"

She turned to him and yelled, "What?"

"Will you *shut the fuck up*!"

Spinelli stared at him in shock. Her mouth opened and closed several times before she was finally able to say, "What did you say to me?"

"I said shut up," Eggleston snapped. "All you know how to do is run your mouth and blame America for everything that's wrong in the world. That's crazy."

"But, Chet," she said, aghast, "you know that America *is* to blame for everything that's wrong in the world! You work for the ACLU! You have to know that!"

"I signed on with the ACLU thinking that I would actually be defending people's civil rights. Instead all I've been doing for years is forcing things they don't want down their throats. And I'm sick of it. I'm sick of listening to all the politically correct crap that's been coming out of my mouth—and yours."

"How dare you!"

"To tell you the truth, Callie, I don't really know how I dare anything anymore, since I handed over my balls to you years ago." Eggleston turned to look at Tom. "You see, she's not just my law partner . . . she's my wife. Not that she would ever use my name or even let me tell anybody that we're married. That would be too patriarchal."

Lauren said, "This domestic drama is fascinating, but you folks better get out of—"

Tom lifted a hand and said, "It's too late. Listen."

They all stood silently on the sidewalk, even Spinelli, and they heard the rumble of engines growing louder and louder. A lot of vehicles were approaching Little Tucson, and that could mean only one thing.

"Here they come," Tom said.

Down the street, the digital clock on the sign in front of the bank changed from 11:59 to 12:00. It was noon.

High noon in Little Tucson.

23

There were at least fifty cars and pickups in the convoy speeding toward Little Tucson from the southeast. Tom was on the roof of the auto parts store, watching the approach of M-15 through binoculars. He had two pistols stuck behind his belt and two more tucked in the small of his back. A lever-action Winchester leaned against the short wall around the roof. In the store below him, Bonnie, Lauren, and Louly waited behind the heavy counter, all of them armed and ready. Callie Spinelli was there, too, huddled on the floor crying in fear. At least she had been when Tom left to climb up to the roof.

He heard something behind him and turned around to see Chet Eggleston clambering onto the roof from the ladder that was propped against the building in the rear alley. The lawyer had taken off his suit jacket and tie and rolled up the sleeves of his white shirt.

"Better get back down there," Tom told him.

"They'll be here in just a few minutes. Stay as low as you can and you ought to be all right."

"The hell with that," Eggleston said. "If you've got an extra gun, I want in on this."

Tom frowned. "You can use a gun?"

"Don't tell Callie this, but I used to go hunting with my dad when I was a kid. I wouldn't do it now, you understand—I really do believe it's wrong—but I can use a gun."

Tom picked up the Winchester and handed it to him. "Here you go, then."

Chet looked down at the weapon almost as if he were surprised to find himself holding it, but then he smiled and nodded. "Thanks, Mr. Brannon."

"You love her?"

Chet looked up. "Yeah. Yeah, I really do. That's what made me realize some things are worth fighting for."

Tom clapped a hand on his shoulder. "Keep showing her that. She'll come around."

Then there was no more time for talk, because *Mara Salvatrucha* was here. The cars came around the curve just east of town and started along Main Street. They slowed, though, allowing a big black limousine to surge out in front. The limo stopped under the red, white, and blue banner. The driver got out, as did the man in the front passenger seat. Both of them were big and strong looking, with enough of a resemblance to almost be twins. They carried assault rifles. The rest of the cars had stopped about fifty yards up the street, in a double line that stretched for several blocks.

Tom had given everyone in town strict orders. They were not going to fire the first shot. If there was to be a battle here today, M-15 would have to start it.

Tom and Chet knelt behind the short wall. The tar on the roof was hot and sticky. They watched as one of the men opened the rear door of the limo and a man in an expensive white suit climbed out. The suit was dazzling in the noonday sun. He wore dark glasses and had a machete in his hand. Most of the members of M-15 came from Guatemala and El Salvador, Tom recalled. It made sense that their leader would, too, and a machete was a common tool in those jungles down there.

The man lifted the machete and shouted, "Little Tucson! Hear me! My name is Ernesto Luis Montoya! They call me the Eater of Babies! You have defied me, and now I bring you death!" Montoya turned to his two lieutenants. "Destroy the town and everyone in it!"

They opened fire, the assault rifles in their hands spewing lead and flame at the storefronts along Main Street. At the same time, the other cars in the convoy surged forward, and the men inside them began shooting as well. Rifles, shotguns, and pistols blared from the vehicles. Meanwhile, Montoya calmly climbed back into the limousine and shut the door after himself. Tom supposed the vehicle was heavily armored and virtually bulletproof, so he didn't waste time shooting at it.

Instead he stood up as the two men on the street below stopped firing to change clips in their rifles. He shouted, "Hey!" and drew both pistols from behind his belt. Their heads jerked up to look at him.

He fired both guns at the nearest of the two men. The slugs smashed into the man's chest and drove him back against the limo, bending him over the hood of the big car. He flopped forward lifelessly. Tom shifted his aim and snapped shots at the second man, but that one had reacted with incredible swiftness, diving behind the cover of the limousine even as Tom fired.

Tom dropped to his knees as beside him Chet Eggleston poked the barrel of the Winchester over the wall and started firing at the cars that were now inching along Main Street, moving slowly so that the gunners inside would have plenty of time to shoot at the buildings they passed. Chet drew a bead on the windshield of one of the leading cars and pumped three slugs through it as fast as he could work the Winchester's lever. The windshield shattered and the car came to a jolting halt as its horn blared. The driver had been hit and slumped forward onto the wheel.

That brought part of the convoy to a halt and allowed the townspeople positioned in other buildings along the street to start fighting back more effectively. Gunsmoke drifted from broken windows and open doors as the defenders poured lead into the cars. Unwilling to stay pinned down, the members of M-15 leaped from the vehicles and began spreading out, spraying bullets ahead of them. Now it would become a classic building-to-building, even hand-to-hand fight.

Tom backed away from the front of the store and grabbed Chet's collar, dragging the lawyer with him. "Come on!" Tom said. "Let's get down off of here while we still can!"

His feet seemed to barely touch the ladder as he climbed down to the alley. Chet was right behind him.

Out in front of the store, several gang members leaped onto the sidewalk and charged through the door. Bonnie, Lauren, and Louly were waiting, all three women with shotguns poked over the top of the counter. The explosions as all three scatterguns fired at once were deafening. The buckshot slammed into the men and pitched them backward through the blown-out windows. Crimson droplets of blood rained down on the sidewalk.

Tom and Chet trotted down the alley to the corner of the building and peered around it cautiously. A couple of M-15 members pounded toward them, trying to get behind the store. Tom nodded at Chet and then stepped out, bringing up his pistols. Chet moved out behind him, the Winchester ready. The gang members saw them, skidded to a halt, and tried to bring their weapons up. One of them actually got a shot off before Tom's slugs bored into his chest and dropped him. Tom heard the wind-rip of the bullet past his ear as it missed him. The other gang member doubled over in response to the whip-crack of the rifle in Chet's hands as the Winchester's bullet ripped into his belly. Tom and Chet advanced up the alley toward Main Street, stepping over the bodies along the way.

All the cars were stopped now as smoke and steam poured from under the hoods of the ones in the lead. Cannily, the defenders had concentrated their fire on those vehicles, forcing the gang to abandon their cars or stay pinned down in them.

Shots snapped and barked all up and down Main Street as the fighting spread. Tom knew that he and the others were heavily outnumbered, possibly by as much as ten to one. Although they were dealing out some damage, in the long run they would have no chance of surviving. M-15 could afford to take heavy losses. Eventually, Tom and his friends would be hunted down and killed, one by one.

Not yet, though. He stepped onto the sidewalk, holding his arms out to the side and firing both guns at the same time, in opposite directions. Two more members of M-15 went spinning off their feet. Luck was guiding his shots; he probably couldn't have made another pair of shots like that in a hundred years of trying.

A gun blasted from the rear of the limousine. Tom felt a giant hand swat him in the side and spin him half around. Before he could get his balance, the second of Montoya's two lieutenants charged out from behind the limo and came at Tom, the assault rifle in his hands blazing. Bullets thudded into the wall next to him.

Chet Eggleston surged forward, shouting and firing the Winchester. The man turned the assault rifle to meet this new threat and Chet went over backward, blood flying in the air. But the distraction he had provided gave Tom enough time to set himself, and he emptied both pistols into the man with the assault rifle, driving him back against the limo's rear fender. The man dropped the rifle and hung there for a moment, a shocked look on his face as if he couldn't comprehend the damage the bullets had done to him, and then he crumpled, falling forward so that he landed with his face pressed to the street.

Montoya opened the rear door of the limo as Tom slowly lowered his empty guns. Brandishing the machete in his hand, Montoya shouted, "Brannon! I know you! I'll cut you in little pieces!" He started toward the sidewalk.

Tom grinned despite the pain of the wound in his side, dropped the empties, and reached behind him to pluck the other two guns from his belt. As he brought them into sight, Montoya's eyes widened and he reversed course abruptly, diving back into the armored limousine that served as his fortress and command post.

Tom didn't waste bullets on the car, knowing the .45 slugs wouldn't penetrate the armor. It would take something like a grenade or a rocket to pierce the vehicle's heavy plating. Instead he turned to Chet and saw that the lawyer had pulled himself into a sitting position with his back propped against the front wall of the building. His shirt was bloody, but he was conscious and had the Winchester in his hands again. "Bring 'em on!" he said with a pained but fierce grin.

Tom was glad to see that Chet was still alive. He said, "You're about to get your wish. Here they come."

About a dozen of Little Tucson's defenders were making their way toward the auto parts store, fighting a running battle as they came. Tom saw Walt Deavers and Pete Benitez and Ray Torres and Wayne Rushing. Francisco Montero limped along, firing the pistol in his hand back at the onrushing hordes of gang members. Ed Crabtree and Ben Hanratty were using rifles. Were those few and the handful of others all that was left? If that was the case, then they had lost ten or twelve men. Fewer than twenty people remained to defend Little Tucson against M-15.

Tom and Chet opened fire on the gang as Bonnie, Louly, and Lauren burst out of the store and added their efforts to the covering fire. The fleeing defenders leaped onto the sidewalk. Tom yelled, "Give me a hand!" to Pete, and the newspaperman paused to help him lift Chet to his feet. Supporting the wounded lawyer, they started toward the door, firing with their other hands as they went.

Moments later, everyone was inside, hunkered around the windows. The shooting died away outside. The defenders holed up inside the store were about to make their last stand, and everyone knew it.

Montoya opened the limo door but didn't come out from behind it where anybody could get a shot at him. "Brannon!" he shouted. "Brannon, you hear me?"

"I hear you," Tom called back, wishing Montoya would step out just a little more.

"Was it worth it, Brannon?"

The haunting question hung in the air.

"Was it worth all the dying? Will it be worth the destruction of this entire town? I'm going to burn it to the ground, you know. None of you are going to get out of here alive. Is your precious gringo freedom worth it?"

Callie Spinelli crawled out from behind the counter, tears streaking her face. Her eyes widened when she saw Chet half sitting, half lying on the floor near the windows. She started toward him. When he saw her coming, he motioned her back and growled, "Callie, no!"

She kept coming, and when she reached him she clutched at him and moaned, "Chet, oh, Chet, you're hurt!"

"I'm okay," he tried to tell her. "I'll be okay . . ."

But none of them would be okay unless something happened soon. All Montoya had to do was give the order, and they would be overrun and wiped out. On the street, Montoya laughed and said, "You stupid gringos. You've always been your own worst enemies! You make yourselves weak, like sheep for the shearing!"

"Oh, Chet . . ." Callie said as more tears rolled down her face.

Then she reached over, picked up the Winchester her wounded husband had put down, and surged up before anyone could stop her.

"Shut your goddamn pie hole, you son of a bitch!" she screamed as she staggered into the open door of the store and clumsily fired twice, both bullets smacking into the bulletproof glass of the open limo door. Lauren tackled her and drove her down out of the line of fire as Montoya's men opened up again, sending a storm of lead against the front of the building.

"Hold your fire! Hold your fire!" Montoya shouted until the shooting stopped again. He laughed harshly and went on, "You hide behind women, Brannon! If it all means so much to you, step out and face me where I can see you!"

Bonnie clutched at Tom's arm. "Tom, no!" she said. "You can't! They'll kill you!"

"Not just yet," Tom said. "Montoya wants to gloat a little first."

"Tom—!"

He stood up, both hands filled with his guns, and stepped into the doorway. "Here I am, Montoya."

"No shooting!" Montoya bellowed to his men.

"No shooting!" He came out from behind the limo door. With a cocky grin on his face, he said, "It is time you and I met face to face, Brannon. You thought to humiliate me, but in the end it is I who have destroyed you."

"Not yet," Tom said. "Little Tucson is still ours. You haven't taken it away from us."

"Oh, but I will, in a matter of—"

"Listen," Tom said. He had heard what he'd been waiting for, a low rumble like the sound of distant drums.

Montoya heard it, too. He looked around in confusion. The sound seemed to be coming from two directions at once. He looked along the street to the east.

Out of the midday heat haze, behemoths loomed, lumbering forward like great beasts out of some dim prehistory. Montoya's head snapped around so that he could look west along the street. The same awesome spectacle met his eyes. As the massive vehicles came closer, the blur of rising heat waves went away, and Montoya saw them for what they were— huge tractor-trailer trucks, eighteen-wheelers, at least fifty of them closing in from each direction, and on the side of each, painted in bright green letters, was the word SAVMART. The only difference in the two convoys was that the one approaching from the east was led by an old man in a bright red 1960 Ford pickup. Inside the cab of the pickup, Hiram Stackhouse laughed out loud, having the time of his life. He pressed the horn ring on the steering wheel, but instead of the normal blare, the horn played "The William Tell Overture"—better known as the theme from "The Lone Ranger".

Like the two halves of the Red Sea after God had parted it, Hiram Stackhouse and his SavMart army came crashing down on *Mara Salvatrucha*.

The gang members panicked and tried to escape, but there was no place to run. Main Street was blocked in both directions, and some of the trucks had split off to circle around and block the side streets as well. They pushed together the cars that had carried the gang into town and crumpled them like tissue paper. Some of the gang members were caught between vehicles and screamed as tons of metal crushed them to jelly. As soon as the trucks came to a stop, the rear doors on several of them rolled up and members of Stackhouse's security force leaped out, wearing body armor and carrying automatic weapons. Their guns spurted fire as they mowed down Montoya's men. The members of M-15 tried to fight back, but for a change, *they* were outgunned. Hiram Stackhouse himself was in the middle of the fighting, unwilling to ask his people to do anything that he wouldn't do. The old Colt revolver in his hand bucked and roared as he traded shots with the enemy.

In front of the hardware store, Tom went after Montoya.

He dropped his guns and lunged at Montoya, ducking under the swipe of the machete in the man's hand. He could have gunned down the M-15 leader, but he wanted to do this with his bare hands. He owed it to his folks, who had died a horrible death at Montoya's orders. He owed it to everyone who had died because of this man's greed and arrogance. He got his left hand on Montoya's wrist and his right hand on Montoya's throat. Banging Montoya's hand against the edge of the limo door, Tom forced him to drop the machete.

Montoya's knee came up toward Tom's groin. Tom twisted aside and took the blow on his thigh, but it was still enough to stagger him. Montoya got his right hand free and slammed a punch across Tom's face. Tom was driven down to one knee, but he kept his grip on Montoya's throat and pulled the man with him. Montoya bulled into him, driving him over backward. Both men sprawled on the hot street, rolling over. They broke apart from each other and came up trading punches. Tom's side was numb now where the bullet had creased him earlier, and his shirt was wet with blood. He could feel himself losing strength. Montoya couldn't win now, couldn't even escape. Hiram Stackhouse had seen to that. But Montoya's sunglasses had come off, and Tom could see the insane hatred in his eyes. All that mattered to Montoya now was killing this gringo who had dared to defy him. When Tom slipped and went down on one knee again, Montoya slammed a vicious kick into his wounded side. Tom cried out in pain as he rolled across the pavement. The world swam crazily in front of his eyes. He came to a stop and pushed himself up on hands and knees and looked back over his shoulder. Montoya had snatched up the machete from where it had fallen in the street and was coming at him, the long heavy blade lifted high, poised to come down in a killing stroke.

"Tom!" Bonnie cried.

He looked toward her, saw something spinning across the pavement toward him, something she had just thrown in his direction. His eyes locked on it, saw the black grip with the twin lightning bolts, saw the blade flickering in the sun as it turned around and around. His father's knife, the one Herb Brannon had taken off the dead German officer in Berlin, the officer Herb had killed to save his own life and perhaps the lives of countless others, because there was no way of knowing how many lives one man's existence touched in his time on this earth . . .

Montoya screamed incoherently as he loomed over Tom and the machete started to come down.

Tom reached out, felt the knife's grip slap into his palm, twisted and came up and drove the blade right into Ernesto Luis Montoya's belly. Montoya froze, the machete stopping in midstroke. Tom stood up, pushed the knife deeper with the last of his strength. He sagged back to the street as Montoya took an unsteady step backward, still clutching the machete. He looked down at his midsection in shock and horror as crimson began to spread on his white suit.

Then blood began to bloom like flowers all over the suit as the defenders of Little Tucson who were now gathered on the sidewalk in front of the auto parts store opened fire. The shots all blended into one thunderous roar as Bonnie, Lauren, Louly, Walt, Pete, Wayne, Ed, Francisco, Chet, and all the others, even Callie, filled Montoya with so much lead that the thing that finally crashed to the pavement next to the limo didn't even look human anymore.

El Babania Comida would eat no more babies.

Bonnie was at Tom's side. She helped him up. Most of the others were wounded, too. They stood with their arms around each other, offering support and comfort. They waited there as the firing around town died away and Stackhouse's security force began the mopping up operation. The old man himself came striding along the sidewalk, a proud grin on his face. He lifted a hand in greeting and said to Tom, "Yep, a can o' whoopass, just like I told you. Works ever' time."

As he looked around at the battleground Little Tucson had become, Tom couldn't argue with that. But he could have added one thing, if he'd had the energy.

A can of whoopass . . . in the hands of an American fighting for freedom. That *would do it. Every time.*

Epilogue

In the aftermath of what became known as the Battle of Little Tucson, well over a thousand lawsuits were filed. The ACLU lost every one in which it was involved.

The President immediately declared the town, indeed all of Sierrita County, to be a disaster area and promised that plenty of federal aid would be forthcoming. Many of the residents refused the offer, explaining to reporters that they wouldn't feel right accepting aid now from the government that had turned its back on them earlier. When told about this, the President pursed her lips and glared for a second before managing to put a phony smile of concern back on her face.

The FBI launched an investigation of the whole affair. So did the Border Patrol. So did Congress. Reports were expected eventually . . . although probably not until after the next election, at the earliest.

The story led every newscast in the nation for a week. Then something happened somewhere else, and it was bumped back to the second segment, then the third, and then the news anchors didn't talk about it anymore. It was old news, which meant it wasn't news at all.

The people of Little Tucson who had left came home. Broken windows downtown were replaced, and bullet holes were plastered over and painted. The dead were buried, the wounded were nursed back to health. Sometimes in the night, people cried out as nightmares haunted their slumber. The lucky ones had someone there to reach out and hold them as they drifted back into a more peaceful sleep.

One day, Tom Brannon saw Carla May Willard on the street and smiled as she waved at him. He didn't blame her for leaving. He was just glad she was back. Little Tucson was her home, after all.

Fred Kelso had the snazziest wheelchair in town, and when Dusty Rhodes retired, Fred took over one of the dispatcher jobs for the sheriff's department. He was good at it, too.

Lauren Henderson retained the post of acting sheriff, but as soon as election time rolled around again, she was going to run for the office. There wasn't much doubt that she would win, too.

Buddy Gorman was in a rehab center in Phoenix. Tom went to see him at least once a month, even though Buddy was blind and only remembered who Tom was part of the time. It helped Jean, though, and anyway, Tom just felt like it was something he needed to do.

Business was better at the auto parts store for a while. Tom was the hero of Little Tucson, after all. But SavMart still sold motor oil and air filters for less, and after a while things settled back into the same old pattern.

Little Tucson went back to sleep, you might say. The Patriot Project was disbanded. There were still illegal immigrants, of course, but the problem wasn't as bad as it had once been. The Border Patrol could handle it for the time being. Folks had their own lives to live again, work to do, steaks to grill, TV to watch, kids to play with. But no one ever forgot completely.

No one ever would.

The villa overlooking the Pacific was the most luxurious in all of Acapulco, a city of luxury. Señor Hector Garcia-Lopez sat beside his pool under an umbrella and looked at the man his majordomo had just brought out to see him. The man was tall, with a face like a hawk and skin the color of old saddle leather. He wore robes and a head cloth, and the heat of the Mexican afternoon seemed not to bother him at all. Like Señor Garcia-Lopez, the visitor's dark beard was shot through with gray. They were like two old wolves, Garcia-Lopez thought, even though they came from opposite sides of the world.

"I was very disturbed to hear of my nephew's death," the visitor said. "The man responsible for it . . . ?"

"Is dead," Garcia-Lopez said. "You have my sincere apologies. Montoya was a useful tool at one time. I had no idea how truly mad he had become."

"I do not blame you, señor. And I do not absolve the Americans of their guilt in this matter, either. But I can wait to take my vengeance until the proper time. Like all my countrymen, I am very skilled in waiting . . . and hating." The visitor smiled thinly. "But for now, we have a business to rebuild, is it not so?"

"Yes, of course," Garcia-Lopez said, but as he looked across the table at the hawk-faced man, he almost felt sorry for the gringos because of the fate that awaited them sooner or later, especially the citizens of Little Tucson. They probably thought it was all over . . .

When the proper time came, they would learn. It was never over.

Lt Colonel Art Jensen is the commanding officer of the 3rd INF BN 32nd INF RGT, 7th Infantry Division. He is ex-Special Forces and Airborne. He is also the direct descendant of mountain man Smoke Jensen himself.

Art Jensen is named chief of the DOD's Special Function Unit—Black Ops, a unit whose mission is so secret that only the President, the secretary of defense, and the secretary of homeland security know of its existence.

His mission is this: to track down and eliminate with extreme prejudice Middle Eastern terrorists operating in the USA—the reputed "fifth column" that threatens America on a daily basis. To this end, Art must infiltrate mosques and get inside the terrorists' lairs, because they're planning an attack somewhere in America that will dwarf 9/11.

Turn the page for an exciting preview of
BLACK OPS: *American Jihad,*
the first in an explosive new series from
William W. Johnstone and Fred Austin

Coming in May 2006 wherever
Pinnacle Books are sold

1

Somewhere in Iraq

The three prisoners, two men and a woman, were brought into the room. They blinked at the bank of bright lights, but they couldn't rub their eyes because their hands were handcuffed. Next to the bank of lights was a video camera, mounted on a tripod.

There were six others in the room, but all six were wearing hoods so they could not be identified by anyone who might view the videotape later. One of the hooded men stepped in front of the video camera and began reading.

"Some time has passed since the blessed attacks against the global infidelity, against America, where our glorious martyrs sent more than 3000 infidels to a fiery hell. Since that time, Americans have conducted a vicious crusade against Islam.

"It is now evident that the West in general, and America in particular, is doing Satan's work on earth, trying with bombs and the deaths of millions of innocents, to destroy the Muslim faith.

"But we are not without our own weapons, and we stand here before these cameras, with three pawns of the great Satan America."

The camera panned slowly across the faces of three terrified prisoners.

"One is Italian, one is Jordanian, and the woman is Iraqi. All are collaborating with the enemy in their fight against our people and our faith. It is for that reason that they have been condemned to die."

The hooded terrorist folded the paper and nodded toward the woman. Another hooded terrorist stepped up behind the woman and, quickly, drew his knife across her throat.

The woman cried out, though her cry was quickly silenced. The terrorist grabbed her by the hair as he continued to saw away at her neck. Two other terrorists held her up until, finally, the head was completely severed.

"*Allah Akbar!*" the terrorist shouted, holding the woman's severed head aloft, blood pouring from the stump of her neck.

In quick order, the heads of the other two prisoners were also severed.

Finally, the three disembodied heads were put on a table while the camera focused on them, remaining for an extended period of time on each one. The eyes of the Jordanian and Italian were closed, but the woman's eyes were opened in horror.

The lights went dark and the camera was turned off. Not until then were all the hoods removed.

"You took a great chance in coming here, *Al Sayyid*," one of the men said, using a title of great respect when he spoke to the terrorist who had read the fatwa.

"I will do what must be done to rid our region of the American infidels," the reader said.

Redha, Qambari Arabia

He sat in the van and watched as the school bus stopped to let her off. She was a pretty girl, a blonde as so many Americans were. She laughed, and shouted something back to the bus as it drove away. Her name was Amber Pease, and she was the daughter of the commandant of the Marine Guards at the U.S. Embassy.

She was fourteen years old, and in her short skirt and uncovered head, her tight shirt and bare arms, she looked like a whore. Didn't the Americans understand the sensitivity of the Qambaris? They knew that women in Qambari Arabia were required to wear burkas but they made no effort to comply. Well, he would see to it that this little harlot paid for her heresy.

It was every parent's nightmare, learning that his child was missing. All the children on the bus reported seeing Amber get off the bus, and two said they had seen a man lead her into a white van. Both children had thought the incident was unusual enough to report it to their parents.

"It was an old Ford van, and it had a big rusty spot above the left tail light, and the license number was 37172," Randy, the twelve-year old son of one of the embassy staff said.

"How do you know?" The military policeman asked.

"I wrote the number down in my notebook," Randy said. "Mom and Dad said you should never get into a car with someone you don't know, and I didn't think Amber knew the man."

Even as the Embassy was providing the Qambari police with information on the van, as well as a description of the man who had taken her, the police found Amber.

"I'm sorry, sir," Captain Hardesty, the military police captain in charge of the investigation told Colonel Pease. "But, we are going to need an official identification. You are going to have to look at the body."

Pinching the bridge of his nose, Colonel Pease nodded, indicating that he was ready. The MP took him into a room at the rear of the police morgue, then pulled back the cover. Pease looked at her, nodded, then turned away with tears streaming down his face.

"How was she found?" he asked.

"You don't really want to know, sir," Hardesty replied.

"How was she found?" Colonel Pease asked again.

"She was," Captain Hardesty started, paused, took a deep breath, then continued. "She was found nude and spread-eagled, with her underwear stuffed in her mouth."

Colonel Pease was quiet.

"We'll get the son of a bitch, sir," Hardesty said. "We have two eye witnesses; we have a make on the van and a license number. We've given the Qambari Police good, solid leads. We're going to get the bastard who did this."

"Thanks," Colonel Pease replied.

With the Americans in Fallujah, Iraq

"Hot damn! We've got ourselves a real juicy target here," Sergeant Baker said as he peered through the thermal sight of a Long Range Acquisition System (LRAS), mounted on a Humvee.

"What have you got, Sergeant?" Lieutenant Colonel Art Jensen asked.

"I've got five Hajs, with weapons, in a building." Sergeant Baker answered. He chuckled. "Look at the poor dumb bastards. Ole' Habib thinks I can't see him. Well he can run, but the son of a bitch can't hide."

It was 0230, pitch black, and the mujahideen insurgents, called Hajs, or Habib by the Americans, were wearing black to fade into the dark interior of the building. They were shadows within shadows, unable even to see each other from no more than a few inches away. But with his thermal imaging optics, Sergeant Baker could see them as clearly as if they were standing in the middle of the street in broad daylight.

"Give me the numbers, Sergeant," Colonel Jensen said.

"Yes, sir, numbers coming up," Sergeant Baker replied, punching them in.

Art looked at the numbers, then keyed the mike.

"Boomer Three, this is Tango Six. I have a fire mission."

The radio call sign, Tango Six, identified Art as the Commanding Officer of the 3rd Infantry Battalion, 32nd Infantry Regiment, 7th Infantry Division.

"Go ahead, Tango Six," Boomer Three responded.

"Coordinates 09089226, direction two zero two degrees. Range niner fi-yive zero meters."

"Ordnance is on the way, Tango Six."

Art looked in the direction from which the fire mission would come, and he saw a few sparks as the mortar rounds climbed into the sky. A second later, a dozen loud booms rattled the neighborhood as a great ball of flame erupted at the target building. The flame was followed by a huge, billowing cloud of smoke and dust.

"Tango Six, can we have a BDA?" the disembodied radio voice asked.

"Battle damage assessment?" Art repeated. He chuckled. "Nothing to assess, Boomer, you brought some heat. The building is gone. Thank you."

"We have enjoyed doing business with you, Tango Six."

"Tango Six out."

Art thought about the five insurgents who had just died. They died because they could not comprehend a technology that could find them from a mile away, then unleash a deadly barrage from mortars that could fire for effect without ranging. In the current operation, scores of insurgents had died, simply because they took one curious peek over the ledge to see what was going on outside. That one, brief second of exposure was all that was needed to kill them, and anyone who was with them.

* * *

The sun rose the next day on a city that was nearly deserted. The melodic call to prayer, enhanced by a loudspeaker, intoned in the morning quiet.

> *Allah u Akbar, Allah u Akbar*
> *Ashhadu all llah ill Allah*
> *Ash hadu all illha ill Allah.*
> *Ash hadu anna Muhammadan Rasululaah*
> *Ash had anna Muhammadan Rasulullaah.*
> *Hayya lasseah, Hayya Lassaleah*
> *Hayya lalfaleah, Hayya lalfaleah*
> *Allanu Akbar, Allahu Akbar*
> *La llaha ill Allah.*

Art stood behind a wall looking over the city with a pair of binoculars. Behind him, Captain Chambers was staring at images on a TV monitor. The images were being projected from an Unmanned Aerial Vehicle, or UAV, circling over the city.

"Anything coming up on the monitor, Mike?" Art asked.

"No, sir," Chambers answered. "Everyone seems to have his head down this morning."

A Humvee drove up behind them and stopped. Two men got out. One was carrying a video camera, and both were wearing sleeve flashes that identified them as TV reporters.

"Is Colonel Jensen here?" one of the men asked.

Art nodded. "I'm Colonel Jensen."

"I'm John Williams with World Cable News," the one who asked the question said.

"Yes, I recognize you," Art said.

"Oh, you've seen me then?"

"Yes."

"What do you think of the coverage WCN has given the war?"

"Not much," Art said, candidly.

"Oh?" Williams replied. "And may I ask why not?" The expression on the reporter's face, and the defensive timbre of his voice showed his irritation.

"Your headquarters is where? Atlanta? The last time I checked, Atlanta was in the United States, yet your network seems determined to find anything negative you can about our effort over here."

"We are a world news organization, Colonel," Williams said. "You do understand the concept of 'world' don't you? We are beyond the chauvinistic hubris that is so prevalent among our sister networks."

"Yes, you and Al Jazeera," Art said. "What do you need, Williams? What can I do for you?"

"I've come down from headquarters to be embedded with your battalion."

"Do I have a say in this?" Art asked.

"Not really, Colonel," Williams replied, smugly. "Unless you want to butt heads with a general."

Art sighed. "All right. Just stay the hell out of the way."

"Oh, and Colonel, if you would, please put the word out to your men that I am here to work, not to sign autographs," Williams said.

"I don't think you will have any trouble with that, Mr. Williams," Art said in a cold, flat tone of voice. "I doubt that you have that many fans among the troops here."

Art turned back toward the street and lifted his binoculars to his eyes. He swept his gaze, slowly, from side to side, looking for anything out of the ordinary.

He saw nothing.

"Colonel, the UAV has made a second pass, still no sightings," Captain Chambers said from his position at the monitor.

Art lowered his field glasses. "All right," he said. "Tell A Company to saddle up. It's time to put out some bait."

"Yes, sir," Chambers replied. He spoke into his radio. "Goodnature Six, this is Tango Six. Get ready to move out. All other units hold your position."

A series of "Rogers" came back.

"Where will the CP be, Colonel?" Chambers asked.

"In my Humvee," Art replied. "I'm going to lead the convoy."

"Yes, sir, I'll be right behind you."

Art shook his head. "No, you take the three spot, Captain Mason will be behind me. Oh, and, take them with you," he said, nodding toward Williams and his cameraman.

"Uh . . . it isn't all that necessary that we actually go out on patrol with you, Colonel," Williams said nervously. "We can get everything we need from here."

Sergeant Baker was chewing tobacco, and he spit on the ground, barely missing Williams' boot.

"So, what you are saying is, you are a pussy. Is that it?" Baker said to Williams.

"I'm not . . ." Williams started, then he sighed. "I would be glad to accompany you, Colonel."

"You and your cameraman can ride with Captain Chambers and Sergeant Baker," Art said.

"That's my Humvee," Baker said. "Over there." He pointed.

The sound of a dozen or more engines starting disturbed the quiet morning air. Art walked over to his own Humvee, got into the right seat and settled down. His machine gunner stood in the back, freed the gun to slide around on the ring, cleared the headspace and activated the bolt.

"Let's go, Jimmy," Art said.

Nodding in compliance, Art's driver, Specialist Jimmy Winson started forward.

2

The Kingdom of Qambari Arabia

The Mercedes sports car raced through the streets of the capital city of Radul, sending pedestrians scattering and frightening a horse that was pulling a cart laden with vegetables. The cart overturned and the farmer watched in horror as his produce was scattered through the street, much of it ruined as it was run over by traffic.

A policeman, seeing the speeding car, recognized the driver as Prince Azeer Lal Qambar, so he breathed a quick prayer that no one would be injured, and he did nothing. It was not healthy to run afoul of the family that ruled Qambari Arabia.

Azeer Lal Qambar was forced to slow down, and then come to a stop. There was a wreck a few blocks ahead, and all traffic had come to a standstill.

Azeer honked his horn a few times, more in anger and frustration than any real belief that the traffic would become unsnarled. When the traffic remained at a standstill, Azeer became impatient, and he left the road and began driving down the sidewalk.

Several sidewalk merchants had spent several minutes earlier in the day very carefully displaying their wares on colorful rugs. They watched in helpless and frustrated dismay as the royal prince drove over their merchandise, destroying much of their inventory.

When Azeer reached the location of the wreck, he left the sidewalk and drove between the wrecked cars and the green crescent-marked ambulance that was there for the injured. Two EMTs were carrying an injured man on a stretcher, but when Azeer roared through, they had to drop the stretcher in order to get out of the way. Azeer skirted just around the dropped stretcher as he honked his horn impatiently, then sped away, leaving the traffic congestion behind him.

When Azeer reached the palace, he was greeted by his father, the Sultan Jmal Nagib Qambar.

"Azeer, I see that you are back from your vacation. I trust it was enjoyable?"

"Yes, Father, it was very enjoyable," Azeer replied.

"I am glad you are here," the Sultan said. "I want you to meet with the American ambassador. He is here to talk about your trip to America."

"Father, why do we not tell the Americans to leave Qambari Arabia?"

"My dear son, without the Americans' appetite for our oil, we would be nothing but another wandering tribe, trying to survive in the desert. We need the Americans, and they need us. It is like the lowly tickbird and the majestic camel. Neither likes the other, but neither can survive without the other."

"Which are we, Father? The tickbird, or the camel?" Azeer asked.

Excusing himself, Azeer went into the office of foreign trade. He was the head of foreign trade, a position he occupied by appointment from his father. In truth, it was merely a position created for him. He knew nothing about foreign trade, didn't understand such things as tariffs, or money exchange, or the balance of trade. He did know that, because of the oil, America bought a lot more from Qambari Arabia, than the QA bought from the U.S.

It was an attempt, on the part of the U.S. government, to narrow the gap in trade that was the purpose of this meeting. The American ambassador was here to extend the formal invitation from his government.

"Prince Azeer, how delightful to see you," Ambassador James said, standing to greet Azeer as he entered. "You have been on vacation I hear."

"Yes," Azeer said without elaboration.

"I trust you had a good time?"

"I had a very good time."

"Good, good," Ambassador James said. He removed a folder from his briefcase. "Here is the official invitation from my government for you to make a fact-finding visit with regard to trading agreements. There are letters of introduction to everyone you might need to see, as well as pre-clearance for customs and that sort of thing."

"You are most kind," Azeer said.

Ambassador James grinned obsequiously. "In our fight against terror, we have had no better friend in the region than Qambari Arabia," he said. "This is just a means of expressing our gratitude toward you and the Royal family."

"Thank you," Azeer said. "I will walk you to door."

It was a dismissive comment and Ambassador James picked up on it at once. He started toward the door. "Please feel free to contact me if you have any questions about anything."

"I will," Azeer replied. "As you said, the friendship between our two countries must be nourished."

As James started to leave, he saw a newspaper lying on the table by the door. Although the paper was printed in Arabic, the photo on the front page, above the fold, told the story. It showed the terrified face of a prisoner who was about to be beheaded. There were five hooded terrorists standing around him. Four were holding AK-47s, the fifth, behind him, was holding a knife.

"I haven't seen that news release," Ambassador James said. "Would you read the caption to me?"

"Of course," Azeer replied. Picking up the paper, he began reading. "Bernie Gelb of Miami, Florida, an employee of Energy Resources, was beheaded yesterday by the Jihad of Allah. In a statement released by Jihad of Allah, it was stated that 'the Jew was executed for crimes against Islam, the heresy of Zionism, and violating the people of Iraq by aiding the American invaders.'"

"Invading? He was helping to restore electricity for the people of Iraq, for crying out loud," the ambassador said.

"Yes, but not all understand the benevolence of America," Azeer replied, putting the paper back down.

"A ghastly thing, to behead someone."

"Yes," Azeer replied. "Much evil has been done by both sides in this war."

"How goes the investigation into the rape and murder of Amber Pease?"

Ambassador James was referring to the daughter of Lieutenant Colonel Amon Pease, the commandant of the Marine guards of the American Embassy.

"I am told that our police are working on the case," Azeer replied. "These things take time."

"We have given you several good leads," Ambassador James said.

"We appreciate your help," Azeer said. "But it will be necessary for our police to develop their case. I'm sure you know how it is."

"Yes," James replied, suppressing his frustration. "I know exactly how it is."

Ambassador James left the meeting nearly boiling over with rage. There were eye-witness accounts as to who the rapist was, and those reports had been given to the government of Qambari Arabia, but they had done nothing about it. And, that was as far as he could go. He knew the United States' relationship with Qambari Arabia was a delicate one. It was his understanding of just how delicate it was, that earned him this appointment.

Redhi, Qambari Arabia

The markings on the side of the yellow bus read, in both English and Arabic: AMERICAN DEPENDENT SCHOOL.

There were eleven students on the bus, ranging in age from six years to sixteen. All were children of the American employees and servicemen attached to the embassy. Fourteen-year-old Amber Pease had been a part of the group until six weeks ago, when she was kidnapped, raped and murdered.

Amber had not been taken from the bus, but as a precaution, a U.S. Marine now rode the bus with the students from the embassy quarters to their school in the morning, and from the school to their quarters in the late afternoon.

It was late afternoon now, and the children were all returning from the school, laughing and teasing with each other, looking forward to the weekend that was coming up. An embassy party was planned, not only for the adults, but also for the kids, and the party was the subject of speculation and conversation.

"We're supposed to have a surprise," eleven-year-old Tamara Gooding said. Tamara's father was an attaché to the embassy. "I wonder what it will be."

"I know," Terry Goodpasture said. "It's the new Harry Potter movie."

"No way! It hasn't even come out yet!"

"Way! We're getting it early."

Two blocks away a man sat at a sidewalk café drinking a cup of coffee. When he saw the school bus approaching, he opened his cell phone, dialed a number, and pushed send. He had done this many times before, in order to be able to time when the signal would get through to the phone he was calling.

He heard the other number ring, one short ring, just as the bus passed a kiosk. At that instant, a huge ball of fire erupted from the kiosk. The blast ripped into the side of the bus. By the time the sound of the blast reached him, and the others at the sidewalk café, the bus had overturned. Fire and oily smoke roiled up from the wreckage.

Smiling, he closed the telephone and walked away.

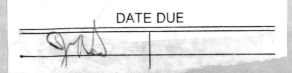

DATE DUE

When You Visit Our Website:
www.kensingtonbooks.com
You Can Save 30% Off The Retail Price
Of Any Book You Purchase

- All Your Favorite Kensington Authors
- New Releases & Timeless Classics
- Overnight Shipping Available
- All Major Credit Cards Accepted

Visit Us Today To Start Saving!
www.kensingtonbooks.com